"Oh?
take
that?'

N

Layla growled. "Stop. ~~treating me like a~~"

She repeated the phrase, enunciating each word through her teeth.

"Sweet Lay, we definitely do not see you as a child," I told her.

"Definitely don't," Novak echoed.

She bristled. "Come on. I'm fine. Everyone's fine. There's no need for this."

"There is every need for this," I argued. "You *left*."

"And *I'm fine*," she countered, folding her arms and drawing my gaze to her breasts. "As I said, I can take care of myself."

"Hmm, that's twice," I murmured, considering her. "Perhaps we need her to prove it?"

Novak's icy gaze narrowed, his expression telling me he agreed even though he didn't speak or nod.

"She also needs new clothes," I added, glancing over her outfit. "We should help her with that."

"Hmm," Novak hummed, stepping forward to grab her shirt.

She glanced down, her arms falling to her sides. "Novak…"

A yank ripped the gauzy fabric down the middle, but he didn't let it drop to the floor. Instead, he pulled the top from her skin and gestured with his chin toward the bed. "Up you go."

She didn't comply, instead choosing to place her hands on her hips and glare at us.

It was a beautiful display of rage and sex, which suited our mood nicely.

NOIR
REFORMATORY
SECOND OFFENSE

USA Today Bestselling Authors
Lexi C. Foss & J.R. Thorn
Writing As
Jennifer Thorn

Noir Reformatory: Second Offense

Editing by: Outthink Editing, LLC

Proofreading by: Jean Bachen

Cover Design: Francesca Michelon, Merry-Book-Round Covers

Published by: Ninja Newt Publishing, LLC

Print Edition

Paperback ISBN: 978-1-68530-021-0

Noir Reformatory

SECOND OFFENSE

Bow or bleed.
A decision all Noir angels must make.
Because I'm their king.

It wasn't my choice. I assumed the position after the prisoners of this nightmare reformatory went after my mates.

Auric is my commander, even if I'm the one giving the orders. He worships the dukedom and the princess, soon to be our queen.

Layla is my crown, my purpose, the sheer essence of life. She's the key.
The key to unlocking the darkness in my soul. There is no reform. No restitution. Only retaliation and fear.

I'll decorate my throne with the broken wings of my enemies. Their blood will run like a river, a red carpet at my feet.

The games have just begun. The players have been cast. And in this world of darkness and sin, all will bow to their king.

Note: *Noir Reformatory* is a ménage paranormal romance spanning six novels. There will be cliffhangers, adult situations, violence, and MM/MF/MMF content.

Suggested Reading Order:

Noir Reformatory: The Beginning — A standalone prequel to the Noir Reformatory universe
Noir Reformatory: First Offense
Noir Reformatory: Second Offense
Noir Reformatory: Third Offense
Noir Reformatory: Fourth Offense
Noir Reformatory: Fifth Offense
Noir Reformatory: Final Offense

PROLOGUE

A NOTE FROM NOVAK

Lies.

Chaos.

Depraved secrets.

Sometimes those we trust the most are the true monsters of our tales. The ones who hide beneath a cloak of white feathers and preach that Falling is a sin. Only the most wicked among us earn their black wings.

Wicked beings like me.

I own my darkness. I adore mayhem and blood and death. But this world isn't black and white.

There's madness, deception, and dangerous twists. Nothing is what it seems. Including me—a Noir with black wings edged with razors.

I used to fight for the cause, rounding up those with ebony feathers and tossing them into prisons meant for reform.

Then I ended up in one of those penitentiaries myself and quickly learned how wrong I'd been.

There is no redemption here. Only survival.

Because purity doesn't really exist. It's a beautiful lie crafted to control the weak.

Which is where our story truly begins.

At the start of a new discovery.

The Noir are not who we think they are. And the Nora no longer represent the salvation I once craved.

Layla is my future now. Auric, too. Together, we will survive this. Together, we will overcome.

Welcome to our new version of hell.

A place where the inmates call me king.

Set in a world riddled with secrets.

Focused on a reformatory that has nothing to do with reform.

Let the blades fly.

CHAPTER ONE

LAYLA

Welcome to the future, Princess Layla.
Which crown will you choose?
—Sayir

My uncle's note had disappeared three days ago, but I still remembered every word. *Which crown will you choose?*

I stared up at the ceiling, pondering the real question lurking within his note. *Who should I believe?*

Kyril, the Noir I'd just met.

Or the world I'd always known.

A warm caress to my cheek had me tilting my head toward Novak. He rested on the pillow beside me, his dark hair spilling into his icy gaze as he studied me in that intense way of his.

Rather than speak, he wrapped his palm around the back of my neck and drew me in for a kiss. One that involved several long, languid strokes of his tongue against mine. By the time he finished, I'd almost forgotten my concerns.

Except that note populated my mind again.

Which crown will you choose?

King Sefid or King Vasilios.

Kyril claimed the latter was my real father. Some figment Noir who was the rightful heir to the throne.

I nearly snorted at the ridiculousness of it all.

This was all just another test from Sayir, likely because I'd failed his last one by mating with Novak and Auric.

Although, if that were truly a sin, surely Auric's wings would have changed from white to black?

I blinked. Then frowned. Then sighed. Because it was all so confusing.

Novak kissed me again, this time with a lethality that required I give him my undivided focus. He was savage. Cruel. Beautiful. *Mine.*

Just like the male on the other side of me. He usually held me while I slept, but he'd given me space to think. Now that our room was fortified again—our door had been knocked off the hinges after the explosion the other day—we could somewhat relax.

But I didn't feel *relaxed* at all.

I felt restless.

Startled.

A right mess of nerves and befuddlement.

Novak's grip tightened on my neck, his kiss bruising.

Then Auric's lips met my shoulder, his teeth skimming my flesh as he placed his palm on my abdomen. "If you're not going to sleep, then we'll make better use of our time," he whispered darkly against my ear.

I shivered.

The two males had given me the last few days to reflect on our mating. Or perhaps to come to terms with what Kyril had said. Or, more likely, hadn't felt at ease enough to let their guard down like this.

But now that order had been somewhat restored within the prison—with Novak leading as the de facto king—they were more than comfortable in our current position.

My body came alive between them, my heart racing in my chest as Novak kissed a path down my throat to my breasts while Auric took control of my mouth.

Oh gods…

This was one way to distract my thoughts.

Yet, a part of me kept repeating Sayir's note. Over and over and over again.

Auric nipped my lower lip, his reprimand clear. Novak took my nipple into his mouth through my gauzy shirt—which I really hoped I found a replacement for soon. The fabric was not made for the chilly weather outside. We were lost somewhere in the mountains, with the nearest ocean being farther than a flight away.

And worse, we were in the human realm.

Or that was what the others thought, anyway.

As I'd never visited, I couldn't say for sure. But the sky was much bluer here than back home.

Home, I repeated to myself, flinching. *Do I even have one of those anymore?*

"Lay." Auric's lips caressed mine as he spoke. "If you don't start paying attention, I'm going to be offended."

"My mind keeps wandering," I admitted, my voice soft and husky. "I… I keep thinking about what Kyril said."

Novak's teeth dug into my breast, causing me to yelp against Auric's mouth.

I arched into them, my heart skipping a beat.

These males… *ohhh*… they owned me entirely, neither of them showing an ounce of mercy. They would utterly destroy me—in the best way—if I didn't comply with their demands.

"Kyril is a pawn," Auric murmured against my mouth, replying to my concern. "One more cog in Sayir's twisted machine." The fact that Auric had locked up the timid

Noir in a cell nearby was a testament to his belief that this was all Sayir's doing.

But was it, though?

A second king—a *Noir* king—living in the human realm. It didn't even seem possible.

Should I believe Kyril? Or was he really working for my uncle?

I opened my mouth to voice my questions out loud, but Auric silenced me with his tongue, leaving me gasping for breath while Novak deftly unfastened my shirt at my neck.

The gauzy fabric whispered across my skin before fluttering to the floor. My pants soon followed, leaving me just as naked as my mates. They no longer slept with clothes on; I'd only worn mine because I'd been too lost in thought to strip.

Oh, but Novak and Auric were both encouraging me to forget now. Their hands and mouths were wicked, their intent clear.

Novak spread my legs to settle between them as he kissed a path downward over my abdomen. He paused to nibble my hip bone, his tantalizing touch destroying all my worries and forcing me to focus on the warmth humming through my veins.

Oh, but Auric wasn't to be ignored, his mouth almost savage against my own as he laid claim to my very soul with his talented tongue.

Gods…

I purred, then trembled as Novak palmed the underside of my thigh, his breath hot against my slick folds.

But despite it all, I couldn't shake the trickle of unease prickling my spine.

Some sort of nagging sensation.

One that tempered the moment, pulling me back to my thoughts even as my body quaked for more.

Ugh!

This irritant refused to allow even my mates to distract me from the dilemma. I wouldn't be able to enjoy them while this weighed on me, and it needed to be dealt with.

"Auric," I said, his name leaving my mouth on a rasp-like groan.

Part protest.

Part plea.

But I had to say this, to voice my concern, to rid myself of the mental burden.

"Think about it," I continued, my purr vibrating through each word. "Even if Sayir is trying to mess with me… *Oh, that…*" I arched into Novak's mouth, his tongue finding a spot I couldn't ignore.

"That what?" Auric prompted, a taunt in his tone.

I swallowed, trying to remember my thought. "That…" I threaded my fingers through Novak's hair, my mind rioting between sensations and concerns. "Even if it's another test, that doesn't mean Kyril's lying."

There.

I'd said it.

King Sefid might not be my father at all.

And that would change everything.

Auric worshipped my breasts while he contemplated my concern. I bowed up off the bed as Novak suckled my tender nub, the joint sensations threatening to shoot me into the stars.

"What should we do?" I asked, nearly mindless from the attention, but the question persisted.

Novak's teeth skimmed my sensitive flesh, making me whimper. "Play the game."

I felt like they were playing *me,* and a sound of wanton

need was my only reply when Novak slipped a finger through my wetness.

Auric hummed in agreement, his thumbs kneading my taut nipples. "He's right. Sayir wants us to learn something from this. Whether it be related to reformation or not, we need to play along. It's the only way to determine our next steps."

Novak slid a second finger inside of me as his way of agreement. My back arched into his touch, only for Auric to press me down beneath him. *So much for my sanity.*

It was like trying to breathe underwater when my mates chose to devour me so completely. All logical thoughts twisted into one another as the two angels thoroughly worked my body into a state of utter desperation.

Auric awarded me a small reprieve as I writhed, only so that he could cup my face before guiding me into a smoldering kiss. His hot arousal branded my hip, ready for more, but he would take his time.

They both would, their intentions clearly meant to drive me insane.

I ached for Novak's tongue to stroke me where I needed him most, but he teased me, working me until my flesh wept for him.

"What about escape?" I gasped out, desperate to resolve the pestering questions revolving around my mind. And yet that query felt entirely appropriate, as though the escape I'd mentioned meant something far more intimate.

An escape into oblivion.

Screaming.

Tumbling.

Panting in ecstasy.

But Auric pulled back, his thumb tracing a path along

my jawline. "We have nowhere to run. Not while you're a Noir."

Novak studied me with raw intensity, licking his lips with promise from between my splayed thighs. This had turned into a new game, one where he would watch me suffer until I fully surrendered myself to them.

"I may never be a Nora again," I pointed out, sliding my fingers through Novak's dark hair once more.

Auric inclined his head in agreement. "Which is why we need to start thinking about what to do if that's the case."

My other hand trailed over Auric's shoulder and slid into the feathery down of his wings. He shivered at the intimate touch, his pupils flaring with dark intensity.

Mmm, it pleased me that I could impact him in the same way he impacted me. Because I knew he wanted to prolong my sensual suffering just as much as Novak did.

Although, this was the sort of suffering I would indulge them in any day.

Oh, how far we've come, I mused.

When we'd first arrived at Noir Reformatory, Auric had been so remote. Callous. Burning with anger over my Fall—as if it had been my fault.

I'd told him it was a mistake. He hadn't believed me.

And Novak, well, he hadn't cared either way. He'd merely wanted to eat me.

So maybe that hasn't changed, I thought, meeting his icy gaze.

My dark feathers fluttered in my peripheral vision, and Auric's blue gaze shifted. The tightening of his lips confused me.

Even Novak stilled as he watched the invisible exchange, and my heart skipped a beat.

Auric had made it clear he still sought my reformation, no matter the cause of my Fall.

Which meant he might never accept me in this state.

We have nowhere to run.

Not while you're a Noir.

Tears pricked my eyes at the futility. *Does that mean he won't truly accept this? Me? Us?*

Auric flinched from his trance, his piercing gaze finding mine.

Emotion trickled through his chiseled features, but not the hard kind I'd grown used to in his presence. No, these emotions were fiercer, yet softened by the tenderness in his eyes.

"We will figure this out," he promised me.

He captured my lips once more, silencing whatever I would have said.

Novak followed suit, clamping his mouth down on my swollen nub as I gasped into Auric's mouth.

I gave in to them with reckless abandon, clinging to Auric's broad shoulders even as a yawning void opened inside of me. Perhaps I would never earn my white wings because maybe it wasn't even a possibility.

I had Fallen, and now I could never go back to the way things were.

As Novak laved his tongue over me, sending me to new heights, I questioned what it was about the past I so yearned for.

"Stay with us," Auric commanded before taking my mouth in a bruising kiss.

Novak growled his agreement, sending dangerous vibrations through my core. This conversation was over, and they would not tolerate further discussion.

For now, we would play Sayir's game.

Novak buried his face between my legs, his aggression

nearly undoing me as I moaned into Auric's kiss. I could let go, just for a little while. We would find an answer to Sayir's plans, one way or another.

I cleared my mind of all my concerns, fisted Auric's hair, and yanked, exposing his throat before I sank my teeth into his flesh.

I wanted to bite.

To claim.

Desire flared inside me as Novak reminded me of his presence, nipping at my damp flesh. My heart pounded as I observed him, my darkness, my mate.

An intense silence engulfed us for a blissful moment, only to be disturbed by a knock at the door.

CHAPTER TWO

NOVAK

ZIAN.

My cousin either had a death wish or pertinent information that couldn't wait until sunrise. I leaned against the door, naked. If he wanted to interrupt me in bed, then he could handle the consequences of such a crude decision.

Layla was the first woman I'd been with since my Fall. She was also my new mate. And I'd only been inside her *once*.

I needed him to hurry the fuck up so I could be inside her again. *Tonight.*

Zian cleared his throat. "Uh, is there somewhere we can go to chat?"

I just stared at him, allowing him to see the refusal in my eyes. He probably didn't want to talk in front of Auric. Too damn bad. Our former commander might have instigated our collective Fall, but I'd wanted to believe him when he'd said it hadn't been intentional. Old hurts weren't easily assuaged, but he'd just been following King Sefid's order. Similar to how we'd been following Auric's command as our leader.

Except I'd broken ranks that day.

And earned my feathers as a result.

Zian sighed. "Fine. We'll do it here, then."

I gave him a look that said, *Speak faster or I'm shutting the door.*

Zian squared his shoulders and glared at me. "We've been discussing our current predicament."

We, meaning he, Sorin, and Raven, I presumed.

Auric spoke up behind me. "As have we."

I frowned, his statement presenting an intriguing nuance.

We, as in Auric, Layla, and I. A new team. A fresh dynamic. Fascinating.

I'd once been part of Zian's *we*. For hundreds of years as warriors, and then a century of it in the reform system. Zian, Sorin, and I had been a team. We'd had each other's backs before Auric's return had changed my dynamic.

Not to mention a certain little Noir angel who scented the room with delectable cherry blossoms, reminding me of our prior engagement.

I gave Zian a raised brow, my standard form of communication enough to get my point across. *And?*

Zian's black feathers ruffled, the vibration an irritating sound that disturbed the air. "We have no desire to sit around and wait for Sayir's next move." His jaw flexed, betraying that he knew I wouldn't like what he was about to say. "We want to go. Tonight."

Auric scoffed. "That's an idiotic idea."

Zian's gaze swerved to the Nora warrior with Layla tucked into his arms. He'd pulled up the sheets to protect her modesty. "Why?" my cousin asked, the word sharp.

"Think about it. Sayir isn't going to let his assets out of his sight, much less waltz around the human world without a tether. We have to play his game, and if we want to win, we need to be smart about it." He kissed Layla's brow. "We're staying."

"Assets?" Zian repeated, clearly not having heard a word Auric had said. "What the fuck does that mean?"

Auric sighed. The proverbial Auric-Layla-and-I *we* had come to the conclusion of Sayir's true motives, at least in theory, but it would be a waste of time to explain it to my cousin.

All Zian needed to know was that I was in charge, the unequivocal King of Noir Reformatory, and he would step in line or learn his lesson the hard way. I hadn't forgotten his treatment of my mate, how he'd chosen Raven over her out in the courtyard when she'd been in danger. While I couldn't blame him for assisting his own mate, it didn't mean I had to like it.

"Or investments," Auric clarified, entertaining Zian's question. "Whatever term he used after the fire at Noir Reformatory. He made it sound like you're all his assets, and we already know that he's tracking us somehow."

Like property, I thought. *Or dogs.*

I leaned against the doorway and wafted my wings, spreading the mixture of Auric's evergreen and Layla's blossom scents through the room. It was the only thing that calmed me when thinking about what Sayir had already done to us.

After the fire in the old prison, the Reformer had knocked us out to transport us to the new prison. No telling what had been done to us during that time.

So yeah, he was definitely tracking us. But could he control us as well? Like how he'd magically been able to put us all to sleep? Did it go beyond that ability?

A growl taunted my throat, my desire to murder the Reformer increasing tenfold inside my mind.

He would pay for his sins, I vowed. *He will bleed.*

"Whatever," Zian muttered. "I don't care. He can track me all he wants. We're leaving. The question is, are you coming with us, cousin?" He spoke the last part specifically to me.

Of course, he couldn't understand. We'd never made a decision or a move without including the other in our plans.

We'd never had diametrically opposed opinions, either. There was a first for everything.

"No," I said, the decision important enough to speak aloud. He was lucky I didn't force his knee and bend him into submission. Letting him leave would give the rest of the prison the wrong idea, and Auric was right. We needed to play Sayir's game.

For now.

A wave of Layla's cherry blossoms wafted over me, sinking into my feathers as her dismay pressed at my back.

Zian's voice grew hard. "No? Why the fuck not?"

"Careful," I warned, unfurling my arms. "If you wish to leave, then go."

However, they would need to keep their exit discreet. And besides, they'd be back as soon as they realized they had nowhere to go.

Zian, Sorin, and Raven all faced the same problem as Layla and I did. Even if we could find a sanctuary in this realm, our black feathers damned us all for eternity.

Layla was innocent. Her feathers had darkened even when she'd done nothing wrong, which made me question my own Fall as well.

But that was beside the point.

"We need a plan," I said, meaning it.

Layla was the key in more ways than one, and we needed to figure out what that meant before making our move.

"A plan?" Zian repeated with a harsh laugh. He spread his arms wide. "Look around you, cous. There's nothing here for us except stone walls and iron bars. The Reformer *will* be back." His arms fell to his sides. "What possible reason would you have to stay?"

"Because there is no logical alternative," Auric countered. "Fleeing without a plan is what Sayir expects from us. We need to be smarter than that."

Zian frowned. "And what do you plan to do when we run out of food?"

A valid question.

Our exploration of this prison had turned up the kitchen and a limited stash of dry goods. The rations would last us a week at most. Another planned obstacle for us from the Reformer, I had no doubt. He probably hoped we'd resort to killing and eating each other like a bunch of cannibals.

Just another arena for a massacre.

"The mountains," I said, glancing at the open window —something the blast had created. We'd fortified it with iron materials from other destroyed cells.

I inhaled, indulging in the scents of my mates mingling with the rise and fall of the evergreen trees outside. The sun peeked at us over the horizon, indicating the late morning hour. I estimated that it was fall or spring in this realm, the cool air and longer nights suggesting we were either heading toward winter or leaving it. I suspected it was the latter.

Hmm, we'll hunt, I decided. I rather enjoyed tracking wild game, something I hadn't been able to do in over a century.

Auric hummed in agreement, his mind likely following mine, not just because of our mating link but because of our centuries of knowing one another.

"If we find out we're running low on reserves, we'll have a logical reason to venture out," he said. "Until then, we stay, at least for a week while we have enough food."

"Fine. So we hang around for a week and then what?" Zian shook his head, frustration evident on his face. "This doesn't make any sense, Novak. We should pack up the food reserves and flee while we have the chance. We're all together now. No supervision. Why are we wasting this opportunity?"

My eyes narrowed, my cousin's tone and commentary testing my patience. He should appreciate the fact that I'd given him the choice to do whatever he wanted rather than demand he follow our lead.

"You're free to leave," I repeated, leaving a growl in my voice that said I would not be giving him a third chance to question me.

Oblivious, or perhaps too enraged to heed my warning, Zian surged forward and jabbed a finger into my bare chest. "Sorin and I waited for you, Novak. We had a chance to escape while you were in solitary, but we didn't take it. We didn't want to *leave you behind.*"

The sting of his words rang with hurt, betraying that this wasn't about a power play. Zian felt betrayed.

He could get in line.

His gaze slid to Auric. A rage built in his midnight irises, making them glint like onyx. "What is this hold that Auric has on you? You're going to refuse our best opportunity for freedom just because golden boy here says so?"

Oh, Zian gravely misunderstood who was in charge.

"Novak," Layla's sweet voice chimed in as if she sensed my mood shifting and wanted to prevent me from doing something I'd regret.

My wings spread from my back in reaction to her, wanting to turn and indulge her beckoning. The motion wafted the intoxicating mix of evergreen and cherry blossoms through the air, calming me once more.

"*Our* decision is to remain here and to consider all of *our* options before acting," I told Zian, enunciating my words carefully.

Zian needed to understand that Auric and I were a team now. Layla was our first priority, and on that front, I would never bend.

Zian straightened as he set his jaw. "I don't know who you are anymore, cousin."

I'm mated now, I thought. *And I am King of Noir Reformatory.* He would come to learn that I hadn't changed. I had merely grown into the role that I was always meant to play.

When I moved to close the door, Zian slapped his hand against it, abandoning any sense of self-preservation in a last desperate move to get through to me.

"You choose them over your own blood," he said as if Auric and Layla weren't even in the room. Their intoxicating scents nearly made me go mad, demanding that I join them in bed.

The statement seemed obvious to me, but I allowed Zian to continue.

"You're choosing the Nora who did this to us," he added as tension bloomed between us.

He didn't understand the nuance of the situation at all. I had blamed Auric for my Fall and for my imprisonment, but Auric had only been following orders. King Sefid had a part in all of this, and it was time we got to the bottom of it.

"Don't you remember? He never once asked for our side of the story before we were carted off like criminals. If he was so unwilling to listen to us then, why the fuck should we listen to him now?" Zian cast a caustic look over my shoulder. "My commander died a century ago. That's just a ghost in your bed."

"I wouldn't presume to be your commander now," Auric said, a hint of violence in his tone. "This isn't a mission. We aren't ranked warriors anymore. We're fighting for our fucking lives, and that means working together despite your hurt feelings."

Zian bared his teeth at Auric but addressed me. "I've been there for you for centuries, through the good days and the bad. We're blood, Novak. Who is he aside from some asshole who shares compatibility with your mate? He directly encouraged our Fall."

He didn't. I told you he didn't, and you're choosing not to believe me. I just stared at my cousin, letting him read the irritation in my expression.

"King Sefid gave that order," Auric said. "I passed it along to my team, as was my responsibility."

Zian laughed bitterly. "What a convenient lie."

"Just because you want it to be a lie doesn't make it one."

Zian grunted. "This isn't about what I want. This is about what we all *need*. Which is to escape while we can, not wait for fuck knows what to happen." His gaze met mine. "I've spent centuries listening to your strategies. I don't understand the one you're using now."

"Because you're too focused on the short term and not considering the long term," Auric drawled. "Some things never change."

My cousin bristled at that. "You want to talk about things that never change?" He took a step forward, but I instinctively stepped in his way, my aim to protect Layla more than Auric. But the shock in Zian's gaze told me he assumed it was for the latter.

"What's gotten into you, man?" he demanded. "You're not even listening to me."

Oh, I'm listening, I thought. *And I'm thinking.*

His words brought up old memories. Former grievances. Archaic pain.

Auric was suddenly beside me, his wing touching mine. "Maybe it's time for you to leave, Zian."

"Why? So you can convince Novak to follow you once more? Do you have any idea how much it hurt for our own commander to not even listen to what we had to say? Did you ever even care?"

This conversation had taken an unexpected emotional turn, one that had my mind whirring with history and thoughts of the day I'd Fallen.

My shock at the sight of those guards hurting that girl.

My fury as I watched the rogue Noir rip them to shreds.

My panic at seeing my own feathers shift.

I'd been... terrified. Confused. Distraught. All emotions I'd rarely experienced. And the one angel I would have turned to for guidance... wouldn't even look at me.

Auric crossed his arms, his muscles bulging menacingly, reminding me of his aggressive stance that day.

I swallowed, trying to pull myself from the memory and ground myself in the present.

But my anger, my terror, my absolute sense of betrayal, clung heavily to my spirit. They were emotions I'd dealt with in my own way throughout the last century, but I hadn't yet faced them in Auric's presence.

"You're upsetting Layla," he said now, entirely oblivious to my mounting ire. "I suggest you leave before you find out what happens when you distress my mate."

My mate? I repeated. *Don't you mean* our *mate?* I thought, giving him an irritated sidelong glance.

Zian moved to push through the door. "I'm not—"

I slammed my palm against the door frame, halting Zian from moving farther into the room. "Take a walk."

Not because I didn't trust him.

Not because I thought he might make this worse.

But because Auric and I needed to have a long-overdue discussion.

I caught my cousin's gaze and held it, urging him with my eyes to make the right decision while I wrestled with my own anger and impatience. *I'll handle it*, I was saying.

But it had nothing to do with his original reason for interrupting us. And everything to do with our past.

I might agree with Auric on staying.

But I did not agree with what he'd done to us. I did not agree with him calling Layla *his* mate. And absolutely did not fucking agree with his prejudices against Noir angels, something he'd hinted at just moments ago when he'd stared at Layla's wings while wearing a frown. *In our bed.*

"Fine," Zian spat, slamming his fist into the wall beside the door. Then he stalked away without a backward glance.

I closed the door and locked it, then whirled around to face the cell.

Layla met my gaze from behind her curtain of mussed fuchsia hair. Her bright sapphire eyes shone, framed by her brow drawn tight with worry. I had intended to distract her with my tongue, and I had almost succeeded until my cousin had shown up to remind us about our current state.

Although, Zian's comments weren't entirely unexpected. Just as he wasn't completely in the wrong, either.

Auric and I bonding Layla was just the beginning, a

temporary glue to bind the two of us above a mountain of history. But I'd seen the truth—no matter what Auric said, he still didn't fully accept Layla as a Noir, which meant he sure as shit wasn't going to accept *me*.

"He's right, you know," I said softly, Zian's comments fluttering through my mind like an errant feather. "You never did ask for our side of the story." Something Auric had already commented on once, shortly after I'd told him what had actually happened that day.

I should have asked you, he'd said.

Yes, you fucking should have, I agreed now.

"Would you have given it to me?" Auric countered, his haughty tone grating on my already frayed nerves.

I considered that. "I guess we'll never know, will we?"

And something about that sparked a fire inside me.

He never really apologized.

How could you possibly think I'd be the type to Fall? I wanted to demand.

Of course, I'd assumed he'd issued that command to orchestrate my demise. But how could I have not jumped to that conclusion? He hadn't even wanted to look at me that day. One glance at my wings and I was instantly dead to him. He hadn't even given me the benefit of the doubt.

I'd accepted some of his commentary on the issue, believing that he wasn't the real culprit here, that he hadn't truly set us up to Fall.

But where was his belief in me?

Why was I choosing him over my own flesh and blood?

Fuck, I'd just turned my cousin away, told myself that I didn't care if he left, all because my dynamics had shifted. My priorities were no longer my own. My life had been irrevocably changed.

By Auric.

His return.

His presence.

His *memory*.

You're choosing the Nora who did this to us.

Don't you remember?

Why the fuck should we listen to him now?

My cousin's words played on repeat through my mind.

"Novak."

I barely registered Auric saying my name.

But I didn't miss his tone or the way his body moved into a defensive stance.

So natural. So definitive. So untrusting.

Just like he'd done the day I'd Fallen. Only, he lacked a sword now. And the air didn't stink of death.

I didn't kill those Nora, I thought. "The rogue Noir avenged his mate, Auric. Why didn't the Nora guards Fall?"

"Novak…"

"They *raped* her for sport." I could see it so clearly in my mind, the carnage they'd left behind. The laughter. The morbid enjoyment. Those tangled red strands of hair, glimmering like flames beneath the moonlight. When that rogue Noir had arrived… I hadn't stopped him. I'd let him go. My wings had changed. And I'd watched the aftermath unfold.

Part of me had even cheered him on.

I could so easily picture Layla in that female's place on the ground. Could so easily sense how that image would impact my own rage.

Would Auric avenge her, too? Or would he see the white wings and forgive them while sending Layla to die in a prison?

"They deserved their fate," I argued, referring to the guards who'd died that day, and the make-believe ones in

23

my mind. Those cruel Nora had paid for their sins in blood. "But their wings never changed."

I'd never understood that part.

"You would have allowed them to live," I said, thinking back to their pristine feathers, the same shade as Auric's. "But you condemned me to hell. You would condemn us all to hell." *Including Layla.*

Even after knowing me for decades that had bled into centuries.

Even after everything we'd shared.

He never once asked for our side of the story.

I met his blue-green gaze, noting the hardness within. It was the same look he'd given me a century ago, one filled with condemnation and underlined with a hint of fear.

"You should have asked me what happened, Auric. You owed me at least that much."

Maybe Zian was right.

Maybe I shouldn't be listening to Auric at all.

"Trust goes both ways," I told him. "And you betrayed mine ages ago."

Why should I trust him now?

CHAPTER THREE

RAVEN

"*He said what?*" I asked, stunned as I lowered the dead rabbit dangling from my grip. Surely I'd heard Zian incorrectly.

"That we can leave without him," Zian repeated, his tone telling me how he felt about that.

Fuck. Zian wasn't going to leave without Novak, was he? *What a feather fluffer.*

Although, I *was* having fun hunting game in the forests surrounding the prison. It felt a little bit like freedom, something I'd never experienced in my eighteen years.

And now we were finally going to escape this shithole.

But of course, Novak had to go and fuck everything up.

After all we'd done for that asshole, he had the audacity to dismiss his cousin—*my mate*—in favor of Auric? The warrior who'd caused Sorin, Zian, and Novak to Fall?

Bullshit.

"Then let's go," Sorin suggested. "Novak can take care of himself."

I nodded, completely agreeing with him. We'd done enough for the silent Noir. If he wanted to stay with Layla and Auric, so be it.

"Not if he's going to let Auric and Layla guide him

around by the balls," Zian muttered as he drew his fingers through his thick, dark hair. He shook his head, his frustration showing. "I can't leave him."

"The fuck you can't," Sorin retorted. "He's made his choice. Let's make ours."

"What about the food shortage?" I asked. "You mentioned that, right?" That alone should be a way to convince Novak to come with us. Not that I really wanted the broody asshole to come along, but I knew Zian wasn't going to leave without him.

Which meant I couldn't leave.

Which meant Sorin wouldn't leave.

Zian glanced at the rabbit dangling at my side. "It seems you and my cousin had the same idea. He thinks there's enough game in the forest for the prisoners to survive."

While I was proud of my kill, one rabbit wouldn't feed us all. Although, in theory, a deer and a decent number of wild vegetables might be enough to buy us another week.

But if we decided to leave tonight, as originally discussed, then we only had to worry about ourselves. And the dead rabbit dangling from my hand would be enough for the three of us when combined with the edible mushrooms Sorin had found in the forest. He had a sack of them slung over his shoulder, the canvas illuminated by the rising sun.

Except now it appeared that we weren't going anywhere until Zian sorted out his familial problems.

That didn't mean I was going to hide my irritation.

"I asked about the food, and they said there's enough to survive the week while we develop a better plan." Zian blew out a breath. "They think Sayir wants us to run."

"So what if he does?" Sorin demanded. "It has to be

better than sitting around here waiting for whatever happens next."

"It's not that easy," Zian replied wearily. "You know Novak. There's no changing his mind once he's made a decision. And he's under some sort of love spell at the moment that has him agreeing with everything Auric says."

I stepped over a fallen log, testing out my footing in the underbrush before I shifted my weight. "Maybe we need to do what's best for ourselves, then, and let him figure this out." I palmed his cheek, reveling in the sharp stubble against my skin. "Sorin's right, you know. Novak can take care of himself."

For the first time in my life, I could taste freedom. I'd been born behind bars, then grew up under lock and key, and not even through any fault of my own. Being in the forest now with the brilliant blue sky high above the green canopy made my heart soar. I couldn't go back to the overwhelming weight of the prison's walls.

More than anything, I wanted to fly away and never look back.

Of course, I couldn't do that without my mates. *Both of them.*

Zian's midnight irises flashed. "I can't leave my cousin behind, sweet bird."

I sighed, my thumb tracing his lip before I released him. "All right. I understand. But did he say what kind of plan he has in mind?"

"No, we didn't get that far in the conversation." His expression and tone conveyed his agitation over that fact, telling me something had happened when he'd gone to visit his cousin. "However, they did remind me that the Reformer is very likely tracking us."

I frowned. We hadn't considered that complication when focusing on our freedom. "Shit. He's right."

And that presented a problem I hadn't wanted to think about.

How could we have been so naïve? Of course we can't run.

After everything we'd learned about my father, also known as *the Reformer* or *Sayir* to some, we knew better than to think anything could be that easy.

"Okay, then we what? We just stay here? Until we have a better plan that may or may not come along?" I asked, incredulous.

Zian blew out a breath and surveyed the forest, his expression haunted. Not a look I was used to on him. I reached out to stroke his feathers, hoping the touch would smooth that look off his face.

"Yes, but no," he said. "We'll… we'll give them another week. See what they come up with. Then go from there."

A bird fluttered nearby, darting from one tree to another. I wanted to join her, my own wings stretching behind me, itching to be used. Instead, I focused on Zian and his need to give his cousin just a little more time.

"I don't see what difference a week makes," Sorin cut in, his long white hair glowing in the early morning sun. "If we're being tracked now, we're still going to be tracked in a week."

"I know," Zian muttered. His expression told me that he hated asking us to stay, but he couldn't let this go. Novak was blood, and no matter what, Zian would go through fire for him.

"Maybe it's time we start thinking about ourselves." Irritation colored Sorin's tone. "We've been following Novak for centuries. Fuck, we're *here* because we followed him. And now he won't even consider our ideas?"

Zian rubbed his chin. "It's not that. He's… he's

considering it, I think, but he's also a master of strategy. I mean, what if he's onto something?" Zian turned toward Sorin, his shoulders squaring with the movement. "He's always five steps ahead, Sorin. He's damn near precognitive in his ability to calculate situations. I might not agree with him right now, but I still trust him."

Sorin let his satchel fall to the ground at his side, the strap slipping to his hand. "Normally, I'd agree. But we both know Auric has some kind of sick hold on him."

A shadow passed over Zian's gaze. "Yes. However, I also think Novak doesn't do anything without thinking it through first. That aspect of his personality isn't likely to change just because he's mated and saddled with the Nora."

I didn't know Novak as well as my mates did, but I trusted Zian—even when I didn't agree with him. The discussion had obviously not gone as planned, and I had a suspicion some things had been said that couldn't be taken back. Yet, despite that, Zian still needed to stay.

And I would stay with him.

"I think it's a bad idea," I admitted out loud. "We still don't really know Layla's purpose, other than being the 'key' Sayir referred to. But staying a few more days shouldn't hurt anything. Besides, we have food." I punctuated my declaration by proudly holding up my dead rabbit. "Although, I fully intend to stash what we find for ourselves. The other lazy bastards can do their own hunting."

"Shouldn't hurt anything," Sorin repeated, his tone implying dubiousness. "Sure. Yeah. Let's just stay and hope for the best."

Zian blew out a breath and palmed the back of his neck. "Okay. Can we give it another day or two, then? Just… let's see what happens and go from there. I'm not saying I won't leave eventually, but I want another chance to talk to Novak. See if I can reason with him or better understand his real motive for staying."

Sorin's dark blue eyes narrowed, the two males communicating in that way they always did—through looks and soundless conversation.

Seconds passed between them.

Then Sorin's shoulders caved just a little, his expression turning hard. "Fine. Two more days, Z. But we're fleeing at the first sign of danger."

"Agreed," Zian replied.

Sorin muttered a curse and shook his head. "For the record, I still think we're blowing a great opportunity to get the fuck out of here."

With that, he hefted the bag up off the ground and onto his shoulder, then stalked off toward the forest line.

Zian and I caught up with him, definitely having more on the agenda to talk about now that we were staying. "Hold on. We're going to have to do something about our sleeping arrangements. We can't keep sleeping on the floor in the hallway."

Our cell had been annihilated in the explosion. We'd been able to salvage the mattress and drag it into the hall, but we couldn't keep sleeping in the open like that, one of us awake at all times. It was supposed to be temporary, until tonight, but now that we were staying, something had to give.

Sorin grunted. "We could try to rebuild, but it seems like a fucking waste of time when we're leaving in two days." He pointedly glared at Zian, underlining that this compromise would not be extended.

"We'll figure it out," Zian assured us. He slipped an arm around my waist and drew me in for a kiss.

I snuggled into his side as we walked, taking the moment to enjoy the breeze and fresh air while I could.

The bird pacing us flitted into the canopy and disappeared out of sight, punctuating the sinking feeling of dread in my chest.

A bad omen, I decided.

One where, no matter what, Sayir would eventually win.

And either way, I would be back behind bars, just like he wanted.

CHAPTER FOUR

AURIC

Rage rippled off of Novak, the look on his face causing me to step between him and the bed. No way was he touching Layla in this mood.

His icy eyes narrowed on me, telling me he saw the protective gesture and didn't appreciate it. I glowered back. *You want someone to take it out on, you use me. Not her,* I told him. He couldn't actually hear me, but that didn't matter. Novak had always been able to read my nonverbal cues, and now was no exception.

And the tick in his jaw told me he was thinking about it. When he dipped his chin in acknowledgment, I looked at Layla. "Go take a shower," I told her.

"What?" She sounded both affronted and surprised.

"Now, Layla." If she stayed in the room, she would suffer the consequences, and they weren't hers to face. Novak and I had unfinished business, a fact that had become very clear during his discussion with Zian.

While Novak believed that I hadn't orchestrated his Fall, he still harbored some blame, as I had been the one to issue the command. It was also true that I had never asked Novak for his side of the story, something I'd already admitted to as a fault. But it clearly still irked Novak. And it definitely bothered Zian.

However, why would I have questioned them?

The visual stuck in my memory like a thorn. My comrades, my friends, scarred by sin.

That was when I'd had to make a difficult decision. They were no longer my equals. No longer my friends.

They were simply my subordinates. They'd disrespected my command. And they'd Fallen.

Things had seemed much more cut and dried back then.

However, my time among the Noir in Noir Reformatory had proven that things weren't quite so black and white. Not that it was an excuse. I hadn't been willing to see the truth before. And now I saw it clear as day.

Novak's gaze promised danger and violence. Not seduction or the drive to dominate, to fuck me into submission, but anger.

Fury.

Murder.

"Layla," I said firmly, keeping my eyes locked on Novak. "The bathroom."

"No," she replied hotly, slipping from the bed to come up behind me. "You both need to calm down and talk about this logically."

"We don't talk, Layla. Not with our voices, anyway."

We spoke through our fists.

With our bodies.

Voices were useless when Novak was involved.

Novak advanced again, his fingers curling into fists. His dark gaze never left mine. The glint in his eye promised pain. Retribution. I could sense his mounting fury in the silence of the cell—a rising tide, a force of nature I couldn't escape.

Layla's tone softened as she stepped toward Novak. "I

know there's history between you, and maybe you need to address that, but we can sit down and—"

Novak's gaze tore from mine to pin Layla with his cold, distant glare. I knew then that he wasn't here anymore—he was buried beneath memories and anger and the sliver of doubt Zian had placed inside him.

My hand lashed out, grabbing Layla by the arm before she could move any closer to Novak. I shoved her behind me.

"Go!" I snapped, then whirled around just in time to block Novak's first punch.

I deflected the blow by reflex, but while I was distracted, Novak's left fist slammed into my face with the full force of his body. I absorbed the blow with nothing more than a twitch in my eye, ducked another punch, and then stepped into him, throwing an uppercut into his abdomen.

My knuckles slammed into his bare stomach, expelling the breath from his lungs. It didn't even slow him down. He lunged for me, his shoulder ramming into my chest, and the two of us sailed through the air as Layla's presence continued to distract me.

The damn female needed to fucking listen to me before she wound up hurt.

I tilted, and my back hit the edge of the mattress. Novak's weight pinned me half on, half off in an awkward pose that gave him the upper hand. His fist struck my face once, twice, everything about him eerily silent and still.

Darkness spotted around my peripheral vision, threatening to take me under.

I didn't want Layla to see us like this, but this was what had to happen between us. What *needed* to happen. It was the only way to calm Novak, to make him see reason, to help him *feel* my unspoken apology.

"Novak!" Layla shrieked, racing toward us like she had a death wish.

"No!" I snarled, then grunted as Novak's fist barreled into my face again. Pain blossomed in my jaw, and I could already feel my eye swelling as blood left a metallic taste in my mouth. "Get out!"

With a roar, I threw my weight forward and rolled Novak off me, tossing him against the concrete floor. I stayed close to him, mostly to ensure he couldn't use his deadly wings against me. He hadn't sharpened his feathers when we'd fought before, but I didn't trust that he wouldn't when he was like this.

I wanted him as far away from Layla as possible, as long as his eyes were void of emotion, empty, like a psychopath on a rampage. If he hurt her in his mindless rage, I'd be forced to kill him.

And Layla would never forgive me.

His head bounced off the floor with a dull thud, and I took advantage of his sudden surprise by punching his jaw. Then I wrapped my arm around his neck, latched on to his body with my legs, and held him in place. His pulse pounded against my forearm, promising me that I wouldn't keep him down for long.

"Don't do this, Novak," I snarled, tightening my arm, cutting off his breath. "Don't lose yourself to mindless anger."

He growled, the guttural sound casting all blame at my feet.

"I didn't know!" I shouted. "You didn't say a fucking word!"

His gaze slammed into me, his eyes saying, *You should have asked. You didn't.*

Yeah, okay, maybe I'd fucked up, but he had, too. He could have stopped me. Could have spoken up, forced me to listen to him, given us a chance to work this shit out before it turned into a century of misunderstanding and blame.

He bucked against me. His head crashed into my nose, sending sparks of agony through my face, and I released him. As his weight disappeared, I rolled onto my side, coughing from the blood trickling down my throat. It poured from my nose onto the dirty floor.

"Novak, stop!" Layla cried again. "You're both being idiots!"

Novak crouched a couple of feet away, his body strung tight with tension. He leaned on his fingertips, his gaze raking over me as he calculated his next move.

"Layla, the bathroom," I rasped, repeating myself for what felt like the tenth time. "Lock yourself inside. This isn't about you."

"It *is* about me. My mates are beating the shit out of each other, and you want me to just *let you*?" Her voice rose at the end, echoing off the stone walls.

Something flickered in Novak's eyes. Recognition, maybe, but it disappeared in an instant and he lunged.

His shoulder caught me in the neck, and we rolled before colliding with the wall. Layla screamed something else, but I couldn't separate her voice from the violence.

Novak and I grappled, hands grasping for necks, wings flaring, legs entangling, our bare bodies pressing together like we were about to either fuck or kill each other.

The line was so thin between the two.

Layla's cherry blossoms assaulted me, stronger as her agitation grew higher. She danced around the periphery of our battle. I couldn't focus on her, too busy trying to keep Novak from ripping my eyes from my head.

The problem we faced wasn't just the history or the lingering mistrust from the wrongs done to both of us. The problem—the biggest problem—was the mate-bond. By bonding with Layla, I'd bound myself to Novak, too, but we'd done it before settling this shit.

A mistake.

One I would correct, if I survived.

Novak grabbed my shoulders and shoved me against the wall. I took the blow to the back of my head, blinking away dark edges in my vision as I punched him in retaliation. Novak grunted when my fist caught him in the solar plexus, and I headbutted him on the heels of the hit. He fell back to the floor, sucking in a breath as blood spurted from his upper lip.

I stood, swiping at the blood raking across my face. Novak did the same, unfolding his powerful body from the floor, his dark eyes still empty, still latched on me. His prey.

Fuck that. He'd chosen to fight a predator.

We circled one another, both of us vying for the right moment. Just the wrong angle of his step, or an opening he couldn't block.

But we were too well matched.

I waited him out, knowing that in his current state of mind, he'd cave first because he wanted blood on his hands to soothe the fury inside him.

Novak leaped, his bare foot hooking in a deadly kick for my head. I managed to avoid the strike, but not the blow from his other knee, which smashed into my torso as I lunged to the side. I swiped at his legs, catching him behind the ankles and sending him crashing to the ground. He grabbed me by the hair and dragged me down with him.

We met one another punch for punch and blow for blow, rolling wildly around the cell. My back hit the wall and my wings wrenched painfully. I repaid him by slamming his face into the floor. Time passed, but it was meaningless. I couldn't sense anything but Layla's overwhelming scent and the heat of Novak's body, and our fucked-up history like a ghost in the room.

Neither of us gained the upper hand.

Neither of us backed down.

Finally, we collapsed in a heap of feathers, both of us exhausted.

We lay side by side, staring up at the cell's stone ceiling as our chests heaved. Novak's head rested on my arm, and one of his legs draped over my thigh. As the aggression faded, my many bruises and wounds throbbed and stung.

"You're an asshole," I told him.

Novak laughed, a low, bitter sound.

He leaned up on his elbows to look down at me. The emptiness was still there in his eyes, a phantom that wasn't done with me yet.

He leaned in and I reacted quickly, my hand latching on to his throat. We eyed one another silently for a long moment, then he pressed into my palm with slow, easy pressure. I kept my fingers digging into his skin, but I let him close the distance between us.

His breath fanned over my face, and his dark gaze flared. Then he licked the blood off my mouth, taking his time cleaning my lips, teasing my tongue.

Even as my cock hardened, I didn't release his neck. I applied more pressure on my grip, cutting off his breath, taking control. We'd released our aggression by fighting.

Now, we'd fuck.

Speak our apologies to each other with our bodies, and to Layla, by screwing until we couldn't think of anything else.

The moment I thought of Layla, however, I realized her scent had faded. It was still there like it always was, a faint hint of her that seemed to seep from the walls and the bedsheets.

But faded indeed.

I released Novak, shoving him away as I sat up and glanced around. The bathroom door stood open. I leaped to my feet and checked inside.

Empty.

Fuck. I ran to the doorway of our room. *She's gone.*

CHAPTER FIVE

LAYLA

My mates had lost their damn minds.

Auric had told me to go and hide in the bathroom like some sort of little girl. But I wasn't a little girl anymore. I was a woman. And I wanted answers. Which was precisely why I'd put on my clothes and sandals and left the room.

If Novak and Auric wanted to waste time by beating the shit out of each other, fine.

Meanwhile, I'd go to the *gift* Sayir had left for me and ask my questions.

The key to Kyril's cell burned in my hand as I slipped it into his lock. I knew I shouldn't be doing this alone, but I didn't have a choice. Auric and Novak were too busy trying to kill each other. And I wasn't about to go find Raven to ask for her help. She was probably furious that Novak had told Zian we wanted to stay.

Maybe I can gather enough answers that will allow us all to leave, I thought, staring at my hand.

It'd been three days since Kyril had mentioned King Vasilios. Auric had locked him up in response, stating we would deal with him later.

It's later, I decided, turning the lock.

Clyde skittered over my feet, causing me to gape down at the mouse. Well, technically, he was a Blaze demon. He was just currently in his mouse form, which I preferred to his dragon-like one.

"Yes?" I asked him.

He squeaked.

"I don't speak mouse."

He huffed a breath in response, then pressed his nose to the door. When he didn't move, I assumed that he meant he approved and wanted to go inside.

With a shrug, I twisted the knob and found Kyril waiting patiently for me on the other side.

Clyde ran straight up to the male and crawled up his leg to his side to perch on his shoulder with a chirp that had Kyril grinning.

"I missed you, too," he murmured, then his vibrant blue eyes landed on me.

I walked fully into the cell and shut the door behind me, nervous and uncertain.

Which crown will you choose?

Sayir's words had haunted me since I'd received the message. Until I knew more or learned enough to understand what the heck was happening, I couldn't choose either. The birthright I'd known all my life—taking the crown from my father—no longer felt like a real possibility.

But the possibility that I had Noir parents right here on Earth?

I couldn't even begin to wrap my mind around it.

Coming to see Kyril seemed like the right thing to do. If anybody could help answer all my lingering questions, he could. He was the wild card, the one with hidden knowledge.

Unless he's lying.

But what else was I to do while Auric and Novak wasted their breath fighting one another on the floor of our cell? If they weren't going to take this seriously, I'd do it without them.

Men. They hadn't even seen me leave.

Oh, they'd be pissed later, but I wasn't all that pleased with them at the moment, either.

Kyril bowed low, his long blond hair almost touching the ground as Clyde clung to his shoulder. "Princess. It is an honor to be in your presence once more."

"Please, call me Layla," I said, a flush heating my cheeks. "We aren't at court. I think if there's anywhere we can speak as equals, it's in a jail cell with matching wings."

Kyril inclined his head. "I wish I could offer you a seat, milady, but…" He glanced around the room. If there had been a mattress here before, it was gone now, likely pilfered by other inmates who'd lost their beds in the explosion. Auric had at least tracked down a blanket for the poor Noir, and the male had made a sad little nest in the corner.

"The floor is fine," I assured him, motioning for him to sit first. Once he was resting on the ground, his back against the wall, I took the opposite side to leave a safe amount of space between us.

I didn't think he was dangerous, but I couldn't ever be sure of anyone's true motives. Not anymore.

Clyde darted down Kyril's shirt and curled up in the Noir's lap, turning three times before his little black eyes closed.

I raised an eyebrow. "So you know Clyde?" Seemed a bit impossible since the little mouse had found Novak in the prison long before any of us had met him. And Kyril hadn't been with us in the old prison.

Kyril smiled as he stroked a single fingertip down the mouse's back. "He bonds to those who serve the crown's goal." His bright eyes flashed up to mine, not having specified *which* crown. "So, to what do I owe the honor of this visit?"

"This is a place where honor goes to die," I warned him. Auric didn't seem to understand that, but Novak did. I tilted my head, lifting my chin as I played the role Kyril needed from me.

To him, I was a royal, and that was a role I knew well.

"Regardless, you claim to have answers, and I'm here because I need to know more." Biting my lip with thought, I picked my next words carefully so that I didn't give him false hope. "I'm not saying I believe you about King Vasilios, or whoever he is, but I'm ready to listen. Tell me more about, well, everything, I guess."

Kyril's smile widened. "I'm relieved you want to know more. I'd begun to think I'd failed in my mission to bring you home."

"You haven't won yet," I said. "Tell me about this Noir king. Where did he come from?"

"King Vasilios came from your realm," Kyril said with slow patience. His finger continued to stroke the little mouse that had begun to snore. "Your own history has been hidden from you, from all of you. It is a true tragedy, one we hope to undo."

We? I narrowed my eyes, not sure if I could buy his act, but the information was still intriguing. "So, he was once Nora before he Fell?"

"King Vasilios didn't Fall," Kyril corrected, his expression darkening. "Perhaps we should start at the beginning. Noir don't Fall, Princess. Noir are naturally dark-winged."

Naturally dark-winged?

Now I knew he was nuts.

Kyril cleared his throat. "Let's go back seven hundred

43

years ago to when Noir kind was decimated by the plague. You see—"

"Noir kind?" I repeated, confused. "Are you saying that the Nora who have Fallen claim to be a separate race? Noir is a name, a consequence of sin, isn't it?" I swallowed hard, sweeping my dark feathers out of my peripheral view. "It's a term for Nora who were once pure, who are no longer deemed worthy to live among their own kind. Nora like *me*." I squeezed my eyes shut, then opened them again.

To call the Noir a "kind" implied they—*we*—were supposed to exist. That we weren't a mistake.

"Noir kind," he said again. "The Noir are a race of angels, not a symbol of sin. He's twisted everything, Layla. The history. The reason for our black wings. It's all a lie."

"He… he being my father?" I guessed.

"Not your father, but King Sefid," he clarified.

"That's what I meant," I whispered. "King Sefid is my father."

"He's not," Kyril promised, his expression genuine. "But we'll get to that. First, you need to be told the truth about the Noir."

I swallowed, my heart beating a little heavier in my chest. "Okay," I whispered, not sure if I believed him or not. It seemed… *wrong*.

Yet, part of me… part of me hoped he was right.

It was too good to be true. A dangerous path for me to even consider. Because it could lead to me accepting what I'd become.

Accepting myself as Noir, forever.

And there would be no going back.

However, it wasn't a sin to listen, right?

"Continue," I said, ensuring he knew I was ready to hear him out.

He dipped his chin in acknowledgment, then cleared his throat. "Once upon a time, the Noir and the Nora lived side by side with a Noir as their king."

"As two separate races," I added, the words phrased as a statement but really a clarification question in my head.

"Correct. Two separate types of angels, but with a significant difference in power. You see, the Noir possess a variety of abilities and gifts that rival all others. A thousand years ago, the Noir were the elite of the elite in every way. Black wings were more enviable than white."

I huffed a humorless laugh. It all sounded like an elaborate dream manufactured by Noir who couldn't accept their predicament.

Yet I thought of Raven and her healing ability.

Of Novak and his blade-like wings.

The Nora had skills, too, but Novak's abilities surpassed them all to the point of scaring me, even as his mate. It was why the others were now bowing to him as king of this prison. Not because he requested it or demanded it, but because he'd proven his superiority during the bloodbath the other day. No one wanted to question his leadership.

"But it wasn't a true utopia," Kyril continued. "Jealousy persisted, namely among the Nora who lacked the extraordinary abilities of the Noir. Then the Stygian Plague happened. I'm guessing you've not heard of it?"

I shook my head, swallowing. "No."

"I thought not," he replied, his wings ruffling a bit at his back. "You see, the Stygian Plague was a lethal disease. It wiped out ninety percent of the Noir over a period of seven years. In the end, those who survived built an immunity to it and chose to flee to Earth for sanctuary."

"What about the Nora?" I asked, choosing to suspend my disbelief of all this for a moment and hear him out.

"The plague didn't impact them," he replied. "In fact, it's rumored that the Nora are the ones who created it."

I gaped at him. "That's impossible."

"Is it?" he countered, arching an ash-blond brow. "Regardless of who or how it was created, it severely lowered our numbers. Which is why we hide among the human population of the world. We're still superior and more powerful, but our numbers are… significantly damaged."

"Hide among the humans," I repeated. "How?"

"Magic," he replied. "We have ways to hide our wings. But that's not the point of this discussion. I want you to understand the history because you are at the heart of it all. You're the heir to the Noir throne, not the Nora throne."

"Right. Because you expect me to believe my father isn't my father." I couldn't help the cynicism in my tone.

"King Sefid isn't your father. In fact, he's rumored to be the one who created the plague."

I sputtered at that, unable to fathom a proper response. *My father? Create a plague?* I almost laughed. "He's the reason Noir are allowed to reform." Clearly, Kyril was insane, or this served as some sort of morbid way to test my faith in the Nora dynasty.

"I only tell you what has been witnessed by me and several others, including your parents. Your *real* parents," he clarified. "I believe that King Sefid was the catalyst, specifically with the goal in mind to annihilate the Noir."

"Why would my father do that?" I demanded, unwilling to even entertain that notion. My father was a good Nora. A decent father. Yes, a little obsessed with my future and wedding me to the best candidate, but that just made him a good dad, right?

"He's not your father," Kyril reminded me gently.

I fought the urge to roll my eyes. "Fine. Let's say I believe you. Why would *King Sefid* do that?" *This ought to be good.*

"You would have to ask him—"

A convenient reply, I thought.

"But I suspect it had something to do with *his* father," Kyril replied.

Okay, well, that was… unexpected. "My grandfather?"

I never knew my grandparents. My parents were already centuries old when I came along. With how long Nora lived, it was common for ancestors to disappear for periods of time and rest.

"My father told me they've been in hibernation." A clever way of saying *ancient sleep*. I never questioned it, because it made sense and fit our culture.

Kyril held my gaze. "King Sefid is the bastard child of a Noir."

"I'm sorry… *what?*" I couldn't even unpack that sentence on several different levels. The absolutely asinine idea that my father had a Noir parent… *Yeah, no. Nope.* "That's impossible."

"Noir and Nora partnerships were once not so unusual," Kyril said carefully. "The Noir were rare. Beautiful. Powerful. Renowned for their charm. They ruled for centuries before King Sefid took the throne. He's since buried all memory of their reign." His gaze darkened. "Betrayal by one's own blood. That is the worst sin of all, the irony. If any Nora should truly Fall, it's King Sefid."

"No," I said, shaking my head. I jumped to my feet and stalked toward the exit, rubbing my palms over my chilled arms. Surely hearing such things would damn me forever.

Because a deep, desperate part of me was starting to believe him.

LEXI C. FOSS & JENNIFER THORN

Which implied I was losing my mind. *Like a proper Noir.*

"I can't listen to this anymore," I said.

"King Sefid didn't appreciate being half-Noir," Kyril went on as if I hadn't spoken or leaped to my feet. "Because his powerful Noir father denied him. He grew up with his Nora mother, always despising the Noir for his father's betrayal, so he decided to betray the Noir in return."

I lowered my wings and glanced over my shoulder as Kyril's features went hard.

"That's the rumor, anyway," he said. "And the reason he supposedly manufactured the Stygian Plague. He wanted to punish that half of his heritage."

"I don't believe you," I told him, whirling around to fully face him. "How could he create a plague that only killed Noir?"

"Easily," Kyril replied with an unconcerned shrug. "Partly through his Noir talents, and partly through Sayir's assistance."

I threw my hands up in the air and started pacing, my heart pounding furiously against my ribs. "Are you going to tell me Sayir is half-Noir, too?"

"Sayir is not of the Noir bloodline. The brothers share a mother but have different fathers. Sayir was born of a Nora male. It is believed he's so enamored of technology and magic from other realms because he feels 'less than' his brother, the king."

I scoffed. "I've never heard anything like this. You said my *parents* witnessed this and can back up your claims? Who else saw it happen?"

Kyril's lips curved down, and his eyes tightened with pain. "Those who fled your realm for Earth remember everything, Princess. We were not tainted by King Sefid's altered history."

In other words, the only witnesses who could support him were rogues and Fallen Nora.

How convenient, I thought.

Yet... Raven had been born with black wings, right?

Except Sayir is her father, so how's that possible?

Maybe Raven was lied to.

But how did a child Fall?

How could a child not be reformed?

And Novak and I, had we really done anything wrong other than disobeying the king? Was that truly a sin worthy of a Fall?

Or was there more?

Gods... the Stygian Plague... another *race*. It was all too much to believe.

"Altered history," I whispered. "You're being serious. You're telling me my father changed the entire history of our race to hide the fact that the Noir once ruled? So, by your account, he not only created this plague, but he manufactured this entirely new history, too?"

I wanted to laugh. Or scream. Or just leave the room entirely.

Yet Kyril's flinch held me captive.

Every time I referenced King Sefid as my father, he winced. Like he couldn't believe I would call that man my dad.

The Noir sighed and stretched his legs out, disrupting Clyde's nap. The little mouse squeaked in protest but curled back up in the next beat, content. "You are aware King Sefid has memory-altering abilities, yes?"

"Of course I am. He's my father," I said, just to make him squirm again. "He can release unwanted or cruel memories to ease the minds of others. It's a *benevolent* gift." And proved that Nora could also maintain powers.

Unless what Kyril said was right and that ability came from his Noir half.

"A gift, yes," Kyril agreed. "Would it be impossible that this gift could be used for nefarious means? That he could wipe an entire population's memories on a larger scale? He's done it more than once."

The blond Noir cupped Clyde in his hands and stood, cuddling the sleepy mouse against his chest. He leveled his serious gaze on mine.

"I know it's hard to believe, but you came here for answers, Princess, and I don't know how much time we have. So I am giving them to you to do with as you will." He straightened, his words as sure as stone. "King Sefid's Noir traits allowed him to develop memory-altering magic. Ninety percent of the Noir were exterminated, the rest chased to Earth, and then he made it so the Nora can't remember that period of time. Nor do they remember the Noir as the royalty they once were."

My lips twisted, my heart beating a chaotic rhythm in my chest. *This has to be a trick. A game. A way to test my resolve to reform.* "Kyril, this is madness."

"Is it?" he asked softly. "Then why are your wings black, Princess?"

There was no judgment in his tone. My knees wobbled, and I sank back to the floor before I lost the ability to remain standing.

Why are my wings black? Because for all intents and purposes, they shouldn't be.

He sat back down, too, as if unwilling to allow me to be beneath him. Clyde made his irritation known with a series of clicks and chitters before he curled up on the Noir's knee.

Kyril spoke again, his tone lower, almost apologetic. "King Sefid's memory magic is potent. He could even make you forget your mates, which he might be inclined to do considering they're not ideal."

His reminder made my chest ache. Now that... that I could believe.

I swallowed an unbidden lump in my throat and blinked away hot tears before they could crest over my lashes. Avoiding his knowing gaze, I murmured, "Nothing about my situation is ideal."

The Noir inclined his head in silent agreement. Out loud, he asked, "Why did you choose those specific males?"

I blinked at him. "Why...?" I asked slowly, uncertain of his intention. I could tell by his scent that we weren't compatible. Nor was he really my type.

"Curiosity," he replied. "It's not what... I expected."

"You say that as though you know me and my desires, but we just met."

"True. But I know you better than you think because of my ties to your family line."

By that, I knew he meant the two Noir he believed to be my parents. "Not that I feel it's any of your business, but Novak and Auric are compatible with me. Thus, they're my mates." It seemed a bit of a succinct reply, but I didn't feel like elaborating.

He nodded. "Yes, but there could be others."

I shrugged. "I doubt it. I went through my entire courtship and found no one to be compatible."

"You only tested Nora," he pointed out.

I scrunched my nose. "Well, I found a Noir mate. Novak."

Kyril just hummed, saying nothing else.

I suspected he knew something I didn't, but I was too exhausted to question him. Besides, it would probably fall along the lines of everything he'd already said, which meant his feedback would border on insanity.

Because this couldn't be real.

His entire story was insane and absolutely counter to everything I'd ever been taught.

Still, there was a disturbing ring of truth in some of what the Noir had said.

Such as my father's talents to alter memories and his obsession with the Nora being the epitome of angelkind and the Noir being the worst of the worst.

But creating a plague to decimate an entire race? Could my father be so coldhearted? So callous?

So terrifyingly powerful and cruel?

Kyril seemed to have all the answers, as unbelievable as they were, but if I was going to find out the truth, I needed to see it for myself.

Maybe… maybe I can meet the ones he considers to be—

An explosion rocked the ground, and I fell against the stone wall, caught off guard by the violence of it. Across the cell, Clyde slipped off Kyril's knee from the force, and in the aftermath, the three of us stared at one another, wide-eyed.

Then growls vibrated through the mountain walls.

CHAPTER SIX

NOVAK

A SECOND QUAKE SHOOK THE MOUNTAIN. IT MEANT THE Reformer was here, that all inmates should cower in terror of his endless deadly tests.

If fear was his intention, it wasn't working. The Noir streamed out of their cells, ready to fight. They'd tasted freedom, and that made it something worth battling for, worth *dying* for. Not just for survival, but for something more.

Perhaps this was an illusion of freedom, but it was a dream I intended to keep, just like my delicate mate, who had a tendency for eliciting my thirst for blood, and for sex, all in one tidy package.

I stormed deeper into the prison and shoved my way past the inmates, ignoring the monstrous growls that emanated from outside. All I had on were pants and a pair of shoes, same with Auric.

After washing the blood off from our fight, we'd searched for Layla outside, thinking she'd gone to talk to Raven and the others.

But no.

That wasn't where she'd gone at all.

Which had left only one place for her to go.

Kyril.

If that bastard had harmed her, I would rip off his wings and hang him by his ankles until he bled out at my feet.

Fuck. Layla had put herself in a cell with him.

Alone.

While Auric and I fought.

Because I'd lost control of my anger.

Damn it!

My nostrils flared at the faint scent of cherry blossoms that went straight to my dick, enticing my current mood, a mood that didn't leave much room for patience.

I ripped the door open, and metal clanged violently against stone. Auric lingered at my back, for once wisely silent. He simmered with an echo of quiet anger, but he knew better than to try to take the lead when Layla's safety was on the line.

I'd shred anyone who even thought about harming her, and then I'd dance in the rain of their blood.

A potent wave of Layla's decadent cherry blossom scent swirled out of the small, sparse room on the sudden burst of air, serving to both calm and enrage me all at the same time.

Her posture was what kept me rooted to the spot. She sat splayed against the wall, her fingers gripping the uneven cut of stone and her brilliant sapphire eyes wide, a vision of glory with her wings of black lace draped behind her. While she appeared to be startled, a quick sweep revealed she was unharmed.

Annoyance slashed her gaze, commanding me without words.

Back down, Novak.

My gaze darted from her to Kyril, a male she had decided to place above me for the time being. He sat across the space from her, his hand resting protectively on Clyde.

Clyde? I raised an eyebrow at the little Blaze demon in his mouse form. I hadn't expected him to be here, especially not with the untrustworthy Noir's hand resting on him like a prized pet.

At least I could trust him to protect Layla.

The Blaze slipped out from beneath Kyril's palm and skittered across the floor to Layla's side, chittering at me to calm down. He'd clearly been here to watch over Layla, which I approved of. His presence calmed the worst of my anger, though it still left questions as to why he seemed so comfortable with the Noir.

The little demon had never given me a reason to doubt his motives before. That could change in the blink of an eye, of course.

"Soften your wings, Novak," Auric suggested, and I realized I'd inadvertently let my blades out as they grazed deep gouges in the stone walls.

"Hmm," I hummed as I complied, surprised that they'd come out. I had precise control over my wings, so this was a first.

Something I'd have to take note of around Layla if my restraint was weakening.

Auric shoved around me, revealing that he'd wanted me to soften my wings for *his* benefit, not Kyril's, so he could tower over Layla. Normally, I didn't approve of him being a judgmental prick, but in this case, we agreed on one thing.

Our mate had fucked up.

"What the fuck were you thinking?" Auric demanded. He spread his wings with authority, sending a wave of fury and wintergreen through the cell, his scent mingling with Layla's in a way that went straight to my groin as another violent shudder rippled through the underground, promising savagery and pain.

Mmm, violence and sex, my two favorite things.

Oh, I hoped Auric would hurry so that we could deal with the distraction outside and then drag Layla back to our cell for a proper *discussion*.

Violence first.

Sex after.

"You want to debate that now?" Layla returned, struggling to her feet. "Here? As the—" Her words died as another tremble rocked the foundation, the growling intensifying outside.

Auric curled a hand into a fist and advanced on Kyril.

I grinned.

However, before he could entertain my thirst for blood, heavy footsteps echoed through the corridor beyond the cell.

Someone barked, "What's happening?"

An answering voice shrieked, "Sayir! He found us!"

He already knew where we were, I wanted to say. Instead, I exchanged a look with Auric, one side of my lips curling pleasantly. *Ready for another fight?* Because I was dying to kill someone or something, and Sayir would do beautifully.

Auric glanced back at Layla and stabbed a finger in her face, his expression equal parts relieved and menacing. "You're not off the hook for this." His turquoise irises swiveled to Kyril and darkened to stunning gems. "Neither of you."

Passing him in three long strides, I reached Layla's side and grabbed her arm, hauling her to her feet—because I most definitely wasn't leaving her alone. Holding her hostage seemed like the only guarantee that she wouldn't slip off again.

Though I did want to tie her up in our bed and make her stay there. Naked. Safe.

From everything but me, anyway.

She weighed nothing in my hand as I pulled her toward the cell door. Another monstrous blast shook the walls around us, and I latched on to the door frame, tugging Layla against my side as I rode out the tremors. More dust filtered down from above. After we passed into the corridor, Auric grabbed the cell door, clearly intending to close it with Kyril still inside.

Not that I had any qualms about that.

"Wait!" Layla cried out. She planted her sandals on the floor and tugged against my grasp. "We can't just leave Kyril here to die." I stared at her, waiting for a reason, because I couldn't think of one. She huffed out a breath. "He's… he's important, Novak."

I shot up an eyebrow.

I was about to disagree—the young Noir wasn't our damn responsibility.

And he most definitely wasn't fucking *important*.

But then Kyril stumbled to the door, both hands up as if surrendering. "Please. I vow to protect the princess with my life."

My fingers still tight around Layla's bicep, I eyed him on the heels of another earthquake. He looked young. Too fucking fresh-faced to protect a puppy, much less a grown female.

And he had managed to elicit my murderous rage, so any pleas he had in mind were only going to convince me to slice his throat and be done with it.

But then Clyde appeared, climbing the boy's pant leg and disappearing into his pocket.

Layla stared me down, unblinking.

And Clyde had clearly made his choice evident, too.

What the fuck is even happening here? I wondered, gaping between them. Layla had called him *important*. Now I wondered in what way she'd meant that.

A series of growls accompanied by a snap of bone caught my attention, followed by screams.

Hmm, if we were lucky, maybe the Noir would get himself killed by whatever threat awaited, and we would be rid of the nuisance.

Or maybe he could prove his supposed *importance*.

Pursing my lips at the little demon's twitching nose poking above the fabric, I snarled, "Fine."

I shoved past Auric—he could keep an eye on the young Noir while I kept an eye on our mate—and then I fell into a jog toward the worst of the noise, moving as fast as I could without dragging Layla off her feet. Auric and Kyril raced along behind us as we navigated the mazelike corridors, dodging falling debris and stumbling when the ground shook under our feet.

We left behind the prison for sunshine, fresh air…

And demon wolves.

Layla gasped, a tremor passing through her beneath my palm.

Five doglike creatures stared at us from the rocky clearing, smoke and fire seeping from their nostrils.

Five creatures with fifteen heads, one of which was busy snacking on an inmate's wings, spraying a weird sort of black-colored blood all over the grass.

Now there's a challenge, I thought, my lips curling at the prospect.

Auric and I had faced this type of creature at Noir Reformatory, and *one* had been bad enough.

They were tough, but not unkillable. Just the right combination to alleviate my current mood.

I exchanged glances with Auric again. *Should be fun.*

"You're a fucking masochist," he replied, unsheathing his blade.

I prefer sadist, I thought, considering how much I was about to enjoy causing this beast pain.

"Novak!" an unfamiliar voice called across the clearing to us.

I dropped Layla's arm, shoving her behind me as the inmate approached. A group of Noir huddled expectantly behind the wild-eyed male as he fell into a low bow.

Because here, I was king.

"What do we do, sir?" the inmate asked, his head still hanging in subservience.

You don't bow and make yourself an easy target, I nearly snapped. *That's for damn sure.*

Auric snorted, probably reading the comment from my expression.

I arched a brow at the inmate, then focused on the advancing four-legged demon dogs. The snacking one was done, the creature having left no trace of gore behind. Not even a drop of blood. Which was strange, considering I'd just seen him spraying that black-like essence everywhere only minutes ago.

Oddly clean with their kills. I didn't recall the monster I'd faced with Auric being so thorough. Although, it hadn't had a chance to do much before I'd slit all three of its throats.

"Sir?" the inmate prompted.

My feathers itched, the stems attempting to harden into those unbreakable, deadly weapons.

If I was losing control of them, perhaps it was because I had too much pent-up rage. Years of celibacy having taken its toll, especially now when I had finally tasted the violence and sex I had long denied myself.

Time to remedy that.

I stared at the inmate, my fingers itching for carnage, then swung my attention to Auric. "You're better at providing orders, Commander," I said, ducking out from our little group and letting my razor-tipped feathers out to play. I hadn't been afforded the opportunity last time, our closed quarters making sharp wings dangerous.

But outside?

Yeah, outside was fair game.

Auric will guard our mate.

Stretching my wings wide, I sailed toward the first monster, baring my teeth gleefully. I'd never complain about having a reason to cut portal monsters into shreds. I'd mow down as many as I could with my lethal blades, and Auric would lead the inmates into battle to take care of whatever was left.

Once in the air, I could see what was causing the whole mountain to shake—the beasts in the back row had turned themselves into battering rams and were beating their bodies against the prison's external wall. Debris pebbled down from large cracks, but they hadn't breached the building.

Not yet, anyway.

Dropping into a free fall, I aimed for the first demon dog, nearly giddy to face a true challenge. His dark fur seemed to swallow all the light around him as if he were made of nothing but smoke and shadows. As I neared, he snapped his massive jaws, his teeth trailing slobber. I artfully ducked his attack, then barrel-rolled past him, swiping out with my razor wings.

Slice.

The satisfying sensation as my trailing wing swept through the beast's meaty neck should have rewarded me with a shower of golden blood.

None came.

Frowning, I studied his remaining two snarling heads and noted the humming electric collars I recognized from back at Noir Reformatory. The beasts continued to beat against the wall, ignoring my presence. Only an external command could override their survival instincts like that. The collars were part of the tech that Sayir used to control the beasts. Each head had its own metal circlet, and as I sailed past, I could taste the tang of ozone on my tongue.

Was it the Reformer controlling these things? Was he nearby? I salivated at the thought. I'd kill him slowly, unlike his pets, and catalog his screams.

Shouts rose up beneath me as the inmates joined the fight.

I ignored them and executed an easy flip, decapitating a second head. I confirmed that these beasts didn't ooze golden blood like the demon dog back at Noir—the head fell heavily to the ground as ash poured from the wounded neck instead.

Strange.

Whatever alterations Sayir had done to these beasts killed my mood. I wanted blood, not ash.

A pity.

I would have to make quick work of them and satiate my violence another way.

Before I could take care of the last head, a second demon wolf roared and broke the creature's trance, causing its beady black eyes to latch on to me.

The final head lunged.

I ducked the thing's teeth but was caught off guard when another snout sent a stream of fire my way. I pulled my wings in and fell, narrowly avoiding the blaze. Heat singed my face, but I ignored it and regained control of my fall before I launched toward the monster's neck. Another slice, and his head flopped to the rocks below.

Swiveling in midair, I glanced back at the first beast—

the one I hadn't yet finished off—only to find the head I'd removed from its body was growing back.

Fuck.

These aren't like the demon dogs back at the reformatory.

Though, I guessed it shouldn't have surprised me that Sayir had made a few modifications after Auric and I had so easily defeated the last one.

I pivoted away from the beasts as they stampeded past me. I scouted the terrain for Auric to warn him and to confirm he'd kept Layla safe.

Too late.

The remaining demon dogs had already cut a swath through the fighting inmates, leaving ashy blood and a trail of bodies in their wake. Half of the beasts were already regrowing heads and limbs, while two more ruthlessly fought against Auric and a group of still-standing inmates. Zian, Sorin, and Raven had shown up as well, showing off their honed skills.

It wasn't enough.

My cousin learned just as I did why decapitation wasn't an option anymore as a head grew back, only for the regrown nub to spit fire at him. Zian lurched out of the way in time, but his gaze met mine, hard and defiant.

What now? he asked with his eyes.

What now indeed.

I caught sight of Layla several feet away, staying out of trouble for the moment, but with these things, that wouldn't last long. Kyril hunched behind her, his gaze on the ground like a fucking coward. A demon dog stalked forward, smoke trailing from its snout with its coal-like eyes locked on them.

Growling under my breath, I pulled my wings in and dove to save my mate, since the useless-piece-of-shit Noir wasn't about to do anything.

"Protect her with my life," my ass. He wasn't important at all. He was just fucking useless.

A demon dog approached Layla, making my blood run cold when she froze.

That wasn't the Layla I knew. She'd faced worse and known when to run from a fight meant for me. Instead, she stood her ground, but her face didn't hold an expression of fear.

Instead, she set her jaw, determined, and shouted a command as she pointed at the beast.

Clyde wound around her leg in his dragon-like Blaze form, obeying whatever she'd just said.

While I appreciated Clyde, he was a minor demon, one who worked through manipulation and shadows for a reason.

I burst my wings with speed, but I knew I wouldn't be fast enough.

"Auric!" I shouted, catching the Nora's attention. Perhaps he could get to her in time.

Auric reacted, but neither of us was fast enough. The beast closed in, his salivating set of maws descending on my mate.

The ground trembled, and shadows lingered on the periphery of my vision, but whatever beast lived inside of me wouldn't come out.

Not yet.

Clyde breathed fire at the creature, and the beast roared in pain. The flames licked over its fur, engulfing its own smoldering stench with a wave of red-hot embers until it burned to a crisp, sending heavy black smoke and ash into the air.

Well, it seemed that sometimes fighting fire with fire worked.

And Layla had figured that out.

I landed just as Kyril stood. He brandished a blade he must have snatched from a fallen Noir, but he didn't point it at me. Flames spurted down the sword from the Noir's fingers, coating the metal. Then he swung the sword and set another creature on fire.

It exploded into flame and ash, then collapsed next to its fallen comrade.

I narrowed my eyes at him.

All right, you get to live. For now.

Following suit, I plucked a dry branch from the forest floor and held it out to Clyde. He breathed flame on my makeshift weapon, setting the bark on fire. Then I strode into the fray and joined the party.

Violence first, I reminded myself, glancing at Layla as she took down another beast.

I grinned.

Sex after.

CHAPTER SEVEN

LAYLA

THE LAST OF THE DEMONIC, THREE-HEADED BEASTS dissolved to silvery ash at my feet, its thick smoke adding to the somewhat mouthwatering scent of fried meat. Not the kind of meal any of us should attempt to eat. Gods only knew what kind of poison Sayir had imbued them with to make them so indestructible.

I tossed my stick on the ground and stomped on the remnants of Clyde's fire to put it out. The charred wood broke apart under my sandal and painted the bare, rocky ground black. All around me, the rest of the inmates followed suit—as if following my lead.

Novak was their king.

So did that make me their queen?

Auric broke through the dusty mist like a specter, his angelic blond hair coated in ash. It gave him an otherworldly look, the soot on his skin contrasting against the sharp turquoise of his eyes, making his gaze piercing.

He sheathed his blade, then placed his hands on my shoulders as he raked his gaze over me.

"Are you injured?" he asked. His fingers slid down my arms, then he gripped my waist and turned me when I didn't respond, my brain too transfixed by his violence and beauty to comply with the question.

"Stop," I choked out, tugging from his grasp.

His overly pushy worry simultaneously warmed my heart and annoyed the crap out of me. Of course I was fine. I knew how to defend myself. I hadn't grabbed a broken stick off the ground and offered it to Clyde for his fire because I'd felt left out.

Clyde was the solution here, and I'd been the first one to see it. He was a demon, and these creatures had been altered from their original genetic makeup—proven when I'd noted ash instead of blood after Novak's first beautifully violent attack.

The creatures breathed fire, but ash suggested that they could burn. I'd acted on a hunch.

And I'd been right.

They weren't demons in the sense that the Blaze was a demon, not after whatever Sayir had done to them. There was something to respect when it came to purity and genuine heritage. Something I found ironic given my current predicament.

What was genuine for me? What heritage did I really come from? Because if I followed the lie, I would be no better than these chained beasts, only to be slain by the fires of the truth.

Novak joined us, stretching his deadly black wings, the edges glinting before they softened.

The effect of his ability unnerved me. I'd had his feathers against my palms… against delicate skin without considering the deadly game I'd been playing.

His eyes glittered with violent promise, telling me that he quite enjoyed deadly games. As I was his mate, perhaps that madness extended to me, too.

"You're sure you're not injured?" Auric pressed, cupping my face in his hands, dragging my focus back to him. Novak stepped closer to me to join in the quiet inspection of my body.

Nothing was wrong with me except for the thick layer of soot and ash covering me from head to toe, just like everyone else in the clearing as they closed in on us.

"Would you stop?" I batted Auric's hands away, my cheeks flaming as I melted beneath his concern. "I'm *fine*. I could just use some new clothes." To punctuate my statement, I patted my hands over my frilly top, sending tiny plumes of ash into the air.

Across from our little group, Raven scoffed. "Typical princess."

"Yes," I snapped, shooting the female my best glare. "I am a princess. And you're technically a royal, too. *Cousin*."

Of course, that followed the assumption that my father was actually King Sefid. Kyril had done a great job spreading doubt all over that theory.

But that was neither here nor there.

Fortunately, the reminder of our heritage—whether right or wrong—shut Raven up. I didn't know what her problem was with me, beyond the fact that I was the Nora princess, but it was really starting to grate on my nerves. We had bigger things to worry about than her pettiness.

Leaving her to continue her silent simmering, I instinctively checked over everyone in our group—my mates and Zian, Sorin, and Kyril. Clyde poked his nose out of Kyril's pocket, telling me the little demon had changed back into mouse form.

Beyond our little team, the rest of the surviving inmates had drawn closer, still carrying the weapons they'd tried to use against the demon dogs.

"Is everyone all right?" I asked, raising my voice to include the inmates I didn't know. The forest floor was oddly free of blood, but perhaps it had already soaked into the soil. Still, I didn't spot any bodies, either, and I would have liked to bury any who were lost.

Perhaps it was ridiculous for me to care about the Noir, but the majority of the prisoners who'd remained behind weren't any of the men who'd tried to kill Auric. In a way, I felt like they needed protecting. And they definitely wanted leadership, considering how they were so quick to look to Novak, and then Auric, for guidance during the attack.

And after Kyril's comments, well, I was a bit conflicted. If the Noir were an actual race and not a perversion of the Nora, then everything I'd ever believed was wrong.

And they were possibly my people. My… my subjects?

As if life couldn't get any stranger.

"Three casualties," a gray-haired Noir replied to my earlier question, his voice tired. "Multiple minor injuries."

"Thank you, uh, what's your name?" I asked.

He bowed, his gray curls bouncing with the movement. "Grahame, Your Highness."

"What about first aid, Grahame?"

The Noir righted himself. "We sent a couple of men to look for supplies."

Auric rested a hand on the Noir's shoulder and pointed toward the mountainside prison. "Take a team back inside and set up a recon area for treatment. You"—Auric snapped his fingers at another younger Noir—"grab a few friends and start digging. We need to bury the bodies." He glanced at the clearing, his brow furrowing as he realized what I'd already noticed. "Assuming they haven't all been eaten."

The inmates nodded fervently and rushed to follow Auric's orders.

Novak looked pointedly at Auric, and the Nora warrior sighed, tossing his blond locks off his forehead. "Don't get used to this. I'm not in charge here."

Novak's expression seemed to say, *I beg to differ.*

I couldn't disagree. I'd seen Auric take charge before, back at the palace when he'd been my guard. But since we'd been at Noir Reformatory, he'd seemed like half of his usual self. Concerned only with my protection rather than leading the charge.

Now he was back in his element.

Zian moved closer to the three of us, crossed his arms over his chest, and glared at his cousin. "Now can we leave? We clearly aren't safe here."

Novak just grunted. The family resemblance between them was obvious. Both men had dark hair and chiseled features. But Zian's eyes were a near-black color, while Novak's were ice blue. And Zian was a hair shorter and more athletic in build compared to Novak's tall, sleek, and muscular form.

Though Zian was beautiful in his own right, he couldn't hold a candle to Novak.

Of course, I could be a little biased, I thought, trailing my fingertips over Novak's hand. An innocent touch, but when his pale eyes met mine, they carried more than a little heat.

Based on the spark in his eyes, he still had a score to settle with me, one I wasn't sure I would enjoy.

But oh, it would be sensual torment, to be sure.

Auric spoke up, ignoring Zian's comment. "We need to better fortify the prison, as well as find Sayir's surveillance. That fucker's watching us. We need to find out how and shut him down."

I agreed.

However, it wasn't just about the surveillance.

"This was all another test, or a culling, or whatever you want to call it," I decided out loud. Novak watched me, his interest piqued. I swallowed as I held his gaze. "Those

69

beasts had collars on them." Which meant they'd belonged to Sayir.

"We faced one before," Auric remarked, his blue-green gaze glimmering with heat. "These were worse."

Novak made a small sound of agreement. The two of them shared a look, seemingly communicating in silence.

Auric frowned, then looked up. "He would have wanted to watch the fight, so the surveillance device must be close."

I followed his gaze, only seeing a pale blue sky past the canopy of trees. "How do we find it?"

The Nora looked at Sorin. "You used to be fond of technology, Sorin. Think you could handle finding Sayir's tech before he sends us another present?"

Sorin didn't respond for a beat, his expression unreadable. "Yeah," he said slowly. "Yeah, I can handle it." His voice held a note I didn't quite grasp—something akin to irritation or violence. A hint of anarchy, perhaps. Like he didn't approve but also knew he was the right man for the job.

Maybe it was because of Auric's former position.

Or perhaps he was pissed that Novak had told them we weren't ready to leave yet.

Unbothered by Sorin's blatant disrespect, Auric pinned Zian with an authoritative look. "You're going to work with me on fortifications. Find a way to keep us safe from another attack. Those beasts were trying to get inside, so we have to make sure future attacks don't succeed."

For a moment, it appeared as though the Noir was going to refuse, similar to Sorin, but he seemed to think better of it. "Sure. I'll handle that," Zian said, only a little sarcastically. "*Alone* is fine."

Auric snorted. "If not with me, then Novak."

My other mate just looked at him, his gaze saying, *Oh?*

"He's your cousin," Auric drawled, waving at the troublesome Noir with a gesture that said, *You deal with him*.

Novak's lips twitched in response, then he grabbed Zian by the arm and steered him away from the crowd in a manner that suggested he wasn't just going to deal with his cousin, but teach him a lesson in respect.

Raven cocked a sardonic eyebrow and planted her hands on her hips. "And what would you like the princess to do, Your Majesty?"

"I'll be helping to distribute the remaining rations of food," I told her before Auric could reply. "To make sure everything is equal."

Raven narrowed her gaze. "Because I can trust you with that."

"Then you can help her," Auric offered. "And afterward, you and I are having a long chat," he informed me, his tone implying that it wouldn't be a good chat, either.

Ugh. "I didn't do anything wrong."

"A conversation we'll be debating as soon as we're done here," Auric countered before issuing additional commands to the other inmates.

Grumbling to myself, I left him to his leadership role.

On my way back, I heard Raven mutter, "The hierarchy leaves a lot to be desired."

To which Kyril replied, "You have no idea what the hierarchy is here."

I left them to their conversation, heading straight for the food pantry deep inside to begin my task of dividing portions and handing out meals as the inmates began to return.

I snacked a little as well, the hours passing quickly. As the last of the inmates came through, I set aside some meager food portions for my mates. But when they finally arrived, it was with a look that told me they weren't in the mood for food at all.

No.

They were in another mood entirely.

I swallowed, uneasy.

Auric gestured with his head, telling me without words that it was time to go.

Hi to you, too, I thought numbly. I'd had most of the afternoon to think about what I'd done, how I'd run off without a word. And while I didn't regret it, I understood why it upset them.

However, I was upset, too.

They'd gone all brutal male on me and had tried to essentially put me in time-out.

"You both—"

"Not here," Auric interjected, already countering my argument.

I sighed. "Fine."

Novak and Auric latched on to my arms when I attempted to move between them and through the doorway, their grips unyielding. Then they proceeded to lead me back to our room with a charged silence that suggested I was about to atone for my sins. Whether I liked it or not.

Inside the cell, they released me, and Auric very pointedly turned the lock.

Imprisoning me inside.

Both males faced me, looming like menacing powers of light and dark.

I'm in trouble.

Two angry mates. Turned on by violence.

And I'm about to be their outlet.

CHAPTER EIGHT

AURIC

CHERRY BLOSSOMS FILLED THE ROOM, A PHYSICAL manifestation of Layla's distress.

My nostrils flared, reminding me that Novak had recently broken my nose. Fortunately, my genetics allowed me to heal quickly.

It almost felt as though my round with Novak in the cell earlier had been a warm-up for the beasts outside.

We'd beat the shit out of each other but hadn't broken anything.

Which meant we'd been holding back more than either of us would ever admit out loud, thus implying Novak hadn't been as gone as I'd feared.

Oh, but he'd certainly been pissed.

And now he was angry for another reason entirely.

We stood shoulder to shoulder, blocking our little mate's only exit. Funny how often we formed a unified front now, though I guessed that was natural when we shared a female who didn't know how to listen.

Bathroom and *Kyril's cell* were very different locations.

She knew it, too.

Because the truth of Layla's situation showed plainly on her beautiful face. In the wrinkle between her brows. The hard set of her jaw. Her sapphire gaze darted behind us as if calculating whether or not she could reach the door before I threw her over my knee and smacked her ass.

She knew she was in trouble. While it worried her, it also pissed her off.

And excited her.

Beside me, Novak drew in a deep breath, scenting the water for blood. His lips curled with danger.

He smelled her lust, too.

And based on the way his muscles coiled, he hadn't received the satisfaction he'd needed from the fight, likely because of the lack of blood.

So he'd take his pound of flesh now.

A worrying mood, one I often protected Layla from. But in this case, I considered letting her taste the sharp edge of consequence.

She threw her shoulders back and tilted her chin up, staring at us defiantly. "I'm sorry I went to talk to Kyril alone," she said, the words rushing out of her with an edge to them. An apology surprised me, until she followed it up with a justification. "But I didn't do anything wrong."

Oh, Princess. You haven't even been punished yet.

The balance of her defiance with her unease felt like a drug. My cock strained against my pants, tempting me to speak with my body instead of with words. I had to fight the urge to toss her onto the bed and fuck her raw, because that wasn't going to teach her a lesson.

And Novak's gaze had turned dark, his ice melting to molten rocks.

No, she wouldn't be playing with us today.

We remained silent, staring her down as I made my decision.

"You guys were busy," she added with a shrug, clearly uncomfortable with the foreboding silence. "Busy doing whatever you were doing, so I did what I did. I just… I had so many *questions*. And neither of you was any damn help."

I took a single step forward, gazing down at her. "We aren't mad that you went to see Kyril."

Novak hummed under his breath, disagreeing with me.

"Fine," I amended, rolling my eyes. "We're partly mad that you went to see Kyril. Only because we would have preferred to be there to hear what he had to say and decide the truth of it."

Layla tossed her arms in the air. "Do you think I'm not capable of deciding what's true?"

"No. I think you're in a prison where Sayir has proved we still aren't safe," I said, keeping my voice low and even. "And you made the crass decision to leave the room unprotected. It was a foolish move, Princess."

She bristled, her fingers clenching and unclenching as her gaze darted between the two of us. "You two were busy trying to kill each other, Auric. If anything, my leaving was a *safe* choice."

"No, it was a naïve choice," I corrected.

She huffed out a breath, her blue eyes turning to liquid. "Stop treating me like a child. I'm a grown woman. And I can take care of myself."

"Oh?" I glanced at Novak. "She can take care of herself, hmm? You hear that?"

Novak grunted. "Yeah, I heard it."

Layla growled. "Stop. Treating. Me. Like. A. Child." She repeated the phrase, enunciating each word through her teeth.

"Sweet Lay, we definitely do not see you as a child," I told her.

"Definitely don't," Novak echoed.

She bristled. "Come on. I'm fine. Everyone's fine. There's no need for this."

"There is every need for this," I argued. "You *left*."

"And *I'm fine*," she countered, folding her arms and drawing my gaze to her breasts. "As I said, I can take care of myself."

"Hmm, that's twice," I murmured, considering her. "Perhaps we need her to prove it?"

Novak's icy gaze narrowed, his expression telling me he agreed even though he didn't speak or nod.

"She also needs new clothes," I added, glancing over her outfit. "We should help her with that."

"Hmm," Novak hummed, stepping forward to grab her shirt.

She glanced down, her arms falling to her sides. "Novak…"

A yank ripped the gauzy fabric down the middle, but he didn't let it drop to the floor. Instead, he pulled the top from her skin and gestured with his chin toward the bed. "Up you go."

She didn't comply, instead choosing to place her hands on her hips and glare at us.

It was a beautiful display of rage and sex, which suited our mood nicely.

"No," she replied.

Novak smiled, stepping forward to wrap his palm around the back of her neck. "Yes," he countered, bending to kiss her as he reached out to me with his opposite hand. I took the shirt from him, aware of his intention.

Layla had said she could take care of herself.

We'd see if she'd meant it.

Just not in the way she'd probably anticipated.

He grabbed her hip, his opposite hand still curled around her nape as he began to walk her backward to the bed.

Her protest turned into a moan as he deepened the

kiss, his tongue whispering dark intents into her unsuspecting mouth.

Goose bumps pebbled down her slender arms, her scent sweetening with arousal.

I finished ripping her top while Novak slid his fingers to the button of her little shorts. She was so lost to his kiss that she didn't even notice him expertly maneuvering her onto the bed. Or perhaps she knew exactly what he was doing and just didn't care.

He pushed the fabric off her hips, his knee on the mattress as he hoisted her into the middle of the bed.

Then he tugged her shorts down her shapely legs and tossed them to me. I caught them with ease, ripping them down the center to create more ropes of fabric.

Novak bent to kiss her aroused center, his tongue licking along her seam and drawing her into a state of contentment as I set the fabric down beside her on the bed.

Then I focused on her ankles, undoing her sandals and letting them drop to the floor.

Novak's gaze met mine, the wickedness in his depths calling to my soul.

Layla threaded her fingers through his hair, guiding his mouth back to her wetness.

He obliged, but not before telling me with a look what he wanted to happen next. Of course, I didn't need his guidance. We were on the same page before this even began.

Layla's cheeks flushed as Novak nibbled her clit, her beautiful lips parting on a sound that went straight to my cock. Mmm, it made me want to fuck her mouth.

But that wouldn't teach our little mate a lesson at all.

No, our sweet princess needed to understand why we operated as a unit. Why what she did was wrong. Why she needed to trust us to protect her, to care for her, to be there for her.

I'd told her to go into the bathroom for her own safety.

Instead, she'd chosen to wander out into the prison without us.

She knew damn well how dangerous that was.

Worse, she'd gone to an unknown Noir—a male we all knew had been planted here by Sayir.

It was a naïve choice on her part, one that could have ended badly for her. Yes, she was fine now. But what if she hadn't been fine at all?

That was precisely the problem.

And what we needed her to acknowledge.

I caught her wrist on the bed and tugged it up over her head. Then I captured her hand in Novak's hair and brought it up to meet the opposite one in the pillows.

Bending, I distracted her with a kiss while locking both hands together beneath one of my own.

She whimpered, her need a palpable caress in the air. But we couldn't all have what we wanted, something Novak demonstrated by lifting his head away from her delectable cunt and grabbing the makeshift ropes on the bed.

Layla looked up at me beneath drowsy eyes, her cheeks a darker red now. I wrapped one hand around her throat as I released her wrists to Novak. Then I kissed her deeply, telling her with my mouth that she'd disappointed me. That I didn't appreciate her defying us. That I wasn't pleased with her choice.

You're ours to protect, I told her with my tongue. *Ours to cherish. And you acted recklessly.*

"Auric," she whispered.

"No, Lay," I replied, nipping her lower lip. "You said you could take care of yourself, remember?"

I skimmed my nose along her cheek as Novak finished securing her hands above her head. He'd tied the makeshift rope to a bar embedded in the wall near the top of the mattress, ensuring she couldn't escape.

"So you can take care of yourself while Novak and I take care of each other," I said against her ear, my knee sliding between her thighs to pin one leg to the mattress.

Novak matched my position on her opposite thigh, placing us both over her on the bed, our hips touching as we stared down at her.

"You can't…" She trailed off on a breath as Novak bent to tuck a piece of her shirt into her mouth, gagging her. She mumbled something unintelligible, making me smile.

"Hmm, now where were we?" I asked, focusing on Novak. "I think you were about to let me taste Layla on your tongue."

Novak canted his head, his dark hair falling into his icy eyes. He didn't negate the claim, merely leaned into me and pressed his lips to mine.

I opened for him on a groan, loving the burst of cherry blossoms that stroked my senses to life.

Fuck.

I fisted his hair, deepening the kiss with a violent tug against his strands and tilting his head the way I desired.

He didn't fight me, simply palmed me through my pants and squeezed.

It hurt in the best way, his grip one I always craved even through my hatred. I was instantly hard for him, and for Layla, our morning fight taking on the role of foreplay and stoking the need inside me to a cataclysmic state.

Our little mate growled, her frustration at being bound and gagged heightening the moment to a near-boiling point.

Then Novak flicked the button on my pants, killing the last vestiges of my restraint.

I cupped Layla's sex, feeling her dampness against my palm as my grip slid from Novak's hair to his nape. "I need your mouth."

He bit my lip in response, the sting telling me he'd drawn blood. Which was precisely what he needed, something he proved by licking the wound as he unzipped my pants.

There were no undergarments.

Just jeans and boots, both of which I kicked off before kneeling on the bed once more, this time between Layla's legs, but sideways. She squirmed in response, my thigh only inches from her core, and she closed her legs around my own.

"Mmm, no friction for you," I noted, gazing down at her weeping sex. "That's okay, though, right? You'll take care of yourself."

She growled, squirming more, but Novak caught one of her legs and pressed it back down to the bed while I hooked the opposite one beneath my calves.

Her expression changed from violence to severe arousal, telling me the restraint was turning her on more than pissing her off. And that was all I needed for this sensual game to continue.

So I looked at Novak, watching as he disrobed to reveal all that lethal muscle and grace. He bent to nibble on Layla's soaked pussy again, coating his tongue with her essence before bringing his mouth to my cock and ensuring I felt all that delicious honey against my own shaft.

Fuck, it was hot.

Layla's legs tensed, her scent blossoming around us in a burst of approval. I shifted my focus from Novak's head to her, meeting her smoldering gaze and noting the stark desire in the depths of her eyes.

"Come on, baby," I said, sliding deeper into Novak's mouth. "Take care of yourself."

Her gaze narrowed as I forced Novak to take me even deeper, his throat well trained and too fucking good. He grabbed my balls, giving them a not-so-gentle squeeze.

Then he took over the pace with his teeth and tongue, driving me to the edge faster than anyone should be capable of doing.

"Fuck, Novak," I groaned, my sense of control slipping again as he forced me to give him my focus.

Twin pairs of icy orbs glared up at me, the violence in his expression driving me closer to the brink of insanity.

He squeezed again, this time harder as he drew his teeth along the underside of my shaft.

Another curse left my lips, my abdomen flexing and burning with intense need. "You'd better fucking swallow," I told him, thrusting forward as he sucked the head deep into his throat.

Layla's slick heat spasmed beneath my hand, her desire a temptation I couldn't deny. I slid my finger through her folds, then slid inside her. The pressure of her tight channel coupled with Novak's skilled mouth stole my ability to think, driving me to a mindless sensation of heat and need.

Then Novak's growl sent me over the edge, his throat a vibration I couldn't ignore.

He seized all my control, my ability to lead, and forced me to follow him for once, taking charge with a sweep of his talented tongue and swallowing everything I gave him.

It hurt in the best way, my body strung tight, my muscles spasming, my heart beating rapidly in my chest.

I was panting. Groaning. *Snarling.*

Because Novak had pushed me into oblivion before I was ready to capitulate to the passion mounting between us.

My fingers tightened in his hair, my opposite hand drenched by Layla's desire and giving me an idea.

An idea I executed in the next breath as I yanked Novak's mouth off of me and shifted until we were both between Layla's legs with him in front of me and facing the beautiful display between her thighs.

"I'm going to make you come all over her cunt," I told him as I went to my knees behind him and pressed my chest to his winged back.

Then I reached around to grab his dick with my wet palm, eliciting a guttural groan from him.

"Feel that?" I asked against his ear, my opposite hand going to his throat. "That's how she feels about you sucking me off. Now let's make her wetter."

He reached backward to grab my hip, holding me up against his ass as I began to stroke him. His opposite hand went to the one I had around his throat and squeezed, telling me to grasp him tighter. The fucking masochist wanted me to hurt him. So I tightened my grip on both his throat and his shaft, which resulted in him throbbing against my palm.

I nibbled on his earlobe while meeting Layla's hot stare.

She looked ready to combust, her cheeks red, her nipples hard points, and her pussy glistening temptingly. I leaned Novak forward to angle his cock toward her slick heat and smiled when her nostrils flared.

"I think she wants you inside her, Novak," I whispered, smiling as her gaze slid from mine to his. "Does that mean she doesn't want to take care of herself?"

He thrust into my hand, his fingers biting into my hip. I

could tell he was close, not because of my ministrations but because of the hungry way Layla watched us. It was such a fucking turn-on, so much so that I was already growing hard again.

A tear slid from Layla's eye, her sensual torment reaching a peak.

Oh, it would be so easy.

All we'd need to do was lean down and massage that little nub. One flick and she'd fly into an orgasmic bliss. Mmm, but she hadn't earned it.

She'd acted without thought.

And she wasn't apologetic about it.

But she would be sorry when we finished.

Very, very sorry.

"I want you to come all over her," I told Novak, squeezing his base and sweeping upward to stroke the sensitive part beneath the head. Layla's gaze dropped to my hand, noting the way I handled Novak, seeing him jump and quiver and groan as I coaxed his orgasm much like he'd done to me with his mouth.

We knew each other well, had spent many decades learning what drove the other one mad.

And it was nice to see that, after all these years, his body still caved to my every whim, just as mine did to his.

His thumb dug into my hip, touching a nerve and telling me he was about to come. I tightened my grasp around his throat, closing off his ability to breathe as I gave him one final harsh stroke. He came apart in my hands, his violence and carnal proclivities pouring over me in a searing blast of heat and *need*.

Shit. I wanted to come again, to slide into his back hole and fuck him while he drove into Layla.

But that would only give her what she wanted.

Not today, I decided. *Not... today...*

I gritted my teeth, the darkness threatening to overwhelm me as Novak came all over Layla's sweet arousal, joining their scents in an intoxicating blend that overtook everything else in the room.

I sank my teeth into his shoulder, needing an outlet for the madness mounting within me. He clawed at my hand, ripping it from his throat to steal a breath. Then he brought his hand slowly up to my head and held me to his shoulder, encouraging me to bite him harder.

So I did, tasting the metallic tang of his blood on my tongue.

Then I ripped my mouth away from him and kissed him deeply, sealing the unspoken bond between us, telling him with my lips that I would never doubt him again.

Only, he didn't repay the favor.

He merely kissed me back as I lazily stroked his cock, drawing out the rest of his pleasure and allowing it to spill onto Layla's mound.

When we finished, we shared a long look, one filled with promises and distrust. This wound between us would take time to mend, but the slight dip of his head told me we were working toward a resolution. We just weren't there yet.

And I couldn't blame him for his caution.

Just as I knew he wouldn't blame me for mine.

Except… I felt his truth deep down. I sensed the goodness rooted deep within his soul. He might be a Noir, but he hadn't Fallen for nefarious reasons.

It had me questioning everything we'd ever been told about the Noir. Which was only made more powerful as I looked down at Layla and her pretty black feathers, sprawled out on the mattress.

She was an angel. A beauty. A sweet, tender soul.

Living proof that everything I knew was a lie.

I released Novak, urging him to move to the side. He did, his fingers trailing up Layla's sternum to trace a circle around her aroused breasts while I leaned down to lick his essence off of her. She moaned, the sound stifled by the fabric between her lips.

That moan turned to a groan as I avoided her clit, my tongue tracing every other part of her as I cleaned Novak's cum from her skin. When I finished, I sat back on my heels, as did Novak, then I canted my head at her. "Well, Princess?" I prompted. "Take care of yourself."

Her eyebrows shot up, understanding finally dawning in those beautiful features of hers and quickly turning to anger.

"What? You don't like being left out?" I asked, feigning surprise. "Interesting." I glanced at Novak. "How did you feel when you found out our Layla had run off to another prisoner's room without us? And not just any prisoner, but the one Sayir admitted was a gift and part of his game?"

"Angry," Novak replied. "Betrayed."

I nodded. "Yes. Me, too. I imagine it's similar to how Layla's feeling right now, hmm?"

"Not nearly as angry or scared," Novak said.

"True," I agreed, reaching down to remove the fabric from her mouth. "Perhaps next time you'll think twice about running off on your own, hmm?"

"Are you kidding me?" Her blue gaze swirled with embers, her ire painting a delicious shade of red over her already pink cheeks. "You're… you're really going to…?"

"Going to what?" I prompted. "Leave you without pleasure?"

Her gaze narrowed. "Yes."

"Pleasure is earned," I told her. "It requires trust."

"And loyalty," Novak added, glancing at me before focusing on her.

"You can take care of yourself until you learn what all that means," I said as Novak deftly untied her wrists. "Now why don't you go take a shower and cool off? Maybe it'll help."

She sputtered in response.

So Novak picked her up from the bed and carried her to the bathroom. "You heard him, sweet cherry. Take care of yourself. In the interim, we'll keep the bed warm." He set her inside, closed the door, and returned to the bed.

I'd thought he'd meant that as a taunt, but as he pushed me to my back and pressed his lips to mine, I realized he'd meant the bed-warming part literally.

Considering I was still fucking hard—probably because I really wanted to fuck Layla—I didn't mind indulging him in another round.

And I told him that as I kissed him back.

Long, hard, wet, and violent.

I bit his tongue.

He bit me back.

And round two officially began.

CHAPTER NINE

LAYLA

EVERGREEN AND LEATHER WRAPPED AROUND ME, CHOKING me like a noose. My body screamed with a need that hadn't been sated, only further angered after my attempts to find reprieve. The lukewarm shower and a self-induced orgasm had only made matters worse.

I hissed a breath through my teeth as I cinched the towel around my body, ignoring the painful stroke of fabric over my taut nipples.

"Damn them," I muttered as I shoved my way through the door.

Heat caressed my cheeks as I glared at the two males responsible for my misery. Novak and Auric lounged on the bed, naked and stretched out like they didn't have a care in the world. By the matching smirks on their faces, they knew what I'd done in the shower, and they also knew it hadn't been enough.

Just as I'd been fully aware of how they'd kept the bed warm. However, their half-mast erections said it hadn't been enough for them, either.

Nothing but *us* would ever be enough.

Yet their expressions told me they planned to continue my "punishment" despite their obvious dissatisfaction.

LEXI C. FOSS & JENNIFER THORN

Which meant they were technically punishing themselves, too.

However, it certainly felt like I was receiving the harsher side of the deal here.

Because even the way they posed on the bed seemed purposeful—Novak with his long, lean body stretched out, his hands clasped behind his head to display his corded muscles. Auric sitting up against the wall, one knee bent up for the best view of his thick, muscular thighs.

And both of them semi-erect, despite their earlier climaxes.

Damn it. Lust swirled in my belly and pooled between my thighs.

They'd left an empty space between them, and Auric patted the blankets, his snarky little smile widening ever so slightly. "Saved you a spot, Princess."

I tugged my towel tighter and glared at him. "You can both sleep on the floor."

The two of them exchanged glances and laughed. So at ease with themselves. With each other. With tormenting me by looking good enough to eat.

"Fine," I snapped, crossing my arms over my aching breasts. "I'll just sleep somewhere else. There has to be an empty bed somewhere."

They stopped laughing immediately, both of them daring me to try with just a look.

Have you learned nothing from this little lesson? Novak's eyes seemed to say.

I briefly considered actually leaving the cell just to make a point but thought better of it. They'd already turned me into a muddled mess of unrequited need for leaving the cell unaccompanied once. Gods only knew what they'd do to me if I did it a second time.

Seething inside over my lack of real options to retaliate,

I stalked to the mattress and climbed into bed, still wearing my damp towel. If they wanted to be petty, I could be, too.

I reclined on my back and tucked my wings in around me, forming a barrier between me and my two cruel mates. I held on to the towel with both hands, my fingers so tightly twisted into the rough fabric that they began to hurt.

Part of me hoped they wouldn't leave me like this. Hot. Wet. Unsettled. I wanted them to rip the towel off my body and make this awful pain go away.

The other part of me didn't want their touch. I'd displeased them, but in doing so, I'd found my answers.

Even if I didn't know what to make of them.

I closed my eyes, attempting to sleep, when the bed shifted. My mates silently settled down on either side of me, wintergreen and leathery smoke cradling me.

As my mates drifted off to sleep, their slow breaths both a torment and a comfort, I resisted the urge to unfurl my wings, move, or even speak.

Because if I opened my mouth, it would be to beg or to say something I'd regret.

I just... need some sleep, I decided.

I had to think of this with my years of training as a royal and not as a sex-starved mate. The answers I'd received from Kyril wouldn't make sense to me without a clear mind, and Sayir wasn't done with us yet.

Which meant I needed to rest, even if I wanted to both fuck and kill my mates.

In that order.

I also probably needed to eat something. But I wasn't very hungry.

Well, not for food, anyway.

Ugh.

Instead of concentrating on the ache between my

thighs, I ran the conversation with Kyril through my mind. It helped as a distraction, giving me something important to focus on.

Was there a detail I'd missed? Some hint that he was lying?

I couldn't think of one.

Which meant he was either insane.

Or he was telling the truth.

I must have drifted off at some point because I woke up pinned to the mattress by a heavy leg. A hand roamed up my rib cage, over the towel, stirring me to full awareness.

Auric's lips closed over my suddenly pounding pulse as he kissed a slow, sensual trail along my skin.

We were alone in bed. Novak's warmth and weight were missing, even though I hadn't heard him leave.

When Auric's mouth reached my ear, he murmured, "I apologize for being so hard on you."

Waking up with Auric wrapped so tightly around me—and naked, no less—was the stuff dreams were made of. But I was still mad, and the press of his hard length against my thigh reminded me how he'd so easily left me unfulfilled. So I kept my mouth shut and did my best not to react to his ministrations.

"I know you wanted answers," Auric went on, his lips traveling back down, cresting over my collarbone.

He fisted my right breast, and I had to fight not to moan and lean into his palm as his thumb brushed over the hard, sensitive peak.

"The next time you need answers, I simply request that you ask for my assistance." He lifted his head to gaze into my eyes. "Agreed?" When I didn't immediately respond, he pinched my nipple.

This time I couldn't ignore the shock of desire that shot

through me. I gasped, my back arching off the mattress, my skin flushing hot.

Traitorous body.

I brushed his hand away and tugged the towel back up. "Where's Novak?"

Auric frowned at my obvious deflection but replied, "Out. Sorin claims to have found evidence of surveillance. Novak's with him to check the perimeter. He's going to bring back some food when he's done."

My stomach growled in response, my hunger making itself known. Those snacks yesterday weren't nearly enough.

Rather than comment on my stomach's reply to his food comment, Auric took hold of my chin with his free hand and forced me to look at him. "Inquiring about Novak won't change the subject, Lay. I asked you a question and I want an answer."

Auric's high-handedness over my comings and goings was growing old. We were no longer in Noir Reformatory with its shitty guards and hundreds of inmates looking at me like a snack.

However, he clearly cared about my safety and well-being—I couldn't very well hate him for that.

Although, I could easily hate him for the horrible afternoon and evening he'd just put me through.

Unless he meant to apologize, and based on the trail of his fingers, I wondered if that was his intent.

"I'll think about it," I hedged.

Auric's lips pressed together in a thin line, and I braced myself for him to lay into me. Instead, the expression fell away and he asked, "What did you find out from Kyril?"

I let out an amused sound and put my hand to my forehead, massaging away the growing tension. How did I even begin with the overwhelming information the mysterious Noir had told me? My father, King Sefid, might have created a plague. Oh, and the Noir were a race, not a perversion of Nora kind.

All of it still seemed absolutely insane.

But I told him anyway.

He listened raptly to every detail, his brow furrowed. I explained about the plague and Sayir's potential involvement, plus my father's innate ability to alter memories, which Auric already knew about. Then Kyril's explanation that those Noir who'd fled our realm for the Earth realm hadn't been affected by the alteration and therefore remembered everything we would have forgotten thanks to my father.

I told him how Kyril had said my parents—the Noir ones—had sent him here. How they believed King Sefid had designed the plague to avenge his mother's honor or to punish his paternal side. Which led to explaining how he was supposedly the son of a Noir and Nora pairing.

And how all of this had apparently happened about seven hundred years ago.

By the time I was finished relaying all the relevant information, I felt lost all over again.

"Do you believe him?" Auric asked, brushing his fingers through my hair.

"I don't know," I admitted. "Do you?"

"That remains to be seen."

"Hmm," I agreed.

Although, waiting for answers to unravel didn't seem to happen by itself. The truth needed to be sought, which was exactly what I intended to do.

Pursing my lips, I considered our immediate predicament.

"It doesn't explain why Sayir sent him," I said. "Or why we're here on Earth and how that's going to benefit the Reformer. So I keep thinking maybe it *is* just a game, but what I can't figure out is what Sayir would gain from this. Or what it has to do with reform."

Auric spanned his hand over my waist, his face thoughtful. "Perhaps it has something to do with trust and rules and not believing in your father."

"Which one?" I quipped, even though I knew what he meant. King Sefid. He was the one we were all expected to obey and revere, something I'd found natural all my life.

Until now.

Auric chuckled, his thumb tracing small circular patterns beneath my breast. "At any rate, maybe Sayir wants to see how far he can exploit our curiosity. Reform us by making us pledge allegiance to King Sefid despite a chance to work against him."

I tried to ignore how good it felt to have the pad of his thumb brush the bottom of my breast and instead focused on his words, because they had merit. "Sure. But if the goal was to make us all believe in my father, then I should have reformed by now because I do believe in him."

We lapsed into silence, my words seeming to echo around us.

"Or," I started quietly, swallowing. "I used to believe in him."

Auric's hand stilled on my torso, and he glanced up at me, adjusting his position to better see my face. "What does your heart tell you?"

I sighed. "That I'm tired," I whispered. "Tired of games."

Auric hummed in agreement. "If Sayir is playing a game, then he's playing it well."

I rolled into Auric just a little, angling my body toward him for a better conversational pose. His fingers ended up on my hip, holding me with a loose kind of possession that made my insides melt.

"If the Reformer is playing a game, then what's the end goal?" I asked. "My ultimate Fall? Or am I already Fallen? Or... what if everything Kyril said is true and Sayir knows it?"

"It doesn't seem true to me."

"It never seemed 'true' to me that I could Fall, yet here we are," I pointed out. "Theories are only theories until they're proven. Maybe we *should* meet with this King Vasilios. At least hear him out."

Auric frowned. "I don't know if that's a good idea."

I pulled back, ready to argue, but the cell door opened as Novak interrupted us. His powerful presence made me go quiet as my gaze dipped down to his torso.

Auric sat up, his fingertips still resting on my hip. "How'd it go?"

Novak grunted and dropped to the end of the bed, his hand finding its way to my thigh. "Found a few surveillance drones."

"Did you dismantle them?" Auric asked.

Novak nodded. "They were decoys meant for us to find. I suspect the Reformer is monitoring us via other means." He glanced down, his fingers sliding under my towel. "Time will tell."

My heart skipped a beat when his fingers brushed my sensitive skin, sending lightning jolting through my body.

Going against all of my impulses, I pulled away and wrapped the towel around myself again.

"What about food?" I blurted out, the ache in my stomach having turned into one of actual hunger sometime in the last however many hours. Time and nights were elusive here, the dark hours longer than the daylight.

Plus, I didn't want to give my mates the satisfaction of

seeing me buckle so quickly. There needed to be some type of groveling for what they'd put me through.

At the moment, I would accept groveling in the form of food offerings.

Novak considered me for a moment. "How much did you set aside for meals today?"

"I set aside meals for the next few days," I replied, frowning. "Why?"

He fell silent, his expression telling me something was wrong. "We're running lower than expected," he said vaguely.

"Meaning someone took more than their share?" Auric guessed, taking the thought right out of my mind.

His gaze went to my Nora mate. "Meaning someone stole the rest of our food supply, and given that yesterday's hunting plans were disrupted by Sayir's beasts, we're officially out of food. That's why I didn't bring anything back with me."

Auric ran his fingers through his hair and nodded, some sort of decision made. "All right. We need to summon the inmates for a communal hunt. Individual provisions will apply as a rule, but what we hunt as a group, we'll distribute evenly. That'll help ensure the wounded are fed, as they can't hunt for themselves due to their injuries."

Novak dipped his chin in agreement.

I glanced between them, rather liking this look on my mates. They were caring for the weak because they were ours to protect. I respected that.

"The Noir have already started gathering," Novak confirmed, his gaze falling to me.

Auric kissed my shoulder. "Then we shall hunt a delicious breakfast for our princess," he decided aloud, grinning at me. "After that, we'll have dessert. As I believe we owe our mate a few apology orgasms."

I started to smile, only a new concern touched my thoughts. "While that all sounds nice… what am I going to wear?"

CHAPTER TEN

AURIC

My preference would have been to have dessert first and forget about hunting entirely. However, Layla needed food. And after the way Novak and I had punished her, feeding her was the least we could do.

I considered it step one of our groveling plan.

Step two involved us devouring her as dessert until she begged us to stop.

Step three was another heartfelt apology where we then told her how we wanted to move forward. Which included her agreeing to not wander off without us.

It wasn't about her ability to take care of herself.

It was about our need to protect her and the fear we'd experienced when we couldn't find her during that initial explosion. I refused to feel that sort of terror ever again.

I glanced at her now, content to see her fuchsia hair glimmering in the dawning sun. *Nearby. Safe. Mine.*

Twigs snapped underfoot as we ventured out of the prison and into the foreign world where the sky ran blue instead of pure whites and grays.

Golden daylight streaked over the horizon, a testament that no matter what happened, what world we were in, another sunrise would inevitably come.

There was no guarantee we'd live to see it if we became complacent.

So I strode on, pausing only when Novak brushed past me, his wing stroking mine as he smirked. He was in a good mood, likely because we were going to kill something and then devour our mate afterward.

Blood, his eyes seemed to say as they sparkled with feverish glee. *Then sex.*

In this, I couldn't agree more.

When we reached the inmates I'd summoned, he silently pulled a dagger from a hidden sheath, twirling it in his palm. While it wasn't unusual to see him with a blade, I wondered why he'd chosen a physical weapon rather than simply using his wings.

The answer came when he tested the blade's sharpness with his fingertip, drawing blood. He grinned, showing teeth, as a shiver ran through his body.

"You're frightening the inmates," I said.

His psychotic behavior was best kept to a minimum while I tried to establish order with our new followers.

"You're grossing me out," Layla added with a curl of her lip.

Novak only chuckled.

I relaxed when Layla straightened, her sable wings fanning regally around her like a cape. It was nice to see her back in better spirits. Although, the tunic we'd found for her to wear left a lot to be desired. It hung on her frame like a beige sack, only covering her to her knees, which made it not all that appropriate for this chillier environment.

Still, she seemed to stand a little taller despite her wardrobe. I could only guess that her excitement had something to do with being able to focus on hunting rather than waiting around and questioning everything.

To be fair, Novak's own glee—such as it was—likewise came from having something tangible to focus on. A simple task. Kill.

We waited for the rest of the inmates to come to us, as a number of them were still trickling out of the prison. Even though the sun was rising, the inmates were not, and they shuffled out into the clearing like zombies, with dark circles beneath their eyes, thin lips, and sagging shoulders, making me frown.

At this rate, Sayir would win. We needed food, then we needed a plan.

A cursory head count told me most had arrived, minus the injured. So I stepped ahead of Layla and Novak, lifting a hand to get everyone's attention. They stopped talking immediately and turned toward us with expectant expressions.

Six months ago, I wouldn't have believed my life would have come to this. I was a commander in charge of Nora warriors—respected, decorated, a royal guard. Now I had a militia of black-winged inmates looking to me, and to Novak, for guidance and leadership.

Fucking twist of fate.

"As you've all surely heard," I began, "Sayir has been watching us. He wants to see us fail." I straightened. "If we fail to work together, that's exactly what will happen. You all protected the prison when the demon dogs attacked." I swept out my finger over the crowd, indicating each and every inmate. "You have proven your loyalty, and so we're creating a provisions rule to help those who cannot help themselves. We will hunt in groups, and for each kill, a portion will go to the injured who could not join us today."

A ripple of unease passed over the crowd, and a few of the males muttered to each other.

"You'll still be responsible for your own food," I went

on, raising my voice over their chatter. "You will hunt on your own and fend for yourselves. You can choose who you hunt with and who you share your kills with, but feeding the injured is mandatory."

I let that last statement settle over the crowd before continuing.

"I'm going to split you into territories," I told them. "You can hunt in your territory and only your territory. We will respect boundaries, and should another attack strike, know that you will be cared for just as you care for those who defended this place."

Silence stretched out, then the inmates surprised me. A roar spread up over them, a cheer of camaraderie I hadn't heard since my days in the army.

They approved of this decision.

The next few minutes fell into controlled chaos as I directed eager groups to different cardinal directions and attempted to map out hunting grounds that would allow everyone a fair shot at game. Then we disbanded, some inmates returning inside the prison to tend to the injured, while the majority of us headed into the woods.

In deference to Novak's familial relationship with Zian, I put them in our territory, though they opted to go off on their own to "forage."

A word that made Novak's lip curl with distaste.

Novak and I flanked Layla as we passed into the dim light of the forest. Somewhere nearby, wolves howled, the piercing sound cutting through the silent morning.

I looked to Novak, surprised. "Odd time for wolves to be out."

He nodded, his gaze roaming the shadows beneath the thick overhead canopy. "Stay vigilant." He twirled his blade and then stepped ahead of us, leading the way while

I took up the rear, making sure Layla remained between us.

The farther we ventured into the trees, the darker the forest became. Slowly, the normal sounds of nature began to dissipate. Insects ceased chirping. Birds stopped singing. The air fell stagnant, not even a slight breeze able to breach the thick overgrowth, leaving the entire landscape as still as death.

"Doesn't feel right," I muttered as I pressed closer to Layla.

Novak grunted his agreement.

I'd been in a few forests in my time. Being a warrior took me to all walks of life and all landscapes of the Nora world. But this place felt... wrong. Abnormal.

Tampered with.

Something cracked in the underbrush to our right. I leaped in front of Layla and unsheathed my blade. Novak's wings extended, razors releasing with a sharp metallic sound, far too close to my face for comfort, as he cursed and tossed the dagger to the ground.

He wouldn't be needing that, it seemed.

Yellow eyes watched us from between the trees.

I stared into the shadows, trying to make out the creature's form. I thought I could see two pointed ears and a snout, all covered in fur. Something seemed to be dangling from its mouth.

"Wolf?" I hissed to Novak.

At the sound of my voice, the creature jumped.

Onto a branch *twenty feet* off the ground.

I caught a glimpse of a long, fluffy tail and four paws that further cemented the idea that it was a canine of some type. Except for the twenty-foot-jumping side of things —*that* was not physically possible for the wolves I'd read about.

Layla gasped, her fingers digging into my elbow. "H-how high can a wolf jump?"

"Not that high," I said.

"Not a wolf," Novak said conversationally. "Stay here."

His unspoken demand was to stay with Layla and keep her safe. I nodded and began surveying the forest around us, opening my senses so I'd know if anything moved before it happened.

Novak stalked toward the creature's location, his gaze on the canopy. Silence surrounded us for a few moments, broken only by Novak's footsteps and Layla's light breaths.

"It's gone," he finally said.

"How?" I replied.

He just shrugged.

When Layla spoke again, her voice was a little more high-pitched than usual. "So we're dealing with jumping wolves? And they're just going to pounce on us from above?"

Slipping an arm over her shoulders, I replied, "Nobody's pouncing." I tilted my head, amending my statement. "Yet."

We continued walking, my blade at the ready and both of us keeping our distance from Novak, whose wings remained sharp and deadly.

Layla had brought along a dagger as well, one she'd lifted off one of the dead inmates during the battle the other day. Seeing her with her fist wrapped around the hilt and her shrewd sapphire gaze darting around the forest warmed my chest with pride.

She'd grown up.

And she really could take care of herself.

She just needed to understand that Novak and I needed to help. She was our mate. Therefore, our instincts demanded we keep her sa—

My boot struck something solid on the ground, sending it sailing over a bed of dead leaves. Layla squatted in the undergrowth and reached for the metallic glint of a cylinder.

As she turned it over in her hand, I realized it was a can of beans from the prison.

She held it up to me. "Looks like someone was already hunting in our territory."

"Not hunting," I countered, frowning at the can. "They were stealing… and running."

It seemed not all our inmates were faithful after all.

Novak sniffed the air, his nostrils flaring. He shuffled in a half circle, scenting the wind with a narrowed brow. "They were attacked."

Standing, I passed the can to Layla and asked Novak, "What do you mean?"

His eyes sparkled with barely restrained glee. "Don't you smell the blood?"

I motioned for him to lead the way.

We found the bodies strung across a small campsite flanked by thick undergrowth and low-hanging branches. Blood soaked the ground, and the coppery tang of it made my stomach turn.

Nobody was intact. Hands, feet, whole limbs, entrails… The camp was a massacre.

Layla walked forward, eyes wide. "Oh gods. What did this?"

Unsure of how to answer, I stooped down and swiped a linen potato sack off the ground. Peering inside, it seemed the food was still there, including a dead rabbit.

"That's Raven's haul from yesterday," Novak said, frowning. "Sorin mentioned it earlier while hunting for tech."

The crack of a twig split the silence, distracting me

from answering Layla's question or commenting on Novak's statement.

I shifted to the balls of my feet and listened intently for further indication that someone was close. Another prisoner, maybe? Or maybe the beast that had caused this carnage.

Something hit the ground near my feet.

It had come from overhead, like a coconut falling from the canopy. Only it wasn't a coconut—

It was a head.

I swiped my blade out, sparing only a glance at the disembodied skull. I recognized it—Grahame, the older, gray-haired inmate who'd been so helpful during the aftermath of yesterday's battle. Then I looked up into the tree.

High above, perched on a branch like a bird, sat a wolflike creature. It snarled and opened its jaws, revealing multiple rows of sharp, vicious teeth. Saliva dripped from its snout and landed on my arm with a painful sizzle.

"Fuck," I swore, flicking my arm to get the acidic saliva off my skin. It left a red welt that immediately began to blister.

Then the wolf lunged.

Layla shrieked.

I stabbed at the falling creature, catching him near the shoulder with a scrape of knife on bone as Novak swiped his wings, catching it on its flank. It yelped and fell away, hitting the ground on all fours before darting into the trees like we hadn't just skewered it.

"The hell was that?" I raged.

Novak grunted. "Not earthly. Not with those teeth."

Branches snapped all around us. I whipped around to see more of the monsters leaping down from the trees, lugging pieces of Noir flesh and bits of food from the stolen reserves. Growling filled the air as they began to stalk toward us.

We were outnumbered.

I fell into a fighting stance, shoving Layla behind me with one arm. She slapped at my hand with an infuriated growl and pointed her blade at me.

"I can *fight*," she snarled.

I couldn't reply, because the wolves attacked.

I slashed out with my blade, catching one on the nose. It yelped and darted left, then lunged at my torso, snapping at my skin. His rows of sharp teeth managed to snag my pant leg but not my skin, and I took advantage of his mistake, shoving my blade into his eye.

The beast released an inhuman screech of pain and bounded away, trailing strange, ash-like blood in its wake. I froze, staring at the trail of ash, but before I could really process what I was seeing, another wolf flew from the shadows toward me.

I took the blow on my left shoulder and fell hard, rolling with the force of it. The wolf catapulted over me and landed on its back with a sharp yelp before leaping to its feet and heading right for me.

My knife zinged through the air and sliced deep into the wolf's chest as it reached me. It snarled and latched on to my blade, attempting to rip it from my hands. But I struck out with a punch, catching the beast's jaw and putting the full force of my body behind the blow.

Nearby, Layla cried out, her blade flashing as she stabbed a wolf's snout before its jaws reached her face.

The sound sent me into a fury. I jammed the dagger into the wolf's mouth, right into the soft palate. He gagged and fell, taking my arm and dagger with him. I ripped the weapon out, relishing the release of dried, ashy blood. Then I shoved off the ground and ran for my mate.

Except… she wasn't in trouble. When I found her, she was on her feet, pulling her knife from a wolf's eye, grinning as she finished her kill.

I was frozen by the sight of her—strong, tall, beautiful, smiling with victory.

Novak paused as well from his slaughter on the southern arc of the attack, lust evident in his blue gaze. He licked his lips coated in bloody ash, and I could almost *feel* his need to go to her. To drop her to the dirt and fuck her like an animal.

Because I felt it, too.

Instead, both of us returned to the fight.

There'll be time for that later.

I leaped onto a wolf's back and took it down, but I rolled too far and it ended up on top of me. I swiped my dagger at its neck, but it headed me off and snapped at my fingertips.

I jammed my arm against its throat to keep its sharp teeth away from my face. Its gaping maw opened, and a string of acidic saliva peeled away from its teeth. It hit my neck with a sharp, painful sizzle, making me growl.

Suddenly, the wolf's substantial weight disappeared. Ashy blood filtered down onto my chest, and I stared up at an unfamiliar face as a male Noir took down the wolf with a clean kill.

Pale brown hair whipped around his face, shading even paler brown eyes. I'd seen the lean Noir around the prison a time or two. A quiet, reserved guy who seemed familiar —not in his looks, but in the way he held himself.

Like a trained warrior.

The male Noir yanked his blade from the dead wolf's rib cage and nodded at me. He watched the now-dead creature collapse to the dirt, then he hurtled away with surprising speed to attack another wolf.

I flapped my wings and shot to my feet, sparing a glance around at the sudden crowd. Other inmates had heard the commotion and came running to help us, even though I'd said nothing about assisting other territories in the event of another attack.

Raven, Sorin, and Zian battled a large wolf. And the brown-haired male who'd just helped me joined a group of fighting inmates several yards away, where he immediately jumped into coordinating their efforts.

I moved to head back to Layla's side, then stopped.

The wolf was gone. In its place rested a pile of ash.

Which could only mean one thing.

Sayir...

CHAPTER ELEVEN

NOVAK

DISAPPOINTING, I LAMENTED.

I had hoped for blood. And it seemed the only blood drawn today had been my own.

Raven kicked at the pile of ash at her feet and cursed under her breath. "This is just freaking great."

Beside her, Sorin stared down at the charcoaled remains of the dead wolves and let out a long whistle. "Earth wolves don't fight like that. They also don't have dust for blood."

I agreed. These creatures couldn't possibly be native to this realm, so while they were potentially modified beasts, they weren't from this world. We had to find Sayir's portals and block them.

"What are we going to do?" Layla asked, her tone holding an edge of concern to it. "Those things just destroyed all the food we had left, with no thanks to the jerks who tried to flee with it all."

"We need to fend for ourselves," Raven cut in. "That was *my* sack they stole. Which would have been protected had it remained with me."

I folded my arms, considering her point of view.

While I'd agreed with Auric earlier that we should share with the weak, I also valued survival. And if the weak were going to take advantage of our hospitality, then I had no desire to feed them.

Although, most of the inmates did come to our aid just now...

Raven held up another linen sack, which she must have found among the stolen goods. Or maybe it was a new one. Hard to say.

"I have some stuff for us." She made a face and poked her finger in a rip at the bottom of the bag. "Some fruit and mushrooms. I *had* a rabbit until those asshat wolves got a hold of it. But there's enough here to sustain us for a couple of days."

Ah, she must have found that sack among the remains, then. Because it held the contents Sorin had mentioned earlier while boasting about Raven's hunting skills. The rabbit he'd been so proud of was, well, no longer edible.

"Us," Layla repeated incredulously. "You mean you're going to deign to share with me, *cousin?*"

Raven rolled her eyes and tossed her long black hair over her shoulder. "By *us*, I mean my mates and me. Not you."

"We share this territory," Layla diplomatically reminded her, making me smirk. "I'll tell you what. I'll give you fifty percent."

Raven's face flushed and she gasped. "Are you insane?"

"Just give her half," Zian sighed, causing Raven to growl. He faced her, standing his ground. "Layla's right. The provisions are in our shared territory, whether or not they originated from us. Rules are rules."

"Fuck," Raven spat. "Fine."

Ignoring the two bickering females as Raven reluctantly separated the supplies, Auric shuffled closer, one hand resting on the sheath of his dagger. "What do you think?"

Sorin and Zian glanced up from the ashy remains, awaiting my reply.

"Another test," I muttered. "Just can't figure out the goal." At this rate, he was going to kill us all. And that felt counterproductive to his intentions.

"And where the fuck are we?" Zian added, one hand gesturing to indicate the thick forest. "I thought we were somewhere in Asia originally, but this tree cover isn't one I've ever seen on that continent."

I shrugged.

I had no fucking clue where we were.

The overly thick forest, chilly temperatures, and mountainous terrain could have been anywhere in the world, for all I knew.

But wherever the fuck we were, we weren't safe. Not from Sayir. Not from his pet projects. And not from each other. Because the hungrier we became, the more desperate we would become.

Raven sighed and tossed what was left of her bag over her shoulder. "I could try to find another rabbit."

Layla shook her head. "One rabbit isn't going to feed us all."

"It'll keep us from starving to death," Raven shot back.

Layla didn't even acknowledge her. She turned to Auric and handed him a can of beans. "I think we should talk to Kyril again."

Auric frowned. "Why? You already listened to a bunch of bullshit from him."

"And if it's not bullshit?" Layla pointed out. "We aren't going to find food if we're stuck in another one of the Reformer's traps. Why waste time trying when we could just figure out what Kyril knows about our situation? The Reformer either sent him here or let him come here to find me. Either way, he knows *something*."

Zian had returned Kyril to his cell yesterday after Auric and I had taken Layla back to our room for our *discussion*. He'd assumed we didn't want Sayir's "gift" wandering around without supervision. And he'd been right. I'd thanked him for the proactive measure this morning.

"Food first," I said. Layla needed to eat something. "Then we'll give Kyril five minutes to talk before I kill him."

Layla rolled her eyes. "You're not going to kill him."

"Hmm" was all I offered.

A few of the inmates who'd been going through the leftovers, looking for food, broke away from the pack and came to join us. One man took point, offering a hand to Auric.

"Hey," Auric said, holding out a hand for a warrior's handshake. The male took his forearm, clasping his grip. "You did well out there."

I watched him step aside to chat with the inmate who'd introduced himself as Tavin.

I'd noticed how well he'd handled the fight, too. The way he'd taken the lead, coordinated efforts with the other men, and terminated the threat.

It was impressive.

He'd fought like a trained Nora warrior, which was probably who he used to be prior to Falling.

However, I wasn't all that interested in wasting time with the other inmates. Auric might want to encourage unity and shit, but in the Noir world, it was do or die. At some point, Auric would have to let go of his Nora warrior preconceptions and come to terms with the Noir way of life.

And if he didn't, I'd just have to remind him where his loyalties lay.

While he busied himself with formalities, I focused on

the rations of food Raven had given Layla. I divided out a few key items that were high in nutrition and could be eaten raw and fed them to our mate.

The scrunch of her nose told me it wasn't her favorite meal, but it cured the ache in her stomach. It abated mine as well.

When Auric finally returned, I gave him some of the food, too. His gaze thanked me. I told him with a look that he could show more gratitude later. Layla's cheeks flushed in response, clearly picking up on my intentions.

"We should go back to the room. Forget Kyril," I suggested.

"Agree," Auric murmured.

Layla's eyes flashed. "No. He knows something."

"What else could he know?" Auric asked. "You already heard his outlandish story, and you're still unsure of what to believe. How is this time going to be any different?"

"What outlandish story?" I interjected.

Layla sighed and told me everything Kyril had told her in his cell as we made our way back to the prison. By the time she finished, I was somewhat in agreement that he could know more.

His story was insane.

Yet… it made some sense.

I'd questioned my Fall for a century. Just as I'd questioned Sorin and Zian's Fall. They'd earned their black wings for taking my side. How was that an egregious sin? They didn't kill anyone. They weren't monsters. They were just loyal to the wrong person. *Me.*

Not the king.

That seemed to be key to all of this.

Which had me glancing at Auric's pristine wings. *Does that mean you're still loyal to King Sefid? Or a natural Nora?*

"We need to know where we are and what's going on. Kyril is the only lead we have," Layla concluded.

I dipped my chin to show her I agreed. Auric stayed silent. And we both followed Layla's lead. Seemed like another way to apologize for our behavior last night. We'd been mean to her, mostly because our concern for her well-being had gotten the best of us. And we'd used each other as an outlet instead of hurting her.

Except the way she'd fallen asleep with her wings wrapped tightly around herself had suggested we'd hurt her in a very different way.

So we'd make it up to her now by doing what she suggested.

Then we'd apologize profusely with our bodies and tongues later.

Auric, Layla, and I bypassed our own cell and went straight to the Noir's locked door, where I handed her the key.

"Zian locked him back up with some food last night," I explained. "He's unharmed." At least according to my cousin, whom I believed.

Layla nodded, gratitude showing in her features. Whoever this Noir was, he seemed to mean something to her. Not romantically, but maybe as a friend.

Which was strange, considering they'd just met. However, Layla possessed a heart of gold, and she wore it on her sleeve. She was inherently good. Sweet. Beautiful. So incredibly worthy.

I ran my fingers through her hair, my lips finding her cheek as I told her without words how proud I was of her for being who she was.

Her skin warmed, then she turned the key in the lock, and I returned to my protective stance.

Kyril glanced up from his nest of blankets, clearly

startled by our sudden entrance. He climbed quickly to his feet and fell into a respectful bow. "Princess Layla."

"Hi, Kyril," she greeted, slipping inside.

Auric followed her while I stayed near the entrance and leaned against the doorjamb. "Did Sayir send you?" I asked, cutting right to the point.

Auric had already asked him this once. I figured it didn't hurt to ask him again.

Although, Layla's irritated glance over her shoulder suggested it annoyed her.

Too bad. I wanted to hear him repeat his answer.

"No," Kyril responded smoothly. "But he knows I'm here. He also knows why I'm here."

"That reason being…?" I prompted.

His bright eyes met mine. "To help Layla find the way back to her parents. That's it. No tricks. No games."

"Except everything with Sayir is a game," Auric pointed out.

"But I'm not involved," Kyril insisted. "I'm here on behalf of His Majesty. Sayir approved the visit."

Layla blinked. "So… so he knows about the Noir on Earth?"

"Of course," Kyril replied, his focus shifting between the three of us as he sighed. "Look, you're all going about this the wrong way. The answer is to speak with Layla's real parents. Then you'll know what I'm telling you is the truth."

Auric laughed, a short, sharp sound that wasn't amused. "Layla's parents are the crown royals of the Nora. Not some secret king and queen of a made-up race."

I wanted to agree with Auric, but something about Kyril's demeanor captivated my attention. He was so calm and collected, calculative and proper. He appeared young, but perhaps I had been incorrect in my assessment of his experience.

He was either a true believer of his story or a very skilled liar.

A little nose poked out of his pocket as Clyde made his presence known. His beady eyes met mine as if to say, *Listen to him.*

I wasn't one to take orders from a minor demon. But I could accept his demonstration as a token of advice.

Hmm.

I dragged my gaze from the demon to Kyril's placid expression. "Who are you really?" I asked, my tone velvety soft and underlined with lethal warning.

You don't want to lie to me, I was telling him. *Or I'll destroy you.*

The Noir grinned, his eyes brightening even more. "I thought you'd never ask," he said pleasantly. "I'm the son of Thoth."

CHAPTER TWELVE

LAYLA

"The son of who?" I asked, unfamiliar with the name.

"Thoth," Kyril repeated, a note of reverence in his tone. "Thoth was the God of Knowledge and Wisdom, and I am his last son, one of the few remaining original Noir."

Did he just call himself the descendant of a god?

I'd been taught where the Nora had come from, but the God of Knowledge and Wisdom had a different name to me. He'd played a crucial part in the origin of our species, and he had fathered children of his own. They all just went by different names.

So Kyril's words rang with truth, but his vision was clearly skewed.

Or perhaps my truth is the one that's skewed.

But… "Wouldn't that make you a thousand years old?" Not that I was one to judge, but he looked so *young*. I'd been operating under the assumption that he was closer to my age, only to find out he was more ancient than my parents.

Well. My Nora parents, at any rate.

However, he had recounted his knowledge of the plague, saying he'd been there himself. Which, by his own account, would have been seven hundred years ago.

"A bit older than that," Kyril replied with a kind smile. "I've been an advisor for King Vasilios for over a thousand years. That's why I'm here, Princess Layla. To teach you, the next generation of Noir royalty. If you'll allow me."

Auric growled, an irritated rumble that came from deep in his chest. "You couldn't have said that when you first arrived?"

Kyril gave him a look. "I did. You threw me in a cell."

Even though his tone didn't indicate any kind of sarcasm, I still had to hide a smile.

Auric shook his head. "You're saying that one of our origin gods was a Noir? The Nora are far superior, so that's blasphemy if you're wrong."

I crossed my arms, my black feathers ruffling. "Your prejudice is showing."

Kyril inclined his head. "You were indeed made to believe such a thing, Auric. The truth is far deeper than the magic used against your people."

"Magic?" Auric repeated.

"My father's ability to manipulate memory," I said softly, bothered by the fact that I'd sort of started to understand Kyril. We'd just met, but I felt as though I knew him. Like I could trust him. Like I could believe in this madness.

It had to be my Fall.

My wings playing tricks on my mind.

However, I couldn't deny that my father, *King Sefid*, was powerful. He served as a leader who would do anything to keep his people safe.

But did that extend to genocide of another race?

I hated to imagine it, but I'd never envisioned myself Falling, either. I'd passed into a universe where things I'd never thought possible had already come to pass. What was one more impossibility?

Novak appeared thoughtful as he murmured, "The Noir were gods. Hmm." He met Kyril's gaze. "Explain."

"It's said that they created the different races," Kyril replied. "That remains true in both our versions of the history. Except that the black-winged ones were the gods, and their children were black-winged, too. Which was why they were much rarer than the white-winged protector angels. The white-winged line was originally created to protect those in power. I assume that's where your warrior sensibilities come from."

Auric scoffed. "If the *black-winged gods* were so powerful, why did they need protection?"

"Because reproduction amongst the Noir has always been difficult. Black-winged children were uncommon. And gods have a tendency to fight. They're territorial by nature. However, adding the white-winged ones, later renamed the Nora, provided a sense of balance among the angels."

"I see," Auric murmured. "So let's pretend I buy that, which I don't, but how do you explain the Nora remaining in charge today with the resurgence of Noir in the population?"

Kyril studied him for a moment, like he was trying to determine the best way to convince Auric to understand. "Have you considered why King Sefid had his brother build these prisons? Why he devised these games meant to pit the black-winged *Fallen* against one another? Could it, perhaps, be a way to distract them from attacking the Nora?"

Nothing changed overtly in Novak's expression. His face remained stoic and empty.

But *I* noticed the change. Just the slightest shift in his stance and a tightening in his shoulders.

"Have you noticed any power growth while in

reform?" Kyril continued, his question directed at Novak this time. "Because one would think a century of imprisonment would make you weaker, not stronger, yes?"

A chill raced over me, and I looked at Novak. "Is that true? Has your power grown?"

Novak remained quiet for so long that I thought he might not answer. But he eventually dipped his chin in confirmation, or maybe it was meant to be a request for Kyril to continue speaking. More likely, he desired to convey both sentiments with the singular action.

"You see, there's a belief among the Noir that the gods will find a way to reinstate their power. It's taken centuries for it to happen, but their genetics are slowly trickling back into the very angels they created to protect them. By causing them to *Fall*. To turn. To change. To be *reborn* as the Noir. We're all descended from the gods, and to them, we will all return."

He paused, then his bright blue gaze met mine.

"Your father is the last of his kind," he said gently. "The God of Resilience, and the only Noir god left. Everyone else is either a direct descendant like me, or an indirect descendant like Novak."

Auric grunted.

Novak bristled.

And I gaped at Kyril. "I don't... That's... This is insane."

"It would sound that way, yes. But I have a way to prove it." His gaze went to Novak. "Let me take you to King Vasilios. One look is all you need. You'll believe me."

My mate's jaw ticked while Auric muttered, "Convenient."

"Why did Sayir approve your visit?" Novak asked him. "If he's created all these prisons as a way to essentially tame the Noir race, why would he let a *direct descendant* in to talk to us?"

"Because his allegiances have shifted," Kyril replied.

"His allegiances?" I repeated. "You mean he's not loyal to my father?"

Kyril flinched again, just as he did every time I referred to King Sefid as my father. "Sayir can't outwardly oppose King Sefid. At least not yet. So he let a black-winged angel into his reformatory knowing no one would notice or care. But my purpose here is to convince you to see your *real* father and hear him out."

"Then why continue the torment?" Auric demanded. "Why send those wolves out here to hunt us?"

"He has a role to play in all this," Kyril answered with ease. "Just like Novak."

My dark-winged mate lifted an eyebrow, his way of saying, *Oh?*

"You wear the Kiss of the Gods mark. Your purpose hasn't yet been realized, but I suspect we'll know soon." His gaze ran over Novak's lethal weapons. "You've been very blessed indeed."

Novak snorted, clearly amused.

Auric just glared.

"Kiss of the Gods?" I repeated. "What's that?"

"Something only King Vasilios can tell us, right?" Auric taunted.

Kyril studied him again, then glanced at Novak. "No. It's a mark bestowed upon an indirect descendant by a direct descendant. You've met someone powerful in your history, someone who found you worthy of greatness."

Novak's nostrils flared as he pushed up off the door frame, a memory darkening his icy irises. He didn't speak, just studied the Noir with a gaze that told me he was evaluating the veracity of his claim.

Auric didn't appear as believing, his expression exuding dubiousness. But he looked at me with a question in his eyes, asking me without words what I wanted to do.

That simple look told me he would follow my lead on this, at least to an extent.

It was a gift of sorts. An apology, too. Maybe one he didn't mean to issue, but it held just the same. He was telling me that he understood why I'd insisted on talking to Kyril, and if it was what my instincts required, he'd agree to my next decision as well.

"I understand why you all are hesitant to believe me," Kyril said, his tone soft. "But I'm not lying, nor am I insane. As I've said, there's an easy way to prove all of this. Let me take you to Layla's parents. They can tell you so much more. You'll also immediately see how much she resembles them." His voice turned affectionate at the end, like an old friend, and he smiled at me.

Could it really be possible? The more I spoke with the Noir, the more I wanted to believe him.

The reason we'd stayed rather than run away was because we had nowhere to go, but Kyril was offering a solution.

Perhaps the wolves and attacks were an incentive to force us out, especially if Sayir couldn't be too obviously involved without revealing his own plans to his brother.

It could all be a lie, but what if it wasn't?

What if… what if this was the path I'm destined to take?

"Where are her parents?" Auric asked, seeming to see the decision forming in my features.

"They move," Kyril replied. "We would need to reach Buenos Aires for me to contact them for their location."

"Buenos Aires?" Auric repeated.

"Yes. The capital of Argentina."

"I know what it is. I'm asking…" Auric trailed off, his brow furrowed. "Are we in South America?"

"Yes," Kyril replied. "We're in the southern Andes Mountains."

"You've known that the entire time and never mentioned it?" Auric sounded furious.

"No one asked," Kyril countered. "I've been treated like a prisoner since I arrived. All it required was a question. I have nothing to hide, and everything I say is the truth."

"Or insanity," Auric muttered, running his fingers through his long white-blond hair. He shook his head and began to pace while Novak continued to evaluate the Noir. He didn't appear angry or violent, just thoughtful. Considering. Planning.

After several beats, he straightened with a nod. "We should pack."

Auric spun on his heel toward Novak. "*What?*"

My dark-winged mate stared at my white-winged one. "We're going to find King Vasilios."

Auric blew out a breath, his incredulity thick in the air. "What if Sayir—"

"He's going to attack us regardless," Novak interjected before Auric could finish speaking, his mind clearly made up. "So let's force him to bring the game to us."

With that, he left the cell.

No more questions.

No room for debate.

Just a command.

One I felt all the way to my heart.

He's right. This is right. This is our destined path.

CHAPTER THIRTEEN

AURIC

NOVAK STALKED OFF WITHOUT A WORD, HIS WINGS RUFFLING at his back.

But I knew what he intended to do.

Scout a flight path.

Which meant he was very serious about leaving. And the more I thought about it, the more it made sense.

If there was even an ounce of truth to Kyril's claims, then we needed to know. He'd also claimed he had proof in the form of Layla's true parents—something I found very difficult to believe. But a small voice in my head wondered if he could be telling the truth.

I thought back to the day King Sefid had called me in to say that Layla had Fallen. He'd expressed true concern. However, rather than keep her safe, he'd sent her to Noir Reformatory, which was the opposite of safe.

Nothing about that place had been about reform.

It was death personified.

He'd sent me along as her guard, but I'd been given no benefits, no direct line of communication back to the royal palace, and barely any respect.

I'd blamed the Reformer, thinking he'd been the orchestrator of all this insanity. However, now I wondered if he'd just been doing his brother's bidding. Or if there was more that we couldn't see playing out behind the scenes.

Are Noir descendants of gods? I wondered, thinking about Novak's warrior display the other day. When those Noir had attacked me, he'd taken to the sky with the grace of a superior being, his wings slicing through the enemies with a precision that had called to my warrior heart. Then the moon had eclipsed the sun as though the heavens themselves were showing their respect as well.

That hadn't felt natural. It'd felt powerful. Too powerful. As though Novak had ascended to something more in that moment, commanding everyone to fall to their knees and bask in the glory of his might.

In all my centuries, I'd never witnessed a Nora orchestrate that sort of reaction. Not even King Sefid.

Swallowing, I took in Kyril's placid features, searching him for a hint of victory. But all I caught in his gaze was a sense of promise. As though he were fortifying himself for the journey to come and vowing to ensure we survived it.

"Where'd he go?" Layla asked, peering into the hallway.

"To the sky," I replied. "He's scouting the right path for us to take on our way out." It was what he'd done as part of my unit, too. His solitary nature made him a natural for such expeditions, as he preferred to work alone. "He'll be searching for any potential traps as well."

Layla frowned. "Why didn't he do that before with Sorin?"

"Because our primary objective has been to guard you," I replied. "Now that we're planning to leave, he's preparing for it."

"I'm starting to understand your mating," Kyril interjected. "Although, your parents may still question them, as Novak and Auric are, uh, not who they anticipated for this journey."

I narrowed my gaze at him. "What the hell does that mean?"

"Just that your mating is unexpected," Kyril clarified. But something about his expression told me that wasn't it at all. He knew something.

"Elaborate," I demanded.

"Auric," Layla murmured, moving toward me and pressing her palm to my chest. "Novak said we should pack. I suggest we start with scrounging up as much food and weapons as we can find."

Her touch against my bare skin abated some of my annoyance, but not all of it. "If her *parents* cared about her mating choices, then they should have tried saving her from this situation earlier. But instead, *I* protected her. As did Novak."

"And I'm sure they will be very grateful for that fact," Kyril answered. "As will the others."

"The others?" I repeated. "The others *who?*"

"Noir," he replied easily. *Too easily*.

"You're hiding something," I told him.

"I have over a thousand years of information in my head. If I'm hiding something, it's because the right question hasn't been asked," he countered.

"Okay," Layla interjected. "I think we know enough for now. Let's just—"

"Who are the others?" I demanded, something telling me that part was important.

"The royal court members. Of the Noir, I mean. Not the Nora."

I studied him, my eyes narrowing. "You're still not telling us something."

Kyril sighed. "There are a great many things I'm not

saying, Auric. But I imagine a lot more will make sense once you meet King Vasilios."

My jaw ticked.

Layla's touch drifted upward to my chin, her fingers drawing my focus down to her. "I want to take a shower," she whispered. "We're both covered in ash."

I considered her request, my attention falling to her lips. She wanted more than a shower. She wanted my apology.

Hmm.

"All right." I could continue questioning Kyril during our trip, find out what he wasn't saying and deal with him then. For now, I had a mate to care for. Novak could join us when he was done playing outside.

"I'm leaving your cell unlocked," I told Kyril as I steered Layla out of his room. "Consider it a show of good faith."

One that I would use as a test to see if he tried to escape or cause mischief.

However, something told me he'd probably remain huddled in his corner.

I didn't trust him in the slightest, but I had a knack for reading people. And he struck me as faithful to an extent, specifically to Layla.

"I still think he's nuts," I muttered after we were several feet away.

"Maybe," Layla whispered. "But some of what he's saying…"

"Makes sense," I finished for her when she trailed off. "Yeah, I know." I hated admitting it, but that didn't make it any less true.

He had an answer for everything, and he uttered each statement with a conviction that confirmed he believed it. Novak agreeing to leave and to find this supposed proof

—King Vasilios, a name I'd never heard before this week
—said Kyril had been more than convincing; he'd been
real.

So either he was insane.

Or…

Or everything I'd known all my life was founded on
a lie.

Which meant I'd been hunting Noir indiscriminately
for nefarious reasons.

My entire world flipped upside down at the thought,
my sense of honor deteriorating in a blink. *What if I sent
those Noir to their deaths? What if they were meant to be revered
instead of imprisoned?*

The Noir I had always known were savage, soulless
creatures, but perhaps they'd been forced into that role. I'd
experienced the so-called reformatory for myself, and it
was a place of survival and chaos with no semblance of
hope to be found.

Anyone would go mad there.

And now that the Noir had been given a chance again,
they demonstrated qualities worthy of a legion I could
command.

Meaning Kyril very well could be onto something.

I swallowed, my mind fracturing beneath the whirlwind
of questions that followed.

Only to be grounded by Layla's touch as she cradled
my face between her palms. "We're going to figure this
out," she promised. "Together."

I glanced down at her, our surroundings beginning to
filter back in. I'd been so lost in thought that I couldn't
even remember walking to our cell.

She stood before me now, her hands on my cheeks, her
eyes on mine.

I memorized every nuance of her delicate features—

her fuchsia eyebrows, matching eyelashes, blue irises, sculpted cheekbones, elven jawline.

So beautiful.

So sweet.

So intoxicating.

I'd loved her for years, had told myself it was wrong, convinced myself that I couldn't have her, yet here she stood with her heart reflected in her gaze.

Even after every cruel thing I'd said and done to her.

She's mine.

My perfect, loving mate.

My Lay.

I had an apology to voice, but my throat no longer knew how to work. I needed her touch, her kiss, her mouth, to remember how to breathe.

Bending, I captured her lips with mine, taking what I needed from her and giving her everything of me in return.

I love you, I was saying with my tongue. *I will love you forever. I vow it.*

Her arms encircled my neck as I caught her hips, lifting her into the air.

She wrapped her legs around me, her tunic bunching up around her thighs.

Shower, I thought, walking toward the bathroom. *My mate wanted a shower.*

Fortunately, the bathrooms in this prison were built for angels—*plural*. The water would be lukewarm at best, but we'd heat it up together.

I kicked off my boots, then tugged the tunic off over Layla's head. Her sandals were next, leaving her naked and clinging to me with her arms and legs.

"Mmm," I hummed, pressing her up against the shower wall and loving the display of her black feathers against the stark white tile. "Think you can unbutton my pants?"

She grinned against my mouth, her fingers trailing down my torso as my palms went to her ass to help her balance. "Maybe," she whispered, flicking open the button. "Or maybe you should take care of yourself."

"I would," I told her. "But Novak and I proved last night that it doesn't work. We can come a hundred times, and it'll never compare to the sensation of being inside you."

Her thick lashes fluttered, her gaze finding mine and revealing a hint of insecurity in her depths. I caught it because she appeared slightly surprised by my admission.

It was then that I realized the true damage we'd done last night, damage she might not have even realized.

By being with Novak and not indulging our mate, a part of her felt not just left out but replaced.

"Oh, Lay," I whispered, cupping her cheek while my opposite hand continued to balance her weight. "You're the center of our world. We might enjoy playing with each other, but you're the one we're thinking about when we come. It's always you. Your scent. Your heat. Your soul. We're mated to *you*, Layla. Not to each other."

"I know," she replied, her fingers faltering a little as she tugged on my zipper.

"No, I don't think you do," I said, pressing my forehead to hers. "We were still hard last night because we weren't anywhere near satisfied. That punishment applied to us, too. We blamed ourselves for not protecting you, for being so focused on each other in our battle that we didn't even notice you leave."

That had been the heart of our anger.

Not just that she'd left to see Kyril alone, but that we hadn't felt her leave until it had been too late.

What if something had happened to her? We would have blamed ourselves more than her.

"Everything we did last night was about preserving *us*, Lay. Our connections. Our need to be a unit and our desire not to operate separately. But I realize now that our actions only worsened the divide between us because Novak and I were on the same side with you facing opposite us."

She finally finished unzipping my pants, the fabric parting around my hips, but I couldn't even think about how close my cock was to her weeping heat. Not when our actions had hurt her so thoroughly.

"We have a history, Lay. But it's nothing compared to what we have with you now." I hoped she could hear the truth in my words. "You're our heart now, Lay. Always. And if that means only being with you and not each other, we'll do that."

I knew Novak would feel the same as me.

Yes, we were attracted to each other.

But I'd meant what I'd said—Layla was our foundation. Without her, that attraction would lose meaning. She was our soul. Our mate. Our reason for reuniting. If keeping our attentions focused on her was what she desired, we'd happily do it. Because what she wanted mattered more than anything else.

"You're what matters most to us," I continued. "The rest is founded in lust and a deep understanding of our limits. But your limits matter, too. Tell me what you need, and I'll make it happen. No matter what it is, we'll do it. I promise."

"I-I like watching you," she stammered, her legs tightening around my hips. "I *really* like watching you together."

"Did it bother you when it was just me and Novak

while you showered?" I asked, needing to know if that was her limit.

She shook her head. "N-no. I... I liked imagining what you were doing." Her cheeks pinkened as though it was difficult for her to admit. "The idea of you and Novak together is..." Her thighs clenched again, her scent bursting between us as she told me with her body what the notion of me with Novak did to her.

"It turns you on," I said.

She bit her lip and nodded. "Yes." A whispered response, but a real one.

"You're upset that we didn't make you come." I voiced it as a statement, not a question, because that had been the entire point of her punishment. However, we hadn't meant for it to turn into this deep-seated hurt inside her.

Looking back, I realized we should have eventually given her pleasure, too. The point had been made the moment we'd tied her up and left her helpless while we played. We'd taken it too far by not indulging her need.

We'd essentially told her we didn't need her to be involved for us to have fun.

Except that hadn't been our intention at all.

The only reason we'd even enjoyed each other was because of her presence in the room, and then we'd gotten off on knowing that she'd yearned for us while in the shower, too. Picturing her touching herself. Coaxing herself to orgasm because of *us*.

Fuck.

It had been impossible not to indulge in each other's needs, and it had stopped us from storming into the bathroom and taking her right then and there.

A need we should have indulged.

I shifted my hold on her to kick off my jeans. The walk-in shower made it easy to send the fabric sailing back into the bathroom. Then I reached to the side to turn on the water overhead. My bigger body took the brunt of the cool droplets, my feathers ruffling in response to the unpleasant sensation.

But Layla had my devotion and undivided attention.

"Can I make it up to you now?" I asked her softly. "Can I make you come until you beg me to stop?"

Normally, I wouldn't phrase it as a question. I'd just tell her my intentions.

However, it seemed important now for her to set the terms. We'd hurt her. Now we needed to make it up to her.

I'd do whatever she desired.

Because she was mine, and my protection expanded beyond the physical to the soul level. A soul I'd carelessly bruised and would now spend an eternity mending.

Never again, I promised her silently. *I'll never make that mistake again.*

Chapter Fourteen

Layla

THE EMOTIONS IN AURIC'S GAZE MADE ME DIZZY. They were so fierce, so protective, so *intense*. I swallowed, my body on fire despite the trickle of cool liquid trailing from his body to mine.

As far as apologies went, his had been… *mind-blowing*.

I hadn't expected that from him. Nor had I realized just how much his actions had hurt until he'd started talking. Because a part of me had been jealous about his relationship with Novak. They knew each other well, had centuries of experience together, and they'd almost too easily kicked me out of their bed last night.

At the time, I'd been so caught up in my dissatisfaction that I hadn't detected the underlying sense of displacement until now.

They'd been able to play together without me. While that normally wouldn't bother me, it had last night because of the context behind it. They'd kicked me out as a punishment, then gone on by themselves without a care in the world.

Which I knew wasn't really true at all.

I'd seen their half-mast erections, had sensed their need for me when I'd returned to the bed.

Yet some secret part of me had felt… left behind.

"Lay," Auric murmured, his palm returning to my cheek as his opposite hand remained beneath me. "I'll give you whatever you want. Just tell me what to do. How to make this up to you."

I swallowed, my heart swelling with each passing minute. I could sense his intensity, his care, his willingness to do whatever I wanted. And I found there was something I needed. Something... I was almost afraid to voice.

"Will you...?" I shivered, my gaze slipping from his eyes to his shoulders, noting his strength and perfectly honed build. He might not have been working out in our room these last few days, but he hadn't lost an ounce of his musculature. If anything, it seemed more pronounced now.

"Will I...?" he prompted softly, his wintergreen scent wrapping around me in an intoxicating caress.

I swallowed again, my lashes fluttering closed. "W-will you make love to me?" It came out on a whisper, the question sounding inane to my ears. Because of course he couldn't do that.

This was Auric.

Strong.

Powerful.

A commander in every way.

He didn't do soft. He was all harsh lines and impossible strength. A warrior in every sense of the word.

"N-never mind," I added, shaking my head. "It was—"

Auric pressed his lips to mine, his touch gentle and so unlike any other kiss he'd given me before. This one felt... *reverent*.

My eyes flew open to meet his, a hundred questions firing in my brain at once.

He didn't speak. He didn't continue kissing me. He merely held me captive with our lips touching without moving. Then he stepped back to allow the water to fall around us, washing away the ash of our fight outside. He slowly lowered my legs until my feet touched the floor, then he reached around me for the soap and began to lather it between us.

No words.

No sounds.

Just the hush of water continuing to trickle over us as he went to work cleaning us both.

Each brush felt like a promise. Each touch stirred goose bumps. And every stroke of his hand caused my abdomen to clench.

I felt worshipped. Cherished. *Loved*.

And all he was doing was washing me thoroughly with water and soap.

He repeated the actions on himself, his eyes never leaving mine.

It was distinctly intimate. A passionate embrace without truly touching. A powerful moment in its silence and intensity.

He rinsed me again, then himself, and slowly reached over to flip off the water when he finished.

A towel came next, his movements careful and concise. My nipples hardened as he drew the fabric around my breasts. Butterflies took flight in my belly when he dried the sensitive space between my legs. Then my thighs squeezed in need of a friction he hadn't provided.

If he noticed, he didn't show it.

Instead, he dried himself, then turned me to pat down my wings.

Rather than do his own, he just ruffled them, flinging water all over the bathroom. I bit my lip to keep from smiling, the action a bit animalistic, yet very Auric.

LEXI C. FOSS & JENNIFER THORN

He bent to capture my mouth with his own, his kiss knowing and slightly teasing.

Then he lifted me into his arms once more, this time cradling me against him protectively instead of having me straddle his hips.

He left the towels behind and carried me to the bed. The door was already closed, but not locked. I almost mentioned it. However, I didn't want Novak to feel like we'd locked him out. That would be counterproductive to everything we'd just discussed.

Instead, I relaxed against Auric and sighed as he set me on the bed. It was gentle, soft, *perfect*, and exactly what I needed. I was wet for him already, despite the towel he'd used on me moments ago, my body begging him to take me and make me his.

But he didn't lie on top of it.

He didn't even lie next to me.

Instead, he knelt near the foot of the bed and lifted one of my legs to kiss my bare ankle.

I trembled, that action decidedly affectionate. He followed it up with another to my calf, then to my inner knee, and up my thigh to the apex between my legs. Rather than kiss the heart of me, he repeated the actions on my opposite limb, taking his time to taste and adore every inch before returning his focus to my mound.

His eyes held mine as he bent to taste me, his turquoise orbs a hypnotic light that held me captive beneath him.

I threaded my fingers through his wet hair as a moan escaped my throat, his mouth whispering sweet benedictions against my flesh and driving me quickly to the point of madness.

All the pent-up sensuality from last night came flooding back, priming my body almost immediately for his tongue.

But he took his time, tracing my seam, licking me deep,

and tenderly circling my clit. "Auric," I breathed, arching into him.

He hummed, his palms holding my thighs and spreading them impossibly wider as his tongue penetrated me deeply.

I nearly screamed, the sensation of his mouth on me ripping me apart from the inside out. My veins burned. My stomach tightened. My lungs restricted my ability to breathe.

Every part of me was on fire, my need to come so much worse than it had been last night.

Auric must have sensed it because he latched on to the most sensitive part of me and drove two fingers into my tight sheath.

I exploded with a scream, his name a curse and a prayer on the wind as my feathers shook from the onslaught of sensation he'd evoked below. It was powerful. Harsh. Beautiful. Intense. Exactly what I needed. And not nearly enough.

He licked me through each quake, then slowly kissed a path up to my breasts, where he paused to give them the same treatment as my lower half. My grip in his hair tightened, my desire spiking with each passing second. "I need you inside me, Auric."

I felt him grin against my nipple, his teeth an alluring contrast to his lips. But he didn't move quickly, just continued to suck and nip at my skin as though he had all the time in the world.

It stoked the flames inside me to burn hotter, had my legs tensing with the need for more friction, and caused the butterflies in my stomach to flutter anxiously.

"Auric," I whispered, unable to hold the plea from my tone. "Please."

His pretty eyes slid up to mine, his pupils blown wide

with masculine pride. But there was something else in his expression. A deeper emotion. One he rarely allowed others to see. An emotion that appeared to be reserved for me.

He finished his path upward, his teeth grazing my throat and my throbbing pulse on his way up to my jaw, where he gently nibbled his way to my mouth.

I sighed against him, overheated and needy and yet oddly content at the same time. "Thank you," I whispered, holding his gaze. "Thank you for... this."

He pressed his lips to mine, his kiss brief, his eyes glowing with more of that unspoken emotion. "Anything for you, love," he said, his voice soft and filled with passion.

I parted my legs around him as he settled between my thighs.

His eyes didn't leave mine, his lips a whisper away from my own, as he slowly slid into me.

It wasn't fast.

It wasn't hard.

It was soft, tender, exquisite perfection.

I felt every inch, every ounce of restrained power, every amazing second.

It wasn't until he was fully inside me that he finally kissed me again, this time his mouth capturing mine in an embrace that demanded reciprocation.

I wrapped my arms around his neck, my ankles locking against his ass while I clung to him as though he were my meaning for life.

And I kissed him back.

I stroked my tongue against his, memorizing his mouth, his technique, his adoration. He responded in kind, his lips unleashing unspoken vows and promises for our future, telling me without words that he loved me, and letting me feel the emotion rippling through his body.

There were no harsh thrusts, just a tender mating of hips. And it was beautiful. Perfect. Exactly what I desired.

He made me feel… loved.

Cherished by him.

Admired.

His.

I quivered beneath the intensity, my climax rushing to the surface beneath a wave of emotion I'd never expected to feel. And this time when I came undone, he was there to catch me, his strong arms wrapped around me in a protective cage that allowed me to fly free with abandon and grace.

His name left my lips.

His heart beat with mine.

His soul drowned me in heated bliss, promising to forever be mine.

Our tongues danced. Our bodies moved. His own orgasm soon followed. And together we went to the stars in a stunning moment of unexpected matrimony.

He's really mine, I marveled, reveling in the sensations and emotions brought on by our embrace. *Auric… is mine.*

For now.

For always.

For eternity.

I love you, I told him with my wings, wrapping around us as we remained joined down below. *I will always love you.*

Even if he didn't feel the same because of my black wings. Even if we found that all this was a dark trick, a horrid game. I'd still love him. No matter what happened. He was mine. I claimed him. No one and nothing would ever change that.

For as long as we both lived.

I'm yours.

Chapter Fifteen

Raven

I can't sleep like this.

I'd been tossing and turning for an hour now, rolling into Sorin only to start sweating against his heat. Then rolling away from him into Zian, where the old mattress dipped so far beneath his body that I felt suffocated from being crammed against his side with no room to move. Even cradling myself on my wings couldn't keep me from feeling the bump between the two mattresses shoved together.

So I was awake, drifting somewhere between sleep and consciousness and praying for a coma, when I heard the brush of something leathery in the hallway.

My eyes popped open, and I stared up at the ceiling overhead, listening intently.

It came again—a slither, maybe the clacking of claws. Mousey Mouse? Or was I imagining it? He didn't necessarily know that we'd moved cells and could be looking for me.

For the briefest moment, I considered waking my mates but decided against it. If it turned out I was just hallucinating sounds because I was so damn tired, I'd feel dumb. And if it was Mousey Mouse, he didn't really get along well with my mates.

I gently climbed to my knees and eased toward the edge of the makeshift bed. Standing, I pulled on a shirt that tied at my neck and slipped on a pair of pants. Then I crept toward the exit.

This new cell had a door that closed, even though part of the ceiling had fallen away during the demonic attack on the mountainside. We'd swept the pile of rubble against the wall, but small rocks and debris still shifted beneath my bare feet as I crossed to the door.

The hallway appeared to be empty. However, the cavernous darkness held a lot of shadows.

Cautiously, I ventured out, glancing left and right, searching the dusty floor for the little Blaze demon.

Instead, I caught sight of white wings with dark tips.

My heart rate kicked up. I eased down the hallway, deeper into the shadows, and they parted to reveal the Reformer.

Standing smack dab in the middle of the prison without a care in the world.

I opened my mouth to scream, to wake up the prison, my mates, a call to arms for everyone to run, but he held up a hand, that mere action freezing me in place. Whether by magic or strength of will alone, I wasn't sure.

He was my father.

So maybe he possessed an enchanted link to my willpower.

What a terrifying thought.

"Don't worry," he said softly in a pitch meant for my ears alone. "I just want to talk."

I glared at him, wondering if I could kill him with my bare hands since I'd left my weapons in the room. *Stupid, Raven. Very stupid.* How could I possibly have thought it was

Mousy Mouse? Ever since I'd found out his real name was *Clyde*, he'd been spending more time with Novak than with me. I wasn't even sure we were buddies anymore.

Sayir held up some kind of bundle. "Are you hungry? I brought you a sandwich."

I eyed the paper-wrapped item as my stomach violently twisted. "Is this another game?" Because I'd bite off his damn hand for something to eat right now.

He smiled, a slash of white in the darkness. "No. Walk with me, young one. If you give me your attention for the length of this hallway, I'll give you more food. Food for everyone in the prison."

In response, my stomach gave a traitorous rumble. I'd eaten only a handful of mushrooms before bed. The idea of biting into an honest-to-gods sandwich felt like a little slice of heaven. Not to mention, food for *everyone* implied I could bring some to my mates, too.

It was a gamble.

But I knew he wanted me alive for a reason. I'd passed all his tests to date, and he'd told me I had to *guide the key*.

So harming me seemed counterproductive to his efforts.

Besides, I could use this as an opportunity to learn more about his motives.

Or die in the process, my intelligent side whispered.

"I have no desire to hurt you," Sayir murmured.

"Uh-huh," I muttered.

His lips twitched in amusement. "You're smart not to trust me. But I know you're hungry."

My gaze dropped to his hand again, my nostrils flaring with a need to scent the item, my tongue drying with the desire to taste, and my stomach curling with a deep yearning for food.

I ground my teeth together. If he wanted to harm me,

he would have done it already. He wouldn't wait for me to follow him into a trap; he'd have set one for me to step into the moment I entered the hallway. Or he would have unleashed one of his pets to attack us.

"Fine," I hedged. "But keep your distance."

Sayir raised one hand in surrender while offering the sandwich with the other. Even though my gut screamed at me to not take the bait, I did anyway. I was *starving*. Besides, it was best to play along and take advantage of his offering.

Unless it poisons me, I thought bleakly. But at this point, I wasn't sure if starving or poisoning would be a worse way to go.

Sighing, I took the offering and crossed the hallway, putting several feet between us so that I was well out of lunging reach. Then I fell into step beside him as I unwrapped my sandwich.

He clasped his hands behind his back as he walked with me, surprisingly docile. He almost seemed to be enjoying my agreement.

"You must be desperate for female company if you're bribing me with food just for a chat," I muttered before I took a bite. *If it's poison, then it's delicious poison, because yum.*

He chuckled. "Perhaps that was true, once. Our kind is painfully lacking in females, something I tried to remedy," Sayir began, peering down the darkened hallway ahead of us.

I took another satisfying bite before asking, "Remedy how?"

His lips lifted in a slight grin. "I created one."

Choking on my food, I paused. "Created one?"

Sayir let out a low hum of acknowledgment. "Indeed. The most beautiful woman I've ever laid eyes upon."

Sneering at him, I said, "You can't find a real female,

so you had to make one?" I wasn't sure where this snarky side came from. The first time I'd met him, I'd been scared shitless. But now that he'd put me through the paces, like, a hundred times, I no longer found him all that intimidating so much as cruel and darkness personified.

Maybe hunger is making me go insane, I mused. *What a delightful development in my life.*

He turned to face me from across the corridor. "Pay attention, Raven. What I'm telling you is important, so I suggest you issue fewer insults and start listening." He tapped his ear, a blade glinting through his sleeve.

As far as reprimands went, it was effective.

"Sorry," I mumbled. Although, I wasn't sure I meant it. However, I did want him to continue because he seemed to be giving me insight into his history. No one had mentioned him creating a female before. Was he talking about my mother?

He studied me for a long moment, then resumed walking. "I was quite proud of my Nora creation. Her strength. Her beauty. She was a compatible mate, too, by scent. Which, I suppose, could be because I made her, but souls don't necessarily work in that way."

I really wanted to say something like, *So you made yourself a sex toy?* But I refrained and took another bite of my sandwich instead.

"Unfortunately, she was taken from me before I could claim her," he went on, his words drifting off as a touch of grief mingled in his tone. Then he refocused, glancing over at me with what seemed to be a genuine smile. "You're lucky to have mates of your own. To be so cherished."

"What does any of this have to do with me?" I asked as I peeled away the last of the paper to finish off the sandwich. Because if he'd lost this female, then she couldn't be my mother, right?

Sayir gazed down the length of the hall. "I wonder what kind of offspring you and your mates will produce. Will your children be true Noir? Gods? Or will they be like the others—indirect descendants? Or Nora weaklings, without supernatural powers…?"

I cast him a sidelong glance. Had he lost his mind? "True Noir? Gods? What the hell are you talking about?"

"You'll learn in time," he murmured. "I've been trying to strengthen the Noir for the war to come, but my efforts have been thwarted at different turns. The biggest breach began at Noir Reformatory with all the outlandish cullings. I designed them to remove the weak, not destroy the Noir population."

He sounded frustrated, his strides turning tense.

"Someone is trying to dismantle my experiments, Raven." His lips twisted. "I'm working on figuring out who the culprit is. Soon, I hope."

Created females? War? Cullings? Experiments? Jeez, he was all over the place with this conversation. I couldn't even keep up with his level of crazy.

"What's the point of this meeting?" I wondered out loud. He wouldn't be here unless he needed something.

Sayir's lips quirked up, and he ducked his head with a little laugh. "Can't a father wish to confide in his only daughter?"

His *only* daughter. Because I'd killed the other in one of his fucked-up games. As much as I'd disliked that bitch, I didn't appreciate the reminder of how she'd died.

"No," I answered him, referring to his question about a father confiding in his daughter. "Not without wanting something in return."

Sayir grinned. "Maybe all I want is for you to understand." He held out a hand, indicating the floor ahead of us. "A gift. And no, it's not poisoned."

I glanced at him sharply. *Can you read my mind?* I demanded.

If he could, he didn't react, merely shifted his gaze to the pile of crates and sacks ahead of us. Pale moonlight spilled through the open door beside the food, and a brisk nighttime wind swirled around us.

"Food," Sayir said simply. "As promised."

I eyed the stack, surprised not only at how big it was but also that he'd already had it sitting here. Waiting for me. "How'd you know I'd walk with you?"

"I think you'll find I know you better than you'd expect. Like father, like daughter, hmm?" His smirk widened into a full smile, and he fluttered his wings. "I'll be in touch."

Before I could argue or make him stay and explain all the crazy things he'd just said to me, he vanished through the open door. A split second later, I felt his presence disappear, even though I didn't sense the electric static of a portal.

Which meant he'd left me with his bribe and with more questions than answers than moments before.

CHAPTER SIXTEEN

NOVAK

A FEW MOMENTS EARLIER...

I'D FINALLY FINISHED SCOUTING OUR EXIT PATH OUTSIDE when I sensed Sayir's arrival. His dark energy sizzled across my skin despite the cool, midnight sky. Everyone in the prison was likely asleep now, completely unaware of his presence.

Except me.

I'd stayed out most of the day and evening, searching for the right direction. His arrival suggested I'd chosen correctly because it meant I'd found a way to circumvent his surveillance.

Unless he was here to confront me on our plans.

Hmm, I doubted it. That wasn't his method. He preferred to maintain the upper hand, to torture us with the unexpected.

So what are you doing here? I wondered, sticking to the shadows as I attempted to follow him into the prison.

He'd appeared with dozens of crates, his portal having disappeared before I could pinpoint it.

If I stayed out here, I might be able to catch him in action.

But then I'd miss whatever trap he was laying inside.

The latter made more sense, as it allowed me to protect my mate, who had likely fallen asleep hours ago.

Or I could just kill him.

But acting rashly never suited.

No. I needed to understand his intentions, figure out this fucked-up game of his, and find answers for Layla. Because whatever was happening here was directly related to her, and if I killed the source, we might never learn the purpose of all this.

Maybe I can kidnap him and torture it out of him, I thought, picturing it in my mind. *Hmm.*

Best to see what I was dealing with first, then decide.

I stuck to the walls, absorbing the shadows and allowing them to help me blend into the night. It was a slow process, one I continued until I heard Raven's voice in the hallway. "Is this another game?" she asked, clearly confronting her father.

I considered stepping out of the shadows, to make my presence known, but then Sayir mentioned food. *An exchange—food for a chat.*

Very unexpected.

Almost as unexpected as Raven agreeing to it.

But she probably saw it as an opportunity to gain resources for her and her mates. I understood that choice because I would make the same one.

Sayir's voice grew in volume, suggesting they were heading back this way toward the entrance of the prison, so I ducked even more into the shadows. It placed me within eyesight of the crates he'd dragged inside, the contents of which appeared to be food.

Their voices carried down the corridor to this open space, despite being several paces away. Sometimes tunnels were helpful in that regard, and this prison had been built into the side of a mountain, so the acoustics were desirable. Although, I doubted anyone could hear them through any closed doors.

Fortunately, their voices traveled to me just fine, allowing me to pick up on Sayir's comments regarding some female he'd created. I frowned, wondering if he was telling Raven about her mother, until he mentioned the female being taken from him.

Is that why you've chosen to go against your brother? I wondered, considering the possibility of a falling-out between King Sefid and Sayir. *Or are you just spouting gibberish?*

Raven retorted with something sarcastic—an unwise move, in my opinion—but Sayir merely issued a light reprimand and continued, the conversation flowing into his curiosity over her future children.

His mentioning of true Noir had my lips curling down because it sounded eerily similar to Kyril's commentary earlier.

Was it all planned? A way to lull us into a state of comfort and encourage us to follow this path?

Does he know I'm listening right now?

The conversation then took an interesting turn as Sayir said someone was interfering with his goals, suggesting that perhaps the wolves we'd been facing weren't sent by Sayir at all, but by another party entirely.

If that was true, then it made even more sense for us to leave.

It also made me think he didn't know I was here and was just having a candid conversation with his daughter.

Except he never did anything without purpose, something Raven commented on as she asked what he really wanted.

But instead of answering… he took flight, leaving her with the supplies.

And left me without an opportunity to grab him.

Damn.

His commentary about the Noir had distracted my focus. Because, apparently, I craved answers more than blood today.

Fascinating.

That was definitely Layla's influence more than my own.

I waited, curious to see what Raven would do.

She crept forward to check the items, lifting a few lids and humming out loud before retracing her steps to her room.

I pushed out of my hiding place to observe the findings as well. Everything was nonperishable, the items all meant to last.

On a trip, I thought, frowning. *So he is setting us up for this journey.*

But I couldn't shake the feeling it was the *right* path to take. Staying here felt too risky. Wrong. Like we were just sitting ducks in a mountain, waiting for Sayir's next *experiment* to find us.

Which only confirmed that killing him now wouldn't have changed a damn thing, especially if a third party was somehow involved. Someone would step out of the shadows to replace him, so it was better to deal with the enemy we knew until we learned more about these supposed interferences.

Some of what Kyril had said made sense. And I very much wanted to meet this supposed Noir king.

Kiss of the Gods, I mused, thinking back to what he'd said. *You've met someone who found you worthy of greatness.*

The rogue Noir immediately came to mind. He'd said something like that to me when I'd let him go that day. Something about being *worthy*.

I'd always known he was the reason I'd Fallen.

But what if it was more than that? Perhaps it wasn't my decision at all, but *his* choice.

I frowned, uncertain of how I felt about that. However, the confusion quickly disappeared behind a mask of stoicism as I heard Sorin and Zian approaching with Raven.

Fluffing out my wings, I made a split-second decision to pretend I'd just arrived and made a show of standing with wide legs while I observed the food pile.

Sorin and Zian fell silent upon finding me.

So I glanced at them with an arched brow, asking without words, *What's this?*

"Uh, hey, cous," Zian said, swallowing.

I cocked my head, curious about his display of nerves.

"It's from Sayir," Raven quickly explained. "H-he gave it to us. But I don't know why."

Oh? I wanted to ask her. I thought it was pretty clear *why* he'd given it to us—to earn her favor with that conversation. But if she didn't want to confide that bit, I'd keep it to myself as well and use it when the opportunity presented itself.

Sorin started rummaging in the bags, making the quick assessment that I had. "It's all nonperishable items. Good for long-term nutrients."

"Assuming it's not poisoned," Zian muttered, casting a glare at Raven.

She lifted her hands. "He gave me a sandwich. I ate it."

"We know," he snapped. "And who knows what's going to happen now."

"I feel fine."

"For the moment," he grumbled back at her.

I folded my arms while I observed their bickering, fully

aware that I would feel exactly the same way as Zian if Layla had naïvely eaten a sandwich from Sayir.

Of course, he was Raven's father.

So maybe he wouldn't poison her.

Although, he had put her in a maze and pitted her against her sister.

So maybe he would.

She looked fine, though. *Fine enough to lie, too,* I thought. Because she hadn't yet mentioned her little chat with Father Dearest, and something told me she wasn't going to in front of me.

She didn't trust me.

Fine.

I didn't exactly trust her, either.

Raven fluttered her wings, the meal seeming to have left her more refreshed than before. A flush had returned to her cheeks, and her onyx feathers gleamed with a healthy shine. I had no doubt sustenance would do the same for my mate, even if I didn't like where it had come from.

Sorin glanced at Zian and then at me. "Do you think Sayir left us these to help us run away?"

I considered the stockpile, then looked at Sorin and Zian.

Perhaps I was wrong, I thought. *Maybe Sayir did see me scouting flight routes and decided to give us some supplies for the journey.*

It would be just like him to ensure we moved down his chosen path.

In this case, I'd take him up on it because the potential end result was too enticing to ignore.

"The Reformer wants us to go with Kyril," I said, meeting Zian's gaze. "To meet King Vasilios."

"King… who?" my cousin asked.

"Vasilios," I repeated. "King of Noir."

He shook his head as though to clear it, then blinked at me several times.

With a sigh, I summarized what we knew. "Kyril says the Noir are a race led by King Vasilios. He claims this king is Layla's true father." I went on to explain about the plague, how Noir had fled to Earth, and ended with, "Kyril wants to take us to King Vasilios to prove his statement."

The three of them stood blinking at me now, perhaps because it was the most they'd heard me speak in a century combined. Or it could be the outlandish story. Either way, it was what we knew.

"I just returned from scouting a path," I added, gesturing at the night. "We leave tomorrow at first light." Which was late morning in this part of South America. Now that I knew where we were, it was easier to understand the light and weather patterns. We were pretty far south, making the nights longer than the days. And we couldn't fly at night, or Auric's wings would be a dead giveaway.

"N-Noir gods?" Raven stammered. "Sayir mentioned something like that."

I arched a brow, feigning surprise. "You spoke to him?"

She swallowed and nodded. "In exchange for the sandwich."

Sorin and Zian both glared, expressing their irritation. But neither of them was surprised, which meant she'd told them upon returning to the room.

Good.

At least she was trusting of her mates.

I could forgive her for not wanting to confide in me, but I could not forgive her if she left Zian in the dark. Her telling him, however, suggested she wasn't playing for the other side, something I hadn't truly considered until just now. But it was a thought I contemplated and discarded in a second. Anyone could see that she loved my cousin.

"How'd he get in?" Sorin asked, searching the hallway. "Where are the guards?"

Gone, I almost said. I'd noticed there was no one outside when I'd returned, something I'd found odd until I'd sensed Sayir's presence. He'd either killed them or cast some sort of spell that had sent them to bed. If he'd meant what he'd said about the experiments not going his way, then I hoped it was the latter. He'd killed so many of his *assets* that there wouldn't be many left to fuck with if he kept assassinating them.

"I don't know. I heard him in the hall and he was just there," she said softly as her feathers drooped. "And when our conversation was done, he simply… flew out the door. I didn't feel a portal or anything, just his disappearance."

That was what I'd sensed as well. Like he was there one moment and gone the next. *Maybe he has a portal on him*, I thought, considering the possibility. *Like a watch that can teleport without a doorway.* That would explain the lack of technology around the prison.

Zian's expression turned concerned as he voiced some of my thoughts out loud. "He's clearly utilizing new portal technology, or multiple portals, ones we can't access."

Sorin rubbed the bridge of his nose as he said, "Which means the Reformer is just playing us again. All the fortifying in the world won't make this place safe."

"Which is why it's time to leave," I said, pulling a velvet bag from the crate at my feet. I untied the strings, and the smell of beef jerky assaulted my senses. Three dozen sticks were crowded inside the small bag—a decent amount of protein—and there were four more similar bags.

The Reformer hadn't skimped on supplies. But why?

To what end? I doubted anything Sayir provided came without a price.

Zian rolled his eyes. "So *now* it's time to leave? What caused the change of heart?"

Dropping the bag back into the crate, I said, "Kyril." That should be bloody obvious by now. *Keep up*, I told him with a look.

"You can't actually believe this shit about Noir gods," Zian scoffed. "We were Nora once, cous. We aren't some different race. We're flawed versions of our true selves."

"Maybe," I agreed. Except I didn't feel flawed at all. I felt very much alive. Powerful. *Godlike*. My feathers itched, even now, and while I was gaining a handle on their penchant to sharpen, something within me swelled. Pressing on every nerve, demanding to be unleashed.

Whatever it was, it definitely wasn't a flaw.

It was real.

And the way Kyril had looked at me said that he knew about my power, too.

Kiss of the Gods.

Hmm.

"It would sort of explain my existence," Raven said, her voice small. "I... I never turned, remember?"

Her mates both looked at her, their expressions taking on a glint of understanding.

I met Zian's gaze with a *See? Intriguing, right?*

Because it was an interesting explanation for all of this. It might be false. It might be true. There was only one way to find out.

Play the game.

I stood and toed the closest crate. "Sayir intended this to feed the whole prison. Needs to be distributed evenly." Which meant he had plans for all of the inmates. I could only afford to handle those directly under my care. The others could tag along at their own risk.

"Yeah," Zian agreed, blowing out a breath. "We'll handle it."

"After that's done, are you coming with us?" I asked, facing my cousin and his mates.

Zian looked to Raven for her input, but her eyes held the answer.

Hope.

She'd spent her life wondering how she'd ended up here. And this trip might just give her the answers she'd long desired.

"Yes," Zian replied, his gaze still on his mate. "Yes, we're coming."

"Tomorrow morning," I said firmly. "First light. We go."

CHAPTER SEVENTEEN

NOVAK

Wintergreen and cherry blossoms swirled in the air as I entered the room. I inhaled deeply, the scent one I would never tire of.

Layla and Auric lay in the bed in a curl of feathers, saturated in sex.

My lips twitched, admiring the view.

Mmm, she must have accepted Auric's apology.

Which meant I needed to deliver mine, too.

Rather than rush the moment, I silently slipped out of my clothes and went to the shower to wash the grime of the day off my skin. The scents inside the bathroom told me Auric and Layla had started here before moving to the bed, their arousal and combined fragrance making my muscles clench with need.

But I took my time soaping myself up before rinsing and thoroughly drying off.

I ran my fingers through my hair, shaking out some of the water after ruffling my feathers, then ventured back into the bedroom to find Layla still asleep. But Auric was very much awake, his turquoise gaze observing my approach as he spooned our mate from behind.

Always protecting, I mused as I carefully joined them. I didn't want to wake Layla yet, as I suspected she hadn't slept much last night, and I doubted she would be sleeping much more once I roused her to awareness.

I studied her delicate face, noting her pinkened cheeks and swollen lips. *Well fucked*, I decided, pleased. That meant Auric had taken proper care of her during my scouting mission.

"She felt left out," he whispered, drawing my focus to him with a frown. "When we came without her."

My brow furrowed. *She didn't like us playing together?* I wondered, confused because I'd scented her arousal. Hell, I'd *felt* it against my cock when Auric had used his wet hand to stroke me.

"We should have let her come afterward," he added, his voice still soft, but I sensed Layla stirring, her nose twitching in response to my joining them in bed.

I considered what he said, thinking through what we'd done and how it might have impacted her. It'd been meant as a sensual torment for us all, a way to solidify the need for us to always work together.

But I'd taken her to the bathroom with the intent of her finishing herself off on her own.

A direct contrast to the goal of our punishment.

Hmm, I thought to myself, seeing that choice in a new light. *We messed that up*, I told him with my eyes.

He nodded, seeming to follow my inner musings just as well as he used to in the old days.

I returned my gaze to her, pondering what he'd said.

So she needed to feel wanted. Desired. Praised for being our mate.

I could definitely do that.

Reaching forward, I tucked a stray fuchsia strand of hair behind her ear. Then I leaned in to press my lips lightly to hers. *Mine*, I told her without speaking. *You're mine.*

My lips whispered across her cheek, unspoken words

following my touch. Her lashes fluttered, her heartbeat kicking up a notch as she pushed herself into full awareness.

I caught her earlobe between my teeth, nibbling gently and eliciting a sweet gasp from her lips. "Mmm, I love that sound," I told her softly as my hand found her hip. "Make it for me again, sweet cherry."

Auric pressed into her from behind, helping me achieve my goal.

Layla's eyes blew wide now, her pretty lips parting on a gasp that melted into a moan.

"That's my girl," I praised her as I kissed a path to her thundering pulse. "Auric tells me you were feeling left out last night. How can we make it up to you, Layla? Would you like to be between us?"

She shuddered in response, her natural perfume spiking with clear desire.

"Mmm, I think she approves of that idea," Auric murmured, his lips in her hair as he kissed the back of her head. "The question is, are we going to take her together or one at a time?"

I studied Layla's expression, seeking the response in her eyes.

But she appeared to be dazed, as though living in a dream. Which I supposed was appropriate, considering her luxurious state between her mates.

My grip on her hip shifted to the sweet spot between her thighs, where I found her slick and hot.

A purr worked its way from her chest, the mating call one that would have made me hard in an instant, except being aroused was a constant state when in her company. Especially when she chose to go without clothes.

Auric palmed her tit, his fingers pinching her nipple and causing her to arch into my hand.

I grinned, my focus still on her lust-drunk gaze.

"Tell us what you want, Layla," I said, my finger gliding through her damp folds as I ventured past her entrance to the little pucker at her back. "Do you want us at the same time?" I asked, my touch circling the place she'd never been taken before, then gently returning to the safe place she already knew. "Or one at a time?"

Her pupils flared, her purr vibrating once more.

"That's not a coherent answer," Auric told her, his palm slipping from her breast to circle her throat. His lips went to her ear as I dropped to take her nipple in my mouth, the delectable little peak too lonely for my liking.

She needed to be worshipped, claimed, fucked, and devoured.

She'd felt left out.

Because we'd failed her in our punishment.

Well, we'd spend tonight making it up to her.

"Do you want me to leave to give you and Novak some privacy?" Auric asked, his gaze sliding to mine. "Or do you want us to fuck you together?"

Her thighs clamped down together on that last question, trapping my hand against her cunt. "Mmm, I'd love to translate that as an answer, cherry, but Auric prefers words." I nibbled her taut nipple, then began a path downward to the sweetness between her thighs.

"Both," she breathed. "Both of you."

"Where?" I asked as my mouth found her clit. "Here?" I thrust a finger into her slick channel, deep enough to hit her sweet spot and coat my finger in her arousal.

I gently withdrew and slid backward to repeat the action in her tight little rosebud.

She jolted in response, her breath sputtering out of her as I asked, "Or here?"

Auric reached up to cup her jaw, drawing her face back

for him to devour her mouth while I continued playing with the dampness between her thighs.

She was so fucking wet.

So fucking ready.

But I wanted this to be about her, not us. I wanted this to make her feel whole. Completed. Owned. *Cherished*. And I told her that with my tongue as I consumed her entirely, licking, nipping, sucking.

She squirmed in response, her back hole tightening against my intrusion as I continued to gently stroke in and out of her.

I drew a second finger through her slickness, bringing her arousal backward to add to the slippery mess. She groaned in response, her legs tensing.

"Relax," Auric said against her lips. "Let Novak fuck you with his fingers. You'll thank him later for it."

Layla shivered, her clit practically throbbing against my mouth.

She feared this, but she also wanted to experience both of us inside her, sharing her, completing her, utterly destroying her for anyone and everyone else.

Just the thought of it made me hard, my dick pulsing in time with her pussy.

It took serious effort to focus on preparing her, my own arousal growing with each passing second. I wanted to be inside her, fucking her, possessing her, making sure she knew she was mine.

But this wasn't about me.

This was about her.

My Layla.

My sweet cherry.

Our mate.

Auric's palm returned to her breast as he continued to kiss her, his fingers helping to make her even wetter, allowing me to insert a third digit inside her.

She flinched and bucked against my mouth, so I latched on to her sweet little nub, sucking and massaging it with my tongue while I forced her to take my thrusts in her untried hole.

A deep groan stirred in her chest, underlined by that addictive purr, her body telling us to mate her. To fuck her. To claim her. To take her. To finish what we started and make her forget her name.

I gave her a final suck, ensuring she was right on the edge of her orgasm before pulling away from her and kissing a path back up her body. "I suggest you fuck her pussy to make yourself wet before you enter her," I said to Auric before taking her mouth away from him and allowing her to taste her own arousal on my tongue.

"She needs to say it first," Auric said as he rolled us on the bed, forcing me to my back as he settled Layla on top of me. Her legs automatically parted over my hips, her damp folds kissing my cock and making me want to thrust right up into her.

Instead, I focused on her mouth, my dry fingers twisting in her hair as my damp hand went to her hip to hold her to me. She trembled again, her nipples hard little points against my chest as I strove for some semblance of control.

This female undid me with such ease, her desire a beacon my body couldn't ignore.

"You have no idea how much I want you," I told her, my shaft throbbing against her. "Your scent drives me insane, Layla. It's like I would break every rule just for a chance to touch you, to kiss you, to be with you. I'd kill everyone who stood between us, too. Fuck, I'd move the world for you, if I could."

I took control of her mouth before she could reply, my need to punctuate all those statements with my tongue a craving I couldn't deny.

She moaned, her fingers curling into my shoulders as she pressed herself against me, the little vixen seeking pleasure from the friction between us. But I couldn't even fault her. I was so far gone for her, too. So destroyed over this female that I barely noticed Auric positioning himself behind her. Except I felt his palm curving around her throat and knew he needed to take charge, just for a moment.

So I released her, allowing him to lead as he pulled her upright into a seated position and pressed his lips to her ear. Her feathers flattened between them as his chest met her back. She visibly quivered, her irises reminding me of wicked blue flames.

"Fuck, that's a beautiful sight," I admitted, my hands going to her hips again as I rocked up against her. Her tits swayed, her body entirely under our control. "Perfect."

Her palms flattened on my abdomen, her nails digging into my flesh as Auric nipped at her earlobe. It caused her to jolt, his bite clearly harder than normal. "Tell us what you want, Lay. Do you want us to fuck you together, or one at a time?"

She swallowed, the movement nearly stopped by his grip on her throat. But he didn't hold her as tightly as he would have held me. No, he handled Layla as though she were a precious jewel, which was exactly right. I could take his aggression and power, just as he could accept my sadism and darkness, but Layla, she was ours to cherish. Ours to worship. Ours to *adore*.

It was why our dynamic worked.

Auric and I provided each other with the balance needed to ensure Layla remained whole and unharmed.

I had no doubt she could take us at our worst, but we didn't want to give her that. We wanted her to experience us at our best.

"Together," she breathed, her folds slipping over my hardness as though to demand I enter her right now.

But that wasn't how this would work, something I demonstrated as I shifted her hips away from mine. Not by a lot. Just enough for Auric to slide inside her and coat himself in her essence.

Her lips parted, a protest leaving her mouth just as Auric thrust home. Her objection blossomed into a scream, her surprise at feeling him inside her causing her nails to dig even more into my skin, to the point of drawing blood.

Fucking perfection, I thought, my dick pulsing in response.

I loved pain, both given and taken, and the way she clung to me hurt in the best way.

I reached for her, needing her mouth.

Auric must have sensed my desperation because he released her throat, allowing her to fall on top of me once more. I caught her with ease, my lips finding hers in the next breath as I took her with a kiss underlined in heat, passion, and a lifetime of anticipation.

I'd waited my whole life for her.

My perfect mate.

My Layla.

Our tongues danced as Auric worked himself inside her a few more times, ensuring he was nice and wet and ready to play.

I felt him leaving, his shaft rubbing against mine along the way and leaving a wet kiss in his wake. Layla tensed in the next second, her breath stilling. "Put me inside you," I said, giving her a distraction. "Wrap those beautiful fingers around my cock, Layla, and help me fuck you."

Auric stilled as he waited for her to comply, knowing as well as I did that she needed this to help divide her focus.

Our beautiful mate didn't disappoint, her hand slipping between us to do as I'd demanded.

Her touch alone almost made me come.

As did her subsequent sigh as she seated herself on me, like I was some sort of lifeline she needed to breathe properly.

"Fuck, Layla," I whispered, forcing her mouth to mine again. "I fucking love being inside you." I shifted upward to prove my point, then slid my tongue in to duel with hers once more.

She would need as much of a distraction as possible for this to work, and it was my job to ensure her focus remained on me.

I slid one hand between us to thumb her clit, aware that I'd left her on the edge only moments ago and using that to my advantage now. My opposite palm went to her head, holding her to me while I claimed every inch of her mouth.

Auric bent to kiss the back of her neck, his wintergreen scent wrapping around us in a cloak of obvious protection as he aligned himself with her back hole.

He started slow, easing himself inside her in a much different manner than he would do to me. If our roles were switched, he'd thrust and make sure I felt the pain of his assault.

But Layla and I were very different lovers.

I would enjoy that ache.

She would not. She needed care. Sweetness. *Devotion.*

I told her with my mouth how much I appreciated her, how much I respected her, how much I adored her.

There was no one else for me in this world. Just Layla. Auric and I shared something else entirely, a friendship born of our warrior past. It was different, a bond that was incomplete without Layla. She was ours. Our mate. Our heart. The center of our souls. And right now, she was the true center between us. I could feel Auric sliding all the way in, his cock throbbing against the thin barrier between us inside her.

"Fuck," I breathed, arching into Layla and fighting my need to take her hard. "I can feel you."

"I know," Auric replied, sliding out of her and thrusting deep inside again.

Layla screamed against my mouth, the sound one of pleasure, not pain, her eyes wide in shock.

"I told you that you would thank him," Auric said, his hands taking control of her hips as he set a pace meant to make all three of us shatter.

I barely had to move, his thrusts coupled with her tightening sheath enough to draw my climax forward with a swiftness unlike any I'd ever experienced in my life.

But I refused to fall apart that easily.

Layla was our priority. I wanted her coming all over me before I gave in to the sensations.

I drew a sensual circle through her slickness with my thumb, coaxing her to join me on the edge of oblivion, but she was already there. Just a little bit of pressure was all she needed to tumble into a rapturous state that squeezed the life out of my cock and drew a guttural groan from Auric.

He started pounding into her, comments leaving his lips about how tight she was, how perfect, how much he loved the feel of her.

I echoed his sentiments, but with less finesse, my words broken and intangible thoughts underlined in a violent craving for *more*.

Which Layla promptly gave us as she fell apart a second time, her body entirely under our command as she tossed her head back in ecstasy. Her feathers fanned out between us, the sight so fucking beautiful that I gave in to the need to empty myself inside her.

I met Auric's pace, pumping up into her, and followed our mate into the heavens on an orgasm that threatened to blind me beneath its intensity.

Auric soon followed, his bellow reverberating through the three of us and sending Layla tumbling into another passionate state that left her pussy fluttering and clenching around my cock as tears streamed down her face.

She kissed me again, her body seemingly lost to her dreamlike state of unending pleasure. I wasn't even convinced she was awake, but she certainly kissed me like she was still with us.

She'd just gone to a beautiful state of blissful unawareness where all she felt was sensation.

We indulged her, prolonging her high with our mouths, hands, and verbal praise.

She shivered. She cried. She sang with passion.

And eventually, she calmed, her purr softening into the heavy breaths of sleep as she passed out with our cocks still deep inside her.

I chuckled as I tucked her against my chest, my fingers brushing through her hair. Auric watched with a grin of his own, then he bent to kiss her shoulder as he gently eased from her. I held her as he left to find a washcloth, the need to take care of her sitting heavily on us both.

I continued to hold her while he wiped her clean.

Then I slowly slipped out of her as well and held out my hand for the cloth.

Only, Auric didn't give it to me.

Instead, he bent to lick my shaft, his eyes glowing with purpose as he tasted the combination of my arousal mingled with Layla's sweet cherry flavor.

He took me in his mouth, sucking and cleaning me in a decadently intimate manner. I groaned as he hit the base, my stomach clenching at the sensation of his mouth on me after having spent a century without it.

I cursed and Layla's breathing changed, telling me his actions had woken her. He responded by pulling away and pressing his lips to hers, allowing her to taste our mingled flavors. Then he tucked her into my side and left the bed again.

I shuddered out a breath, my heart beating a mile a minute in my throat. I was still sticky with sex, as was the apex between Layla's thighs.

But Auric returned with a new washcloth, one not tainted by her opposite side, and used it to finish cleaning both of us up.

He ended his caretaking routine by bringing me a third cloth for my hands.

Then he tucked us all into the bed, his wing stretching out over Layla as he spooned her from behind. I followed suit, extending my own wing to cover her, and smiled when Auric locked our feathers together.

"When do we leave?" he asked me, his voice soft with the need for sleep.

"At first light," I told him, my tone equally as quiet. "Sayir even left us some food."

"Mmm," Auric hummed groggily, halfway to sleep already. "Map a path?"

"Yes," I told him, my hand settling over Layla's as I inched a little closer to her.

Auric's wings locked with mine even more, his possessive mood seeming to take over the room.

"First light," he repeated. "Okay."

"You going to ask about the food?"

"Tomorrow," he mumbled.

"Tomorrow," I agreed, grinning as I caught Layla's gaze. She was still blissed out on sex, but there was a soft, happy quality to her expression that told me she was truly content. "Good night, sweet cherry," I whispered to her.

"Night," she murmured back on a yawn.

No more words were needed. No more strokes or kisses or soft touches. We were in this together. Bonded by our connection to Layla.

So it didn't matter where this journey took us tomorrow.

Because, with them, I would always be home.

CHAPTER EIGHTEEN

LAYLA

I COULD BARELY KEEP MY EYES OPEN AS I STARED AT THE amber horizon. Novak hadn't been kidding about leaving at first light.

He and Auric were up before the sun this morning, the two of them ensuring the Noir were left under reasonable leadership before we departed.

Auric had tapped Tavin for the job, saying his skills with the wolves marked him as worthy. I'd suggested letting the Noir come with us, but Novak had pointed out the dangers of that and also said we couldn't afford the distraction.

Because he knew I'd end up feeling obligated to protect them all along the way, and we weren't sure how long this journey would take.

I'd been too tired to argue.

Just like I'd accepted the gift of new clothes without comment—a pair of jeans and a long-sleeved shirt with an open back. I wasn't sure where Novak had found them, but I was grateful for the additional coverage.

He'd also found me a pair of proper shoes, which were much more efficient than my sandals.

All of it had come in handy for our all-day flight. It

protected my skin from the sun and helped me fight the chill of the wintry air.

But now my wings were beginning to ache with the strain of flying all day. Being stuck inside Noir Reformatory with only the occasional chance to fly had weakened me.

Although, if I was tired, then Raven was even worse off. She'd been born in the system, meaning she'd never experienced long flights, let alone short ones. She'd already nearly fallen out of the sky more than once.

Zian and Sorin flanked her now, barely keeping her aloft, and I could have sworn I saw her eyes droop closed more than once. She was a fighter and fierce as a warrior, but she could hurt herself at this rate.

I hadn't realized we would be in the air this long. Of course, it was naïve to think it wouldn't be a long journey to our destination; how could it be anything but? Even if the Reformer had deposited the prison in the earthly realm specifically to put me near my "parents," nothing he did was ever easy.

Raven dropped abruptly, losing altitude quickly. Sorin's hand shot out to grab her, and on the other side, Zian snaked an arm around her waist, dragging her back up into their wind stream.

I angled my wings and soared closer to Auric. "We need to stop."

He glanced over at me with a placid expression. "Why?"

"Because we've been flying for too long," I said. "We need a break."

"You need a break?" he clarified. On his other side, Novak angled toward us and moved closer to listen in, though he remained higher than the rest of us.

Always watching and guarding, I mused.

Even though I didn't necessarily need a break myself, I replied, "Yes. Let's rest for the night and fly again tomorrow."

Auric raised an eyebrow, his wings flapping once with a burst of air that nearly tossed me aside. "Or is this because your bitchy cousin can't hack it?"

"*I'm tired*," I insisted, biting out each word through my teeth. Maybe it was the fact that Raven was family. Or supposed to be my family, anyway. Noir king notwithstanding. Or maybe it was because I knew she'd be too proud to ask for a break, and even if Sorin and Zian tried to force her to stop for the night, she'd argue just to not appear weak.

I understood because I'd want to do the same.

If I asked for a rest, she could recuperate in dignity. I was the princess. Sometimes it came in handy to act like one.

Kyril soared closer, Clyde clinging to his shirt with tiny dragon claws. The Noir straightened out slightly beneath me and looked up at us both. "It would be easier for all of us if we took a break. We still have a ways to go."

Raven and her mates lingered far behind us, nothing more than dots in danger of blinking out entirely. We had to slow down, or stop, or we'd become separated.

"Your wings are about to light up the night, too," I pointed out. The reason Novak had wanted to fly during the day was to appear as nothing more than birds in the sky to any watching humans. That would be at risk if we flew too late into the evening; most birds hid at night for a reason.

Auric's lip curled up. "Are you growing soft, Layla?"

I rolled my eyes. "Just tired."

He growled, a half-playful, half-furious sound. One arm lashed out and caught me around the waist. With a mighty heave, he yanked me against his chest, closed his wings, and let us free-fall past Kyril in a blur of white and black feathers.

For a chaotic few moments, the two of us plummeted toward the earth below. We dipped and spun in a terrifying and dizzying array of colors. It reminded me of the day I'd arrived at Noir Reformatory, when a useless guard had allowed me to fall out of the airship with my wings still bound. Auric had risked his life to save mine that day.

Way before we reached maximum velocity, Auric's wings spread wide to stop our fall.

I grunted against the sudden upheaval and tried to figure out which way was up. Instead of releasing me, Auric squeezed me tighter to his hard chest. A chuckle rumbled through me.

"Are you done insulting me with your claim of being tired?" he asked, a note of amusement in his tone. "Or should I teach you another lesson?"

I squirmed against his grasp. "Let me go. You made your point."

He released me, and I did a quick barrel roll to level out and throw my wings wide. I caught a glimpse of Novak overhead, irritated to find he had an amused glint in his azure eyes.

These males and their need to dominate me would be the death of me.

Auric addressed Kyril when the Noir drifted into range. "There's no safe place to land. We're in the middle of the mountains. Forest thick enough you can't walk through it without a machete."

"Are you scared?" I teased.

He bared his teeth at me. It would have looked ferocious if I didn't know the softer side of him. "What if we encounter those damn demon dogs?" he asked. "We need to see where we're going."

"The terrain won't change," Kyril told him. "We're in the thick of a deep forest that doesn't appear to end."

Novak had been hovering above us for miles now, like a predator stalking his prey. I suspected Kyril felt uneasy with his eagle-eyed observation, but I didn't exactly have the chance to reprimand my mate.

Novak, unfortunately, was a man of his own.

Auric spread his wings and soared beside us as he asked, "How much farther?"

Kyril shrugged. "I'm not… sure. Ten miles. Twenty. Maybe more."

Raven slipped downstream again as she caught up to us, the relief on her face evident. Sorin and Zian caught her by each arm and hauled her higher in the air, but it was clear to me that if we didn't stop soon, she wouldn't be able to continue. By the looks on their faces, they knew it, too.

"Let's descend," I said, loud enough for them to hear me.

But on our way down, Raven dipped dangerously, falling out of her mates' hands and tumbling heavily toward the forest below. Auric's shock betrayed that he hadn't realized how far gone Raven would be after a flight like this.

Closing my wings, I fell after her and grabbed her by the waist, her black wings opening in front of my face as I hauled her back into the air. I angled her toward the ground, trying to carry half her weight with my own wings so we didn't slam into the dirt at full speed.

We landed in the forest canopy, branches swiping at us all the way down to the ground. I took the brunt of the force on my legs and rolled, trying to keep Raven from hitting her head. Unfortunately, my momentum won, and we both hit the dirt on our sides, rolling apart.

I slammed into a tree with my hip, narrowly avoiding pinning my wing in the process.

Breathing heavily, I lay still in the silence to gather my bearings. Close by, Raven let out a slew of curses that would have made my mother blush.

One by one, our mates touched down on the thick, leafy undergrowth. They had to pull out their daggers and hack through the heavy brush to reach us. Auric's warm hands wrapped around my biceps, and he hauled me to my feet, setting me against the tree to look me over.

"That was stupid," he chided.

I glared up at him. Luckily, Raven's mates burst through the underbrush a moment later, relaxing when they found Raven relatively unharmed. They went to her, Zian offering me a grateful nod.

"Any injuries?" Auric asked when I didn't respond.

"No, just some bumps and a freshly bruised ego," I assured him, rubbing my palm over my blue-jean-clad hip. "I can handle myself, remember?"

Novak drifted to my side, but his gaze remained on the forest around us. It was dark here—nearly midnight black and crowded with overgrowth. "Too thick down here."

Auric nodded his agreement. "We'll have to cut down an area to rest. It'll provide coverage, at least."

"But we won't see anyone coming," Novak pointed out.

The hard line of Auric's jaw said he understood, but given that we were literally grounded, there wasn't much choice in the matter.

Kyril approached us through the haphazard path Novak and Auric had cut through the brush, Clyde still riding on his shoulder. "Ah, I'm glad to see everyone's all right. Well, if you're looking for a place to camp for the night, there's a small clearing on the other side of the trees there," he said, pointing into the brush. I could just make out the rosy glow of fading sunlight. "First one I've seen in miles."

Apparently, it had been a lucky fall after all.

The clearing was fairly large and open to the evening sky. We stepped out into it, the scene putting me at ease. A thin mountain stream snaked along the edge of the grass. We all dropped to our knees for a drink, except for Novak, who kept watch.

I cupped crisp, cold water in my hands and drank deeply. Despite the cool atmosphere, I'd worked up a sweat —particularly when I'd snatched Raven out of her free fall and navigated us both somewhat safely to the ground. So the water soothed my hot body and refreshed my senses.

I bent for another handful when I realized all the sounds of the forest around us had disappeared.

My head snapped up, and I caught Novak's gaze on the other side of the stream. He held up a hand, indicating I should remain still, then one by one, everyone else paused and went on alert.

The last time the woods fell silent, we were attacked by demon wolves.

Novak motioned for us to stand. We moved as a group, following Novak's lead back into the center of the clearing, where we had the best vantage point of both the ground and sky.

Auric drew his knife and put an arm out in front of me, holding me between the two of them. Kyril and Clyde stepped up behind me, while Raven and her mates drew in behind him.

Deathly quiet met my ears.

I waited, breath held.

Something clicked. Whirred.

Then the ground began to erupt all around us.

My immediate instinct was to fly, but Auric slammed his hand into my chest and roared, "Down!"

I didn't question him. All of us fell to the dirt as something metallic zinged above us. Craning my neck to look up, I realized that what was erupting from the ground wasn't some kind of explosive, but razor wire.

A ton of it.

As the wires shot up into the air, the lines dragged nets with them that sizzled with static, and the contraptions yanked out of the ground, tossing dirt and clumps of grass everywhere.

"That son of a bitch!" Auric snapped. "He knew! He knew we'd land here!"

Raven, who was huddled near my knees with her eyes on the sky, replied, "How? There's no way!"

"Up!" Novak shouted before anyone could respond.

I shoved against the ground with both arms, wings flapping frantically as I took off from a horizontal position. When I pulled away from the dirt, I realized why—the nets were huge, and one of them was about to erupt from right beneath us.

I shot into the sky, darting around a whizzing razor wire before the net could grab me. Auric and Novak flanked me, slashing out with their daggers in an attempt to slice the nets.

Except they were electrified.

Auric yelped, and his hand convulsed as sparks shot up his knife. His blade fell to the ground, and the netting swung into him, dragging him back to the ground.

"No!" I shrieked, darting toward him. Shouts rose up from our companions, and I felt the barest hint of heat from Clyde's fire as I flew toward Auric.

Novak launched after me, shoving me away with teeth-rattling force. I whirled head over heels twice before I could right myself, only to find him downed beneath the netting, too.

Without warning, white-hot fire sizzled through my body.

The netting hit my back, and electricity filled every one of my senses. My wings seized, sending me plummeting several feet to the ground.

I landed on my side, too filled with pulsating agony to even notice the blow. Excruciating pain weighed down on me, and I screamed.

I'd failed.

We'd failed.

And we'd literally fallen into Sayir's trap.

CHAPTER NINETEEN

NOVAK

THE ELECTRICITY DIDN'T PISS ME OFF NEARLY AS MUCH AS hearing Layla scream.

I'll kill him.

I gritted my teeth and planted my hands on the grass, shoving against the netting with all my strength. My muscles protested from the sudden launch, everything convulsing from the steady stream of static energy being forced into my body.

The stench of burning flesh and fabric tinged my nose, a reminder of how screwed I was as the involuntary twitching in my fingers and legs tossed me back to the ground with little effort.

Beneath Layla's frightened shrieks, I could hear the rest of our party shouting to one another. Auric called for Layla, a rare note of fear in his tone. Not an emotion the Nora warrior had ever expressed in my memory.

Layla had changed us both.

Now we had something to fear. Not the loss of our own lives, but the loss of hers, which would be so much worse.

Ignoring everyone, I blindly thrashed against the electric constraints, roaring to the heavens as my feathers hardened into blades.

I wasn't about to let Sayir take my mate away from me.

Her screams broke off in a piteous sound that hit me in the chest, cracking my heart open from the inside.

I pushed harder, lifting off the ground.

Sweat stung my eyes.

The electric netting burned my bare skin, searing holes into my clothes. Jagged wounds tore across my skin wherever the wires touched, drenching my skin with hot blood. A sensation I'd craved for so long, only to be denied by monsters of ash.

Oh, the irony.

The yawning void in my chest continued to open after Layla's terrified screams cut off. Power writhed in that void, something terrifying and heady awakening in my soul. I thought I could feel Layla at the other end of that sensation—feel her agony, her fear, almost like I could sense her reaching out for me. A connection to her that felt more natural than breathing.

Flaring my nostrils, I drew in her scent, overpowering the burning stench with her cherry blossom sweetness. Gulping it in, I burst with it, feeding from it, oozing that power from my pores.

Then I let it loose.

Raw power exploded within me, launching me from the ground and shredding the net holding me captive.

It fell from me in pieces, sparking as the electric current cut off. That strange, staticky hum abruptly ceased, and as I straightened, Auric and Kyril shoved aside the nets holding them down.

I'd cut the power to the whole grid.

I sprinted toward Layla's slumped form. Her chest heaved, but she didn't utter a sound.

Nor did she try to move or attempt to stand.

My heartbeat thundered in my ears—my own pain and blood meant nothing.

She needed me.

Before I could reach her side, an almost imperceptible metallic *chink* echoed through the clearing.

I sensed the air pressure change before I spotted the threat.

A flat, curved blade whirled toward me like a boomerang.

I ducked, but not quickly enough. The blade sliced through my feathers, taking a few with it despite their hardened state. Agony ripped down my spine in punishment.

A second blade hurtled toward me, nearly invisible in the growing dusk.

I leaped out of the way, then dodged a third that seemingly came out of nowhere.

Another metallic *snick* sent four more barreling through the clearing. I kicked out at one, knocking it to the ground, then I darted up into the air to avoid two more, while the fourth caught me on the boot. They came so hard and fast that I didn't have a chance to do anything more than rely on my instincts alone to avoid being shredded.

The sharp smell of ozone filled the air. Suddenly, the blades stopped. Those already in flight halted and fell to the ground, and I landed, too, whipping around to check on Layla. She was flat to the ground, her hands tucked around her head—unharmed.

Thank fuck.

Auric landed next to me and tossed one of the curved blades down. Blood poured from a superficial wound in his palm. "What the hell is happening?"

"A trap," I said. "Just for us."

I glared down at the curved blade still stained with his blood. It had two wickedly sharp ends, and the curve was honed to a sword's sharpness. Too perfect to be made by human hands.

Something wasn't right about this.

Beneath my boots, the ground shook menacingly, distracting me from the thoughts building in my mind.

I turned, softening my feathers before placing my back to Auric's. Kyril helped Layla to her feet, and I motioned them both over to us, putting them in the relative safety between us. Raven, Sorin, and Zian righted themselves as well and moved closer to join our party.

Blood trickled from a cut on Sorin's cheek, but he and his mates seemed otherwise unharmed.

The ground shook again. Huge, massive thuds, one after another like the slow, methodical footsteps of something much bigger than any of us.

Our group pressed in tighter, all of us back to back as we surveyed the trees for the source of the noise. I kept my feathers soft, but I was ready to harden them again the second I broke free of the group. I opened my fist, readying my hand to grab my dagger as well.

To my right, limbs and branches began to crack and fall, and crunching joined the thuds, all of it growing louder.

Louder.

Closer.

"Hold," Auric ordered when Zian flared his wings as if to escape. The razor wire had just been a precursor. If we tried to fly, Sayir would cut us down.

We knew how this game worked.

We'd played it before.

A massive wolflike creature appeared in the shadow of

the forest, our challenge sent by the Reformer for his sick pleasure.

I frowned, searching for the twist, because there was always a twist, something different to keep us on our toes.

It roared, then erupted from the trees like a bomb, shoving aside full-grown trunks as if they weren't even there. Splinters and shattered branches rained down on the ground as it stalked into the clearing. It was larger than any demonic creature we'd encountered before. However, it still had the same vicious three rows of teeth and glowing yellow eyes as the wolves that had attacked the prison.

Its gaze latched on to me, then it bounded across the clearing in one leap.

Right for me.

Whipping my blade from its holster, I stepped back onto my left foot and planted my feet, ready to use the beast's own momentum against it. In the two seconds it took to reach me, I noticed that its movements were jerky. Its knees bent in strange, anatomically incorrect directions. The monster seemed to flicker like a bulb that had been shorted out.

My suspicion grew, but I didn't have time to think about it. The overgrown wolf pounced on me.

I jammed my dagger up between its tree-trunk-sized legs, catching it in the chest as I ducked beneath its body. Dragging my knife out of the wound, I hit the ground in a roll, wings tight to my back. I managed to clear the beast's claws just in time for Sorin, Zian, and Auric to jump in.

Rolling back to my feet, I spared a glance for my blade, unsurprised to find the remnants of ashy blood dripping from the edge. I lunged forward, slashing out at the wolf's snout as it whirled on me again. The creature's eyes latched on to me and flickered out of existence before wavering back in.

What the actual fuck?

The beast lunged for me again, tossing Auric and Zian off its back as if they were nothing more than flies. It bounded to me, slamming into me with its huge barrel chest. I absorbed the hollow blow and flew back, hitting the ground on my ass. My dagger flew out of my grasp and into the trees.

I scrambled to my feet, chest heaving, and activated the blades in my wings.

As the wolf circled back, coming for me again, its legs bent left at a ninety-degree angle before popping back into place. It was like a computer glitch—a jagged error in the picture.

Virtual reality, I thought, staring down the monster. *Or a forced hallucination. Is any of this even real at all?*

Time seemed to slow. I pieced together what I knew so far. The way the Reformer had tracked us. The way he'd known our every move, listening to us, surveilling us. I'd assumed his methods were exterior, but my eyes told me something wasn't right with this picture.

The Reformer had bugged *us*.

Narrowing my gaze at the oncoming wolf, I said, "You're not really here."

I stood my ground as the wolf charged me, even when Auric and Zian screamed at me to move.

The wolf roared, an earth-shaking tremor that sent leaves falling from nearby trees. The beast reached me… and went right through me.

I whipped around to follow the wolf, but it was gone. Everything around me blurred and shifted, a painting melting away.

Mind over matter.

Sayir had implanted us with something that affected our ability to understand reality. Whether he'd spiked our food or surgically placed something inside us, I couldn't say.

Either way, it was time to figure out where the tech was and how to remove it.

Because the game had changed.

And we'd just figured out the rules.

CHAPTER TWENTY

AURIC

How? I marveled, rubbing my eyes as I tried to understand *how* Novak was still standing.

The beast had just gone through him.

Right. Fucking. Through. Him.

At this point, I wasn't even sure I could believe my own eyes. That wolf had hit him hard enough to knock him on his ass. Hard enough to rearrange his bones or detach his skull from his spine.

But he hadn't even flinched.

Novak whirled around, looking after the still-running monster with a glint in his eye. He looked like a wild animal himself—more feral even than the demon wolf. A self-satisfied smirk touched his expression from whatever revelation had made him stand his ground in front of a literal killing machine.

"It's not real!" Novak shouted, his voice rising over the beast's snarls and thunderous footsteps. "Don't believe it!"

Raven, who had fallen in her haste to escape the monster's path, climbed to her knees and screeched, "Are you *insane*? That's fucking *real!*"

I couldn't disagree with her. Ashy blood tinged my nose. Musk and violence vibrated through the air. It was a difficult thing to do, to pretend a monster didn't exist when it was about to rip out my throat.

But Novak's mind worked differently.

I'd seen him in action a century ago. And now, after years of surviving the reform system, his instincts were honed to a fine point. If he said not to believe my sight, then I'd fucking listen to him.

"It's not real," I repeated, shoving my knife back into its sheath.

A split second passed where nothing happened. Then the beast whirled on me as if angered. It ran, the ground trembling with every quaking step.

Not real, I pushed into my mind, clinging to the proof of what I'd just seen Novak do.

The beast marched on me, about to prove me wrong.

But then everything began to dissolve.

The clearing disappeared, replaced by a rocky slope of thin tree cover. Even the sky looked different—a little bluer, a little cloudier. Everything appeared *just* different enough that my gut instinct told me we weren't where we thought we were.

I couldn't spot the glints of razor wire anymore, either. All of it had been a mirage.

So I launched into the sky to take a look at our surroundings.

We were still in the mountains, but we hadn't flown nearly as far as it had felt during the long-ass journey today. In the distance, I could see the protruding, broken pieces of the prison jutting out of a slope, reflecting the red sunset.

Novak appeared beside me, his smoky scent tickling my nose as he followed my gaze toward the horizon. "*Fuck.*"

"Yeah. My best guess is we were flying in circles. Controlled by, uh, the virtual reality?" I waved a hand around to indicate the vision that had faded away. "Sayir meant for us to land here. He kept us in the air until we were too worn out to notice none of it was real. Fucking psychopath."

Novak grunted and gave a single nod, his whole body dipping in the air with the gesture. He was covered in burns from the electrical netting, raw lines that crisscrossed his body. His shirt and pants were shredded and half hanging off him from the damage, but then I noticed it wasn't razor wire that had done that to him.

I glanced down at my own blade, finding it wet with his blood.

We'd done this to ourselves.

"Question is, how'd he control us so thoroughly?" he asked, his gaze following mine to the damning evidence.

I shook my head, glaring back at the prison we'd left so many hours ago. "I don't know."

We landed back in the clearing, where the rest of our team had pulled themselves together after breaking through the alternate reality theater.

Layla rushed me, throwing her arms around my neck and burying her face in my chest. I cupped the back of her head and glanced over her head at Novak.

He motioned to the nearby creek—which obviously *hadn't* been an illusion. "Let's wash up."

I guided Layla to the stream, and we settled next to one another, while Novak stepped carefully over the running water to be across from us. He began to wash the worst of his wounds in the crystal, cold water as everyone else wandered over to join us.

Kyril sat beside Layla and crossed his legs, reaching out to touch her shoulder. "Princess, are you all right?"

I had to rein in my protective tendencies. I wanted to chop off his hand for touching her—wouldn't be the first time I'd done it to an offending party, either. But Kyril, for all his mysterious past and crazy stories, hadn't made any inappropriate moves toward Layla. If anything, the way he treated her was brotherly. Maybe even a bit fatherly, given his age. I'd learned not to judge an angel by their young looks.

She nodded and placed the tips of her fingers on his knuckles in a show of solidarity. With a wan smile, she said, "Yes, Kyril. Thank you."

Always a princess, no matter where she was or whom she was with.

"So," Zian said, plunging his arms into the stream up to his elbows. "What the hell just happened?"

I snorted. "We were played by Sayir. *Again*."

"How?" Raven demanded.

"A bug," Novak said, splashing his hands in the stream to clean them. He didn't bother to look up, but I could see the gears turning in his mind. "Tech of some kind that he placed inside us. Or something in the food."

Shock rooted me to the ground. "Are you sure?"

Novak's pale blue gaze shifted to me. "Have a better hypothesis?"

Her expression said she didn't.

Kyril clutched at his knees while Clyde perched silently on his shoulder. "I suppose it's possible that Sayir could have planted microchips inside all of us. I was hardly in his presence, though, for him to have time to do that."

Raven chuckled bitterly. "Makes no difference. The Reformer will do what he wants, when he wants, and we're nothing but toys in his twisted game. He could have knocked you out and implanted it." She clenched her fists. "And if it was the food…" She trailed off, her annoyance palpable.

Because that would somewhat tie the blame to her as the one who had accepted the food.

But something told me this had nothing to do with the sustenance and everything to do with being tagged somehow.

Layla held out her hands, looking down at them as if she didn't recognize them. "My uncle put a… a *piece of technology* inside me?"

"He's not your uncle," Kyril murmured.

But no one was listening to him.

We were all too focused on the fact that we'd been fucked over—yet again—by the Reformer.

"At least we know what we're up against," I muttered.

Novak grunted in agreement, then swiped his wet hands over his face and neck.

I followed suit, cupping my palms beneath the water to splash it on my cheeks. I thought of the day after the prison had burned to the ground, when Sayir had flown in, furious by the breach in instructions. He'd put the entire population of the prison to sleep and claimed it to be "magic." But it wasn't—I could see that now. It was technology.

Which further proved this wasn't related to the food at all.

Kyril spoke up. "Sayir has always enjoyed dabbling in sciences. Prior even to the plague."

I sat back up and nodded, swiping the excess water off my skin as I replied, "It makes sense."

Sorin, who'd taken a spot beside Raven on the opposite side of the stream, said, "So, theoretically, everything has been virtual. Nothing more than some kind of projection."

Raven's brow wrinkled. "Even the events back at the prison? The demons visiting at night? The purges that killed so many inmates?"

"The Nora guard turning to ash," I added pointedly, meeting Novak's gaze.

Novak grunted. "Was he really Nora, or was he a Noir meant to look like a Nora?"

I frowned because it sounded exactly like something the Reformer would do. "The same could go for all the guards. Maybe they weren't Nora at all."

Layla slipped one hand into the water and let it idly float on top as she murmured, "Maybe nothing's real at all."

The group lapsed into an uneasy silence, everyone considering what we thought we knew and comparing it to what we definitely knew.

Which seemed to be very little indeed.

Novak, however, zeroed in on Raven. He rubbed his fingers over his chin, his shrewd gaze stuck on her. Studying. Calculating. Finally, he dropped his hand to his lap and said, "You might be the key."

She arched an eyebrow. "Just because Sayir is supposedly my fath—"

"No," Novak interrupted. "Your power. You could find the tech inside us."

Zian's eyes widened, and he nodded. "Damn. You're right," he said, focusing on his mate. "You could use your healing power to find the weak link. The foreign object that shouldn't be there, some part of us that we can't heal."

She shook her head. "I don't think it works that way."

"You've leveled up in the short time we've been with you," Zian reminded her. "I don't think we can discredit anything you can do."

Raven flushed from the compliment. "Okay. I guess I'll give it a try."

Sorin stood abruptly. "I'll go first." He held out his arms, giving her access to his full body.

Still looking skeptical, Raven stepped up to him, then pressed a soft, meaningful kiss to his lips. She gave him a wistful smile before she pulled away and held her hands over his chest.

On my end, it didn't appear to be all that impressive. She walked around Sorin slowly, her palms a couple of inches above his skin. Her expression didn't change. There was only the barest hint of magic in the air, a nudge that indicated something otherworldly was happening. Otherwise, she simply circled him in silence.

With a gasp, Raven halted behind him, her palm resting against the back of his neck. Her eyes fluttered open. "Here."

"Then get rid of it," Sorin demanded.

Zian unsheathed his dagger and cut into Sorin's skin without hesitation. He made a small slice, then pressed on the edges of the wound until something metallic popped out with a rush of blood. Pinching the object between his thumb and forefinger, he held it up for our perusal. No larger than a grain of rice, which explained how we'd never even noticed.

Novak crossed his arms, his expression schooled back into its usual emptiness. I knew he didn't want to be proven right, because being bugged was a new kind of invasion of privacy, but at least we had the upper hand now.

Raven, who had pressed her hand to her own neck while Zian worked, let her arm fall to her side. "It's in the same spot on me."

"What about me?" Layla asked, turning her back to her cousin.

Raven's fingers hovered near her nape, her expression grim. "Yep."

For a few moments, Raven made a circle around our

group, verifying that the bug was in the same spot on all of us.

So we set to work digging them out.

Novak handled his own chip while I cut carefully into Layla's skin. She let out a little protest of pain, then seethed, "I can't *believe* he did this. I'm going to kill him with my bare hands."

"Get in line," Raven replied. She leaned her head forward for Zian to dig out her own bug as she hissed, "At least he's not your father."

"True," Layla agreed, wincing as I pinched the wound to release the chip, "but I don't even know *who* my father really is."

I tossed Layla's bug in the water as Novak came up behind me. Without preamble, he dug his knife into my skin to free me from my tracker.

"When did he even bug me?" I wondered out loud. "I was awake on the plane here."

"But you slept in the prison," Sorin replied. "We all did. Even Kyril did in this new one, right?" he asked as he removed the bug from the blond Noir's neck.

"Yeah, I did," Kyril muttered, sounding affronted. Considering he was supposed to be Sayir's sort-of guest, I could understand the irritation.

Hell, even as a non-guest, I was fucking pissed.

"What now?" Layla asked.

I glanced upward, taking in the midday sky, so different from the night that had just been coming in our altered reality, and frowned.

We really had only one option here.

"We need to fly," I said grimly. "We can't afford to rest any longer. Once the Reformer realizes his trackers are gone, he'll come for us. And soon. We need to run."

CHAPTER TWENTY-ONE

RAVEN

WHY DID I HAVE TO HAVE A SOCIOPATH FOR A FATHER?

I soared on the wind a few feet above Zian and Sorin, but below Layla and her mates. We'd been back in the air for hours—after having flown for a full day already—and I was running out of steam fast.

Again.

I'd received a temporary boost of energy after removing Sayir's tech earlier because apparently the damn thing had been amplifying my exhaustion. All that time I'd struggled to stay aloft, fearing that I wasn't strong enough to keep up with everyone else, had all been a fucking lie.

The monsters hadn't been the only hallucinations.

It'd been subtle, a little voice inside my head that had fed me doubts and lies until I'd believed them.

The moment Zian had popped the offending chip from my neck, I'd experienced an intense adrenaline rush.

But the boost had been fleeting.

I felt just as exhausted now as I had when we'd been caught in the electric nets inside Sayir's little "vision."

As if it wasn't bad enough that Sayir had implanted us with trackers, those little bugs had been recording *everything* we did. Hadn't he seen enough when I'd been a captive?

Not only that, but he'd also used the tech to literally control our surroundings.

How long had I been in what amounted to a damn simulation? My whole life? Since birth?

I started losing altitude in an unexpected drift, forcing me to flap my wings twice to right myself.

The effort it took felt much worse than usual, and I sucked at the oxygen to regain my strength. But the air up here felt so thin that I could hardly breathe.

Just like being incarcerated my entire life had kept me from being a decent flyer, I'd never had need of the atmospheric membranes in my lungs, either.

After Sorin and Zian had explained the biological details to me, I'd figured out how to open them so they maximized the amount of oxygen entering my blood, but because I wasn't used to utilizing them, it was wearing me out faster.

Trying to balance both flight and breathing had turned out to be difficult, to say the least.

If Sayir wanted to strengthen the Noir for some future revolution, his methods left much to be desired. Every day at Noir Reformatory had been hell. Even the bugs had kept us from being the strongest we could be.

So was this how he justified his behavior? Putting us through the wringer as a way to embolden us for his war?

I dipped again—this time fast enough to alert my mates as they rushed up from beneath me. Wobbling ever so slightly, I straightened out and fluttered my wings, my heart lodged somewhere in my throat.

Gods, I'm tired.

Not even just physically exhausted, but emotionally, too. We had no way of knowing what was coming or what Sayir had in store for us. I wasn't naïve enough to think that severing our technological ties to him would keep us safe from him for long.

I still felt like he watched my every move no matter what I did. No matter what kind of trackers I pulled from my body, he'd always find a way under my skin.

Zian and Sorin both nudged up beneath me, boosting me with the wind coming off their much stronger wings. Sorin's golden hair flicked into his eyes as he glanced up to meet my gaze. "You okay?"

I lifted away from them, still embarrassed by the way I'd fallen out of the sky earlier. I was determined to prove my worth. "I'm fine."

The two of them exchanged glances, and Zian asked, "Do you believe her?"

"Of course not."

Ignoring them, I lifted my eyes to the darkening horizon. I could keep going. I could make it.

I had to. We had no choice but to keep flying.

I wasn't weak. Not by a long shot. But the unfortunate truth was I had never been trained for flight.

I'd been caged by four walls and fenced yards for every moment of my life. My lack of flying prowess wasn't a fault in my character or in my genetic makeup. It was something my father had designed, a weakness he would exploit.

My eyelids felt like weights dragging my eyes closed. I blinked quickly and slapped at my cheeks, hoping it would wake me up. A jolt went through me, and then I started to shake. First my limbs, then my body, followed by my wings.

I'd been straining myself for too long.

I couldn't keep my eyes open anymore. I couldn't keep my wings moving.

As I started to lose altitude again, I suddenly understood what Sayir had wanted from me.

This was what he fought to avoid. He wanted me strong

enough to handle anything, to survive. The bug's instinct that had made me feel weak had been a test, and I'd failed him in this instance, unable to fly an inch farther.

Right before I passed out, my last thought was *I must do better. I will do better.*

And then everything went dark as I plummeted to the ground below all over again.

CHAPTER TWENTY-TWO

LAYLA

W E'D ESTABLISHED A CAMPSITE SHORTLY AFTER RAVEN'S second fall.

Sorin and Zian had kept her aloft, but their strength wouldn't have held up forever, so I'd been grateful when we'd located a place to stop for the night.

"Hey," I said as I joined Raven at the fire. She poked at it with a stick. The embers reflected golden specks in her dark eyes.

She was going to pretend like she couldn't hear me?

Fine.

I nestled onto the ground next to her, close enough for my wing to brush hers. She flinched away.

"Are you okay?" I asked, worried about her. She'd been through a lot already, and finding the trackers had only made all of this worse. She probably needed to talk about it, because whatever Sayir did affected all of us, and he seemed fixated on her.

Because she's his daughter.

Which, of course, only made this worse and that much more awkward.

She glowered at me as she broke the stick in half. "Did your father cut you open and put a tracker in your body?"

"No," I said slowly, taking up half of the stick as I drew

scribbles in the dirt. "But he did send me to prison, where I almost died, so there's that."

She frowned. "Yeah, there's that."

I glanced up at her. "Is the tracker what you're really upset about?" I doubted it. We all had endured several of Sayir's games. While it was an invasion of privacy, I guessed Raven's current anger ran deeper.

Her feathers fluttered as her dark gaze lowered with defeat. "I just keep falling for it. He offered me food, and I took it like a rat begging for scraps. Shouldn't I have learned not to take anything from him by now? Not to trust him?"

Sighing, I tossed my stick into the flames. We both watched as it cracked under the heat. "Sayir wanted us to come here. Perhaps he even wanted us to find the trackers. He has so many layers to his tests and games that it's impossible to know his motives or intentions. All we can do is survive."

But for Raven, it was more than survival.

It was personal.

Sorin interrupted us, tossing a log onto the fire. He knelt and rummaged through Raven's pack before producing one of the offending sandwiches.

"I'm not fucking eating that," she snapped.

He glanced at me, pleading with me to help.

I leaned in, giving Raven a soft smile. "It's just food. No sense in letting it go to waste now." We also hadn't eaten since before we'd left the first time, which had only provided us with enough energy for one flight, not two.

I slipped my hand into my own bag to pull out a similar item and made a show of taking a bite.

It didn't taste amazing or anything, but it certainly sated my hunger a bit.

I took two more healthy bites while she watched, her

expression skeptical. She probably expected me to fall over dead at any moment. Maybe even hoped I would.

But all I did was eat.

A third swallow.

Then a fourth.

And finally she snatched the sandwich from Sorin's grip and tore a bite through the bread. She chewed aggressively, her throat working when she eventually swallowed. She stared into the flames, anger flexing her jaw.

Sorin sighed and pressed his lips to the crown of her head. "That's my sweet little dove." He kissed her again before joining Zian in making a nest, ignoring Kyril and Clyde already asleep in a small ditch covered in moss.

Novak and Auric likewise worked on a nest for me, and I longed to lie down with them, but something haunted and broken lingered in Raven's gaze. I couldn't leave, not until I pushed her to talk about it.

But I gave her some time first, both of us eating in an oddly soothing silence.

When we finished, we shared some water, then glanced up at the stars overhead. It was a clear night. Beautiful, yet foreign.

I shivered, the air chilly despite the open fire.

Snuggling up to Auric and Novak sounds good right about now, I thought. But something was still very much troubling Raven.

"Did Sayir say anything to you?" I asked, running my thumb over the hem of my long-sleeved shirt. "Anything to suggest that there might be more trackers?"

"No," she said. "I checked everyone. We don't have any more trackers." She shook her head, finally meeting my gaze. "He said a whole lot of crazy. I don't know what to believe. He said someone was trying to dismantle his experiments, but he didn't know who it was. There's a war coming. And he wondered about my future children. If they would be gods."

"Gods?" I repeated.

Earlier, before we'd left the first time, Novak had told Auric and me how he'd secretly overheard Sayir and Raven's conversation. But he hadn't mentioned the gods part, only the experiments and the weird commentary on the woman Sayir had created and lost.

It was clear to us that either Sayir and Kyril were working together—something I very much doubted now because of the tracker in Kyril's neck—or there was a grain of truth to the matter that the Noir came from gods.

"Maybe Sayir's trying to bring them back," I said slowly, thinking through everything we knew.

Raven stared at me like I'd grown two heads. "Them who?"

"What the Noir used to be." I didn't know if the Noir were once truly gods, but I'd seen some of their incredible abilities.

There were also already two races of angels—Valkyries and Nora.

Why couldn't the Noir be a third race? Just like Kyril had already said.

But all Sayir's odd experiments, the potentially fake Nora guards, the female he'd supposedly created, him wanting Raven to mate, all these bizarre games… Maybe it wasn't about creating soldiers but about inspiring Noir gifts to shine through.

Noir gifts like the one Novak possesses.

He'd been the one to see through the hallucinations. He was growing in his abilities, something that Sayir likely wanted to see come to fruition.

Raven's wings shrank to her back as her shoulders

slumped. "He said he knew me better than I'd expect. Like father, like daughter." She flitted her gaze to me, the desperation there frightening me. "Am I really like him, Layla?"

Raven's question distracted me from my thoughts, her true fear coming to light.

She worried she was like her father, or might one day become him.

I broke the tension of the moment with a harsh laugh. "Of course not. You're strong and passionate, and you don't put up with any shit." I glanced at Sorin and Zian, who'd finished their nest, their gazes on their mate. "You have a capacity to love with all your heart and to be loved in return. Sayir definitely can't say the same."

She glanced over her shoulder, peeking at her mates. She hummed a little in response. Feathers rustled as she climbed to her feet. "Thank you, Layla."

I knew she meant it, and I felt like we'd finally crossed some invisible barrier between us. We definitely weren't friends. But maybe… maybe she no longer saw me as an enemy, either.

We were both victims of Sayir's "experiments." And because of it, I could relate to her in more ways than one.

I watched as she nestled into a cocoon with Zian, disappearing into a shadow of dark feathers while Sorin ventured into the forest. I wasn't sure where he was going, but I didn't really care. I was too damn tired.

Turning back to my own nest, I found Auric missing as well. Novak sprawled out on the soft collection of moss and blankets as he stretched his arms behind his head. His ice-blue gaze beckoned me to rest with him.

Sleep sounded pretty awesome right about now.

I joined him, cuddling against his side as we listened to the rest of our companions settle down for the night. It was late—well past midnight after flying for gods only knew how long.

"Auric took first watch?" I guessed.

"Hmm," Novak confirmed.

His palm spread wide over my back, his thumb brushing rhythmically along the thin line of bare skin beneath my shirt. The touch soothed me in a way I couldn't describe. It wasn't just sexual, but possessive. Not dominant or demanding, but comforting.

Novak's black feathers tickled my skin as a cool breeze wafted over us, and I snuggled deeper into his body for warmth. He curled around me, his confidence and power an aura I could easily lose myself within.

Kyril was right about one thing—Novak was special. Maybe he wore that Kiss of the Gods mark. Or maybe it was all him. Whatever it was, I felt safe because of it. Because of *him.*

"The stars are different here," he murmured.

Such a poetic, romantic thing to say. Coming from a male who didn't speak often, I knew these words were just for me.

I turned into him and lifted my head to rest on his shoulder so I could look up at his face. The starlight heightened his features—deepened the shadows, highlighted the angles, and turned him into something closer to a work of art than a living creature. "Different how?" I asked

He glanced down at me, his blue eyes brilliant, glittering pools of intensity. "Brighter, as if this world is young and new."

"Did you stargaze often? Before you Fell?" I asked, my lips lifting at the thought. He didn't strike me as the type, but Novak was full of surprises.

"Only when I couldn't sleep." He paused, and I

imagined that was often. "It wasn't uncommon for warriors to sleep outside during missions," he said, his voice low, meant only for my ears. He faced the sky again. "I spent many nights alone, staring up at the stars. But they're different back home. Older. Dimmer."

Back home. The words struck me. Would we ever make it back home again?

Worse still, would there be a home for me to go back to? One where I belonged?

Squirming, I pushed my troubling questions aside and focused on his comments instead. "If we really are in the human realm, then the brighter display of stars makes sense. Their realm isn't as seasoned as ours, right?"

"Hmm," he said, a noncommittal response.

"I like it here," I decided out loud, snuggling closer to him. "Sometimes different is good." I listened to his strong heartbeat, glad to have him for my mate. "You're different," I pointed out. "Whatever comes next, I hope it's different, too." I was tired of the same old game. Sayir and his tricks. A wall at every turn. *Different* was exactly what we needed.

A low, rumbling chuckle vibrated against my cheek. "Careful what you wish for, little blossom."

We lapsed into a short silence, both of us studying the human sky as if it held all the answers. I was never much of a stargazer in my life at the palace, but I had a passing knowledge of our most prominent constellations. Here, though, I recognized nothing. We were far from home. The reminder sent an echo of loneliness through me for the life I'd lost.

On the other hand, I'd gained two amazing mates and the promise of a new life—as long as we could find a way to slip out of Sayir's grasp. If anyone could defeat the

Reformer, surely three ex-Nora warriors and a current one could.

Tracing my fingertips over Novak's hard muscles beneath his shirt, I asked, "Do you miss being a warrior?"

A smirk tilted up a corner of his lips. "I'm still a warrior. Just on a different playing field."

I returned his grin; he wasn't wrong. Watching Novak fight was a thing of beauty.

Our eyes met, and his arm tightened around me. He tugged me in for a kiss. Slow. Languid. Thorough. I sank into him, my hand resting on his chest where I could feel his heartbeat. When we finally broke away, I was breathless, and Novak wore the self-satisfied look of a male who knew he could arouse his mate with only his mouth.

"Don't get cocky," I murmured, my neck heating up from his knowing gaze.

He hummed again and brushed away a lock of my hair. His eyes held a world of affection that I still wasn't used to, though I definitely looked forward to a lifetime of indulging his brand of adoration.

Staring at him in the starlight, so beautiful he made my heart hurt, it was easy to believe he could be a god. Like those black-winged Noir gods Kyril had told us about.

I thought back to my conversations with Kyril and all the lore he'd relayed to us. The idea of an entire forgotten history had taken root in my mind, though I wasn't sure if I believed any of it. Not yet. I rested my chin on my hand to look up at Novak again. "Do you believe in the gods?"

He shook his head, and his long, midnight hair spilled around his head like a dark halo. "No. I never believed in anything divine until I met you." He gave me a slow, toe-curling kiss. His tongue ran across my lower lip as he added, "I never understood worship until now."

Cocking an eyebrow, I grinned and asked, "Worship?"

"Worship is a form of obedience," he declared. "Your body commands me to obey." He drew in a long breath, running his nose along my neck. "You torment me when I fail in my worship."

"You aren't exactly the obedient type," I teased.

He lifted a hand and brushed two fingers over my cheek. "Certainly not," he agreed with a wolfish grin. "Perhaps I just need the right motivation to obey orders."

A flush heated my cheeks. I slid my fingers higher on his chest to caress the bare skin at his collarbone. "Worship me, then."

He obeyed without question.

His lips captured mine, hot and demanding, and the heat in my cheeks spread through my veins.

Novak rolled me until he was above me, pinning me to the ground with just his upper body. His tongue whispered sweet benedictions into my mouth. Warmth rose between us until I panted with need, so hot I wanted to tear the clothes from us both. I fought the urge to moan, to press my hips against his—we weren't exactly in a private place.

When Novak broke the kiss and looked down at me with those lethal ice-blue eyes, my breath caught in my throat.

"Kiss lower," I demanded.

But Novak just grinned and lay back, tucking me against his side as he murmured, "It's time to sleep."

I let out a small mewl of irritation. "You're no fun," I grumbled, snuggling closer to his warmth. "We need to work on your obedience."

His chuckle rumbled against my cheek. "Sleep, little blossom. Morning will come soon."

I knew it would, too. Which left me disappointed because it would mean prying myself away from my mate.

Letting go of this comfort and warmth to fly into an unknown destiny.

For now, I sank into his arms, content to listen to his strong heart that sang to me with every beat.

Because Novak was mine and I was his, and Auric would watch over us both.

No matter where the future took us.

CHAPTER TWENTY-THREE

AURIC

Sorin paced past me, and I fought the urge to berate him for not attempting to sleep. We both knew he needed it, particularly as his weak-winged mate was relying on his strength to fly.

Yet the asshole had shown up only moments after I'd sat down to begin the first watch, stating two guards were better than one. I had a feeling it had nothing to do with that and everything to do with his obvious distrust of me.

But what the hell did he think I was going to do? Go to sleep and let a mountain lion come in and maul everybody? Sayir wasn't going to let up now, not when we'd finally found our trackers.

I had come to the conclusion that Sayir wanted us to survive, but to achieve his end goal—whatever that might be—our lives needed to be on the line.

With each test, we learned something new, and if this was really about honing our skills, then the experiments would only become more challenging.

Survival came at a price, and no matter what kind of game Sayir played, we could be assured that it would be a deadly one.

Now was not the time to be at each other's throats.

So Sorin really shouldn't be here distracting me when I

also needed time to think. Time to plan and attempt to jump ahead of the latest game the Reformer had set out for us so we didn't wind up as casualties in the grand scheme of his madness.

Sorin muttered something as he stepped across my path again.

"Enough," I barked. "Sit. Down."

Sorin tossed me a flippant sneer. "I no longer report to you, *Commander*."

"Good thing, too, or I'd be forced to remind you of why I'm in charge."

"Except you aren't in charge," Sorin replied, circling on his heel to start pacing back the other way.

Sarcasm dripping from my tone, I asked, "Would you like to be in charge, then?"

He huffed with amused laughter. "I'd be better at it than you. I wouldn't ruin your life and make your wings turn black."

There it is. The truth of the matter in plain language.

Neither Sorin nor Zian had forgiven me for their Fall.

Hell, Novak hadn't, either. Not really, anyway. Because he would never forgive me for not asking him what had happened. Just as I might not ever forgive myself for the same reason.

I sighed and let my head fall back against the tree trunk behind me. "You wrongly blame me, Sorin. I'm just as much of a victim as you are." At least in the sense of falling for all the lies in the world. None of us knew the truth from the fiction anymore.

His jaw ticked, his blue eyes glittering with barely controlled fury.

Apparently, that had been the wrong thing to say.

"A victim? You dare call yourself the *victim* here?" He scoffed. "I must have misunderstood how hard your life was after our Fall, what with your white wings, getting your dick wet by a princess, and dragging Novak around by his cock while you're at it."

The image of anyone dragging Novak around by his dick made me chuckle. If anything, it was the other way around. Although, I'd never admit it out loud. But that male sure as fuck knew how to rile me up. Especially when he added Layla to the mix.

Unfortunately, my amusement only seemed to piss Sorin off more, making me sigh again. "If you hate me so much, why did you follow me out here?"

Sorin met my gaze directly without hesitation. "I don't *trust* you to keep us safe, Auric."

Of course you don't.

Sorin sat down several feet away against another tree and shifted his focus to the horizon. He crossed his arms and gazed out into the murky forest in silence.

Turning away from Sorin, I glanced back toward our makeshift camp. I'd settled on a slight incline some distance away so I'd have a decent view of my companions and the forest around them. I could just make out Novak and Layla lying in their makeshift nest.

As though he could sense my stare, Novak bent to pay homage to Layla's mouth.

Speaking of leading another by their cock, I thought, my pants suddenly tighter than they should be.

Because I knew *exactly* what he could do with his tongue, and I could feel the desire between them from all the way out here. I wanted to join them and be a part of whatever bonding moment they were sharing, but I also wanted them to have their time together.

Just as Layla and I shared our sweet experiences.

Novak pulled away after a beat and stared down at

Layla with an adoring look. She spoke, and he grinned, and then they curled up together and went still.

Layla was already proving to be a good influence on him. She'd started sanding down his rough edges and teaching him how to open up. He seemed less lethal, at least between us. He had leagues to go before he could shake off the sociopathic side of him—if he ever could— but for now, he was growing.

Layla, on the other hand… What kind of influence would Novak be on her?

She'd accepted him as a Noir so easily. I wasn't sure I could do the same. I'd known Novak in his past life, when his feathers had been white and his morals had run parallel to mine.

Now, though…

Now he was a different angel. One I'd been trained to distrust and dislike.

I've accepted Layla as a Noir, a small voice inside my head reminded me.

And it was true. Layla was new to the Noir world, and she was still *herself*. Nothing had changed but the color of her feathers. Black or white or even fuchsia like her hair, the color of her feathers had nothing to do with how deeply she owned my heart. She always had. I'd been an idiot to take this long to see it.

My only concern now was how to hide her feathers— and mine—should we choose to remain in this world. And because of that, Novak seemed to think I wouldn't accept her as a Noir, or him for that matter, but I was just being realistic. We couldn't live out our lives with things as they were now.

That thought was what had given me pause the other morning when she'd mentioned her wings. I'd been distracted by the consideration of what to do, but I strongly suspected that she'd misunderstood my hesitation.

Given how cruel I'd been to her before about her Fall, I couldn't really blame her for jumping to conclusions.

But wasn't that the crux of all our problems? The fact that we all anticipated the worst, especially when it came to the Noir?

Maybe redemption was a lost cause I should abandon. I'd been taught to expect and respect reformation, when in reality, maybe it wasn't even possible. Maybe it wasn't even *necessary*, if Kyril was to be believed.

I rested my hand on the sheath of my dagger and stared up at the stars.

Damn, life had become so complicated. A part of me missed the days when my world had been as simple as black and white.

Then again, I'd never go back to a life without Layla. Or Novak.

Nearby, a twig cracked, followed by a low scuffle.

I bounded to my feet in seconds, blade drawn as I stalked toward the origin of the sound. Sorin, to his credit, had moved just as quickly, and the two of us crept through the woods together without a word.

The last time we'd heard cracking twigs in the forest, we'd been up against Sayir's giant demon creature. Just because we were disconnected from his grid didn't mean he couldn't send us new—and *real*—threats. I doubted that everything had been a complete fabrication.

But we didn't find any of Sayir's minions stalking the forest. We found a female deer and her stag. They stood like silent wraiths in a patch of moonlight, leaves from the canopy overhead casting shapes on their tawny bodies.

The stag chuffed at us, pawing at the ground.

Sorin and I remained still. I didn't exactly want to be

gored by a territorial male just because his female had wandered too close.

The deer took off, leaping elegantly through the forest as if the trees weren't even there. Her mate took off after her, and they vanished into the darkness.

"Could have been dinner," Sorin said, holstering his blade.

I shrugged. "Maybe. Or we could have been impaled by an angry mate for threatening his female."

Sorin snorted. "Finding a mate does change things. I've experienced that firsthand."

"Yeah," I agreed, my thoughts drifting to Novak and Layla curled together on the ground.

As if he could read my expression, Sorin raised an eyebrow and added, "I never expected Novak to find a mate. Not after you destroyed his ability to trust anyone."

I rolled my eyes. *This again.* "What happened wasn't my fault. Don't try to lay that blame on me."

"So who's fault was it, then?" Sorin snapped back. "Novak's? Because he saw the corruption in the order you gave us? I'm not placing the blame on him. He isn't the reason our lives have turned to shit."

"No, he's not."

"That only leaves you," Sorin pointed out. "You're the one who gave the order. You're the one who didn't question what happened."

This was the third time they'd brought this up.

You didn't ask.

I fucking know I didn't.

Just as I knew I probably wouldn't have listened.

But none of that erased the past, and I was really fucking tired of everyone just assuming I walked away without a single hint of remorse.

"Do you really think that situation didn't scar me, too?" Because it had. Far more than he could ever understand.

"Yeah, I do," he snarled. "You didn't fucking care at all. Just issued the damn order and sent us off to face our fates. And you know what happened? We spent decades trying to repent. *For nothing.* And what were you off doing, *Commander?* Living the dream, yeah?"

"You know nothing about my life or my regrets."

"I know enough," he seethed. "You destroyed our lives, and you've never once apologized for it. *And you never fucking asked us what happened.*"

I was prepared for his attack, so I stood my ground and absorbed the blow. The pain balanced me, chasing away the anger to reveal the hurt festering beneath.

"I lost my best friend that day," I said, my voice coming out quiet, tinged with sadness from an old wound that still burned. "And knowing now that Novak Fell because of my order? Well, it's not the best feeling in the world. So yeah, I might not have suffered with you. But I'm still suffering, Sorin. Just in a different way."

Sorin was quiet for a moment, perhaps because my honesty had stunned him. But then he cleared his throat and said, "Well, it doesn't feel any better to be one of the ones who Fell."

I couldn't blame him for his anger, because everything he said rang true.

I just hadn't been ready to accept that the Noir weren't the only ones who needed reformation. That evil Nora could exist, too.

That maybe there was a whole world we didn't yet understand with a history that had been hidden from us throughout our lifetime.

"I know I should've talked to him, Sorin. That's the part that guts me. I *knew* him. I *knew* Novak wouldn't Fall lightly. But I was too angry... too *shocked*... to think beyond my own fury. Too indoctrinated to consider that there might be an alternative." I ran my fingers through my hair and blew out a breath. "But talking to him wouldn't have fixed it. Because I'm not sure I would have *heard* him."

It was a truth I had to experience to believe.

Which I supposed was one positive that came out of our time at Noir Reformatory. In addition to the obvious. *Layla.*

Sorin started to reply, when his attention caught on something over my shoulder. He blinked.

I whirled around, expecting a wild animal or some other threat.

Instead, I found Novak leaning against a tree, blending into the shadows as if he were made of them. Based on the look on his face, he'd overheard everything.

And all the pent-up anger and blame laced between us was once again darkening his expression.

Great. Just fucking great.

CHAPTER TWENTY-FOUR

NOVAK

I HELD AURIC'S GAZE, UNNERVED AND YET NOT SURPRISED by what he'd just said.

It really wasn't new information. We'd discussed the past several times now. However, not once had he admitted that he'd known I wouldn't Fall lightly.

He'd said a lot of other things.

But not *that*.

Time and silence stretched between us, reminiscent of the century we'd lost while he'd been playing guard to the crown.

While I'd been fighting to survive prison.

When that gunshot-like crack had awoken me from a light doze, I'd gone into protector mode. Even though I'd known Sorin and Auric were out here on guard, I'd slipped away from Layla and followed after them.

It wasn't that I didn't trust Auric to handle any threat, but a part of me had known something was wrong. Something that had to do with me.

I'd drawn up behind him, where the two deer were frozen, startled by our presence. Neither he nor Sorin had even noticed my arrival, too riveted by the angry stag. And then, while they were distracted by their bickering, I'd overheard his confession...

I lost my best friend that day.

Yeah. So did I, I thought now.

We continued to stare at one another in potent silence, both of us speaking volumes without uttering a sound. Like we always did.

Sorin glanced between us, a knowing expression settling on his face. He nodded and pointed a thumb over his shoulder, back toward camp. "I'll just go back to my mates, yeah? You guys can handle the guard from here."

Without looking at him, Auric nodded.

We listened to Sorin's footsteps fade through the trees until they vanished beneath the drone of nighttime insects.

In the shadow of night, Auric resembled a ray of sunlight. A golden god with his flaxen hair draped around his rugged face and his white wings shining in the starlight. So untouchable. So unapproachable. Especially to a Noir.

But not to me.

He looked down at the ground and cleared his throat. "So, you heard th—"

I didn't give him a chance to finish.

Instead, I took two large steps, grabbed him by the back of the neck with one hand, and yanked him to me.

Our lips crashed together—*hard*.

Auric's arms circled my back, dragging me closer as he yielded to my kiss. I fisted my other hand in his golden hair and devoured him, letting my mouth tell him the things I wouldn't use my voice to say. I dug my fingers into his skin, relishing the pained grunt that passed from his lips into mine. I disappeared into him for several moments, ignoring everything but the way he made me feel. The way he seemed to be just as perfectly fit for me as Layla was.

Finally, I ended the kiss and pressed my forehead to his. We stood like that for a brief moment, chests heaving, hands on one another with absolute possession. Then I released him and stepped away.

He knew me. Better than anyone.

The only thing that had been keeping us apart was his failure to admit that he'd been wrong. Not just in his failure to ask me what had happened, but in his easy acceptance of my Fall. As though he hadn't been surprised at all that I could become a Noir, even after everything we'd been through today.

But now he'd finally admitted his faults. That his prejudice had allowed him to misjudge me. And moreover, he *regretted* it.

I thought I would have relished this moment. Instead, I found myself wanting to put the pieces back together.

A sensation I never would have expected.

We sat down on the ground beneath a tree, facing our sleeping companions. I leaned against the bark beside him, pulling up a knee to rest my arm on. We fell into a companionable silence, our shoulders and thighs touching in unspoken solidarity as we observed the still night around us.

Time passed comfortably. We didn't need to speak to connect. I listened to the crickets and distant insect songs, but none of it was as musical as the sound of Auric's slow, steady breathing beside me.

"Hmm," Auric hummed after a time. "Remember that time in Calston?"

I didn't have to think hard to remember *that* mission. A grin lifted the corners of my lips, but I didn't reply.

"We waited four days for that mark to show," Auric went on, amusement in his tone. "Thought I was going to go fucking crazy."

"Didn't you?"

Auric laughed. "If you're referring to the possible heat stroke incident..."

I shrugged, flashing him one of my rare full smiles. I could still remember him with his pants tied around his head, ranting about how the summer sun needed to fuck off.

I could still remember, too, how that night was the first time we'd ever been intimate with one another. We'd been so bored and hard up for sex after months without it and had indulged each other. It had been explosive. A battle of wills where neither of us had won, and we'd both come out on top.

We shared a smile loaded with innuendo.

"Care to revisit old memories?" Auric asked.

My immediate desire was to say *yes*, then to take him down to the dirt and fuck him hard, to indulge in a battle of wills once more just to see which alpha would come out on top. But the sun was already starting to come up. And we had responsibilities.

We also had Layla to think about.

And while she didn't seem to mind our connection, I didn't want to risk her feeling left out again so soon after our last mistake with her.

So I caught his eye, promising we'd continue this another time. "When we're free from all this."

"And Layla can watch," he replied, pretty much reading my mind.

I nodded. "Then we'll indulge her afterward."

He grinned, and that look alone was almost as intoxicating as his suggestion that we fuck. "This isn't over between us," he said, the words loaded with promise.

I bared my teeth at him. "It never is." *And it never will be.*

CHAPTER TWENTY-FIVE

LAYLA

SIX DAYS.

That was how long we could go with minimal rations. With no sign of civilization or any hope that we were on the right track.

Still, we ventured onward because every sign suggested we were one step ahead of Sayir.

For now.

I glided alongside Kyril on a warm current while Auric and Novak flew above us like predators ready to strike. If it made Kyril uncomfortable, he didn't show it.

Raven had improved in speed and agility, too. Although, I'd noticed that her mates had given her their share of rations for the past few days to keep up her strength.

Our flights had run shorter every day, all of us wearing down, and I gnawed on my lip as my wings protested such extended use.

Aches and spasms ran up and down the length of each arch, and it felt as if every feather burned with fire. My entire body screamed for rest, every muscle overused to supply my wings with the strength required for flight.

I wasn't sure how much longer we could go on like this.

"What are we looking for again?" I asked Kyril, even though I knew the answer.

"Water," he informed me.

His responses never changed, and I never caught him in a lie, but that didn't mean he was being entirely truthful. I had hoped our weariness would provide some sort of proof if I caught him in a conflicting answer, but none ever came.

What worried me more was the line of concern along his brow.

"Are we lost?" I asked.

He glanced at me, his bright blue eyes reflecting the sunlight as he grimaced. "Perhaps, but once we find water, we will inevitably find civilization." His nostrils flared. "There is a faint scent of salt. We're going the right way."

I inhaled deeply, but any hint of salt and sea could have been a trick of the mind by now. I was so tired, so *sore*.

The idea of running into "civilization" didn't appeal to me, either.

He'd talked about this before. It seemed contradictory to seek out the indigenous population, given that humankind didn't know about us and we didn't yet have the means to hide ourselves from them. But it sounded like the Noir of this world had learned how to blend in, which meant that once we found humans, we would likely find others of our kind.

Or at least the Noir who Kyril claimed existed here. *Like my parents*.

"They're not all bad," Kyril said, and even without context, I instantly knew he meant humans. "I've lived among them for some time."

"Hmm," I said, taking a page from Novak's book not to commit to anything verbally. I preferred to listen to

Kyril and digest what he had to say because it usually came with a punch.

"King Vasilios and Queen Gaia have lived among humans for centuries," he continued, mentioning my supposed mother's name for the first time ever in conversation.

Vasilios and Gaia.

Dad and Mom.

Maybe. Maybe not.

The heat and exhaustion were clearly messing with my brain and my ability to reason.

So I continued to refrain from speaking out loud.

"Hiding our wings was the first step to true immersion, something many Noir were too proud to do until Sefid found us," he said.

I swallowed hard, my throat dry from thirst and unending flight. "So my father came here?" I asked, referring to Sefid.

Kyril nodded. "The Stygian Plague killed ninety percent of the Noir, but that wasn't his primary goal. His intent was true extermination. He hunted us down even when we weren't a threat, even when we escaped to an entirely different realm."

He dropped in altitude before catching a warm current again and returning to my side.

"He sent the Valkyries. We almost didn't survive." His blue eyes found mine. "Sefid had his chance. He could have killed your parents twenty-one years ago, on the day he took you. Instead, his pride won out, and he gave them to his brother to play with. He wanted them to suffer a fate worse than death."

My eyes went wide. That was a lot of information to take in. Particularly the part where he so casually mentioned my supposed kidnapping.

I swallowed. *Going to… ignore that part… and ask about an, uh,* easier *topic…*

"The Valkyries?" I asked, my voice higher than usual as I attempted to picture the terrifying warrior species that differed from both Nora and Noir. "You mean to tell me they know about all of this?"

Kyril nodded in response to my question about the Valkyries. "The plague didn't work on them, nor did the memory alterations. However, the heart of their existence is strength, and in their eyes, the Noir had failed. Sefid had earned their respect, so they took his deal."

"What deal was that?"

"They would stay out of his way, and when called upon, they would fight for him to exterminate what Noir were left."

I felt Auric's and Novak's eyes on me, but I ignored them. Every time I spoke to Kyril, I learned something new. His strange words held truths to them, I could feel it, and whether or not he was right, it would help me piece together where I had landed in this web of deceit and lies.

"And Sayir?" I asked. "How did Vasilios and Gaia escape him?" Escaping from the Reformer had proven difficult. While three hundred years seemed like a lot of time, it seemed implausible that Sayir would have let them out of his sight.

"He let them go," he said matter-of-factly, making my eyebrow shoot up. He glanced at me, a soft smile on his face. "He's an ally, Princess. Why do you think he brought me to you? He needed you to know the truth, to be reunited with your true family, and that's exactly what is going to happen."

I scoffed. Now I knew he was mad. "May I remind you that Sayir nearly succeeded in killing us, *again*?"

Kyril shrugged, the motion making him dip in the sky.

"Age and grief can change an angel, Layla. He's been through a lot, and while his methods can be misguided, he does what he believes is right." He glanced down at the canopy of endless trees below. "Do you remember the first time you took flight? How it felt?"

I remembered it all too clearly. My mother had taken me to the highest balcony overlooking the sea and encouraged me to jump. Sheer terror had run through me, even though I'd known in my soul that I was a creature meant to be in the skies.

I had plummeted, but my mother had been only half a second behind me in case I failed. However, she hadn't intervened even when the water had rushed up to greet me. As was customary, the mother taught her children to fly, but in the end, it was a skill an angel had to learn alone.

My father had watched the lesson, his hard gaze on me as though he hadn't cared if I'd broken on the waters below.

Snapping out my wings had been painful, but the joy had come a moment later when I'd soared up into the embrace of the sky.

"It was both horrible and exhilarating," I said honestly.

He chuckled. "Yes, as it was for us all. And in a way, that is how Sayir views the strong among us. It takes a moment of fear, and a brush with death, to unlock your potential to fly."

I fell silent at that thought. Because it sounded eerily familiar to the revelation I'd had the other night while talking to Raven.

When I'd thought about *why* the Reformer might be trying to push the Noir. *To inspire any gifts or talents to make themselves known during their fight to the death.*

Kyril's gaze snapped up and his nostrils flared. "There," he said, pointing.

Salty mist hit my nose a moment later on a warm updraft.

We'd found the sea.

The memory of learning to fly for the first time rushed through me, and I found myself wondering yet again if I would break into a thousand tiny little pieces.

Or if I would soar into the sunlight with a smile on my face.

CHAPTER TWENTY-SIX

AURIC

OCEAN.

And, more importantly, *food*.

The mouthwatering scent of roasted boar settled over our group as we gathered around Novak's bonfire that evening. It felt different to camp tonight, and not just because we'd found something more substantial than rations to eat, but because we were finally making headway.

Perhaps Kyril was onto something. I'd been letting him lead, unsure about the decision until now.

Flames roared high over the deserted beach we'd chosen for rest. A rocky overhang against the side of the ocean cliff would give us shelter for the night, while the open air allowed us to have a nearly one-hundred-eighty-degree view with a sheet of rock at our backs.

No room for Sayir to attack without someone noticing.

Unless he suddenly figured out how to control the sea.

None of us had gone on a hunt expecting to come out with actual food, so we were pleasantly surprised when we managed to track down a wild boar and kill it—and it didn't turn to ash.

Progress.

Maybe we'd be free of Sayir's tangled web yet.

Now, the boar roasted over the spit while Novak and Sorin took turns rotating it and bickering over how long it needed to cook.

Raven and Zian lounged on the other side of the fire, nearly obscured by the flames, while Layla was sandwiched between me and Kyril.

My mate's eyes glowed with excitement as she asked, "Skyscrapers? What does that mean?"

Kyril chuckled. He had one palm resting on Clyde's back as the little Blaze demon slept on his lap. I had no idea where the beast hid during our flights. "Maybe we'll see some if we venture farther into the human realm. There aren't any giant skyscrapers in Buenos Aires, but there are many in other cities throughout this world. They're thin buildings as tall as mountains. The humans build them when there isn't much space to grow *out*. Thus, they grow *up*."

"Fascinating," Layla said, her eyes wide. She'd grown more interested in humanity since we'd found water. "But I can't imagine not having land and nature right at your doorstep."

"Well, many humans in the cities keep small gardens on their balconies," Kyril pointed out.

He continued talking, but I tuned him out. I glanced sidelong at Layla, unsure of how I felt about this developing friendship between the "son of a god" and my mate—not that I'd completely bought into the "son of a god" tale.

On the one hand, I could fully appreciate how learning about humankind could be fun and exciting for the princess. Even my knowledge regarding the race was limited to military intelligence.

However, on the other hand, her fascination for Kyril grated on my nerves.

As if she could sense my gaze on her, Layla's wing stretched ever so slightly beside me and rubbed against my own in a subconscious show of intimacy. The touch grounded me and cooled my unfounded jealousy.

Kyril didn't react, only continued talking about vehicles in the human realm. Layla clearly had no sexual feelings toward him.

But still, I watched him closely. Especially after his weird commentary regarding her mating choices. I still felt like he wasn't telling us something.

Which could also just be my paranoia since everything he claimed seemed so outlandish.

Their conversation had moved on to space exploration by the time Novak came to join us. He sat on my other side, listening intently as Kyril described a rocket ship.

"Taller than you can even imagine," he told Layla, a glint in his bright blue eyes. "It spews fire from its tail as it shoots into the sky. A rocket took humanity to their moon," he added, pointing up at the thin sliver of light in the sky. The moon was a crescent now after so many days of journeying, barely casting any light at all in the inky night.

Novak glanced at me, one eyebrow rising half an inch.

I shrugged. "I told you they've advanced in the years you were locked away."

Sorin sat back on his heels and glanced at us over his shoulder. "Dinner's ready."

We split up rations of the boar, then packed the leftovers away for the rest of the journey with a layer of salt to keep it fresh.

Kyril continued to share stories of the human realm while we ate, though I hardly listened at all.

There was a camaraderie to our group that I hadn't noticed before. Maybe because we'd been traveling together for roughly a week. That was about the amount of time it took to break in a new squadron of fresh Nora.

Except this squadron was unlike any I had ever led.

By the time we finished eating, we fell into our shared chores with surprising efficiency—extinguishing the fire, cleaning up our mess, laying out our nests. Then Novak clapped me on the shoulder, kissed Layla soundly, and headed off for the first watch.

I went down on my knees, throwing an arm over Layla's waist, and yanked her against me before she could situate herself in our makeshift nest.

Her lips tasted of salty meat tinged with her distinctive cherry blossom scent. I took my time tasting her, enjoying the feel of her against me. A feeling I'd never actually thought I'd know and, now, couldn't get enough of.

But after a few moments, I released her before we ended up giving our companions an unwanted show. This journey would come to an end soon enough, and then I would thoroughly make up for missed time.

Rolling onto my back, I tugged her on top of me. She fit perfectly on my chest, her head nestled beneath my collarbone. I could feel her rapid heartbeat next to mine, her bright-colored hair tickling my nose.

"Your heart is racing," I murmured, pressing my lips to her head. I spanned her waist with both hands, anchoring her in place.

"Is it?" She lifted her head and tucked her arms beneath her chin so she could meet my gaze. "I suppose I'm nervous."

"About meeting your supposed parents?" I assumed aloud.

She bit her lip in confirmation.

"We don't know for sure that they actually *are* your parents," I reminded her.

"But what if they are?" she countered. "Will you be able to accept the fact that I'm Noir? *Fully* Noir and not just a Fallen Nora?"

I cupped her face in my hands, holding her firmly as I lifted my head and stared deep into her beautiful eyes. "I'll accept you regardless of your feathers," I told her solemnly. I'd come to that conclusion what felt like ages ago. It didn't matter if her feathers were black, white, pink, or spotted. She was my Layla. "You're mine. I'm yours. No classification can ever change that."

Tears sparkled on her lashes in the little bit of moonlight shining down on us. Something settled between us that I didn't quite understand at first—some kind of deep hurt that darkened her gaze and pinched the skin between her brows.

It was a hurt I'd created. One I'd put in her eyes along with the doubt in her heart, all caused by the callous way I'd treated her when we'd arrived at Noir Reformatory.

As a result, she had no idea how much I cared for her.

I pulled her up for another kiss, vowing with my mouth that somehow, someway, I'd show her just how much she meant to me. No matter what it took.

"Rest, sweet princess. We'll be finding more answers soon."

CHAPTER TWENTY-SEVEN

LAYLA

MY HEART NEVER SEEMED TO SLOW DOWN. IF ANYTHING, ITS rhythm increased the closer we came to our destination.

We finished the last leg of our journey under a clear, brilliant blue sky. Though the sun shone like gold against the horizon, the thin upper atmosphere was chilly. Moving was the only way to stay warm.

While Raven and her mates flew some distance behind us, Kyril remained with me, and Clyde hid deep in his pockets.

The Noir had us flying incredibly high the last few hours of our journey, stating a need to remain hidden in the clouds due to human technology monitoring the airspace.

Auric side-eyed him while he asked, "Radar?"

"Among other tech," Kyril agreed. His light voice was almost indistinguishable from the wind in my ears, the air so thin up here that I wanted to scream yet probably couldn't inhale enough air to make it happen.

Auric seemed unconvinced. "How is remaining unseen going to keep them from noticing us on their equipment?"

Kyril tapped his temple with a small, secretive smile. "All Noir living in the human realm have been equipped with a jammer. A type of low-frequency microchip that interferes with human technology. Otherwise, we'd never be able to fly at all. But we need to have some distance for it to work properly."

As we continued in silence, I noticed the look that passed between Auric and Novak. I noticed it because I felt the same internal suspicion at Kyril's easy declaration.

He had… a different kind of bug?

Like what Sayir had done to us?

I dipped to join my mates, lowering my voice to say, "He's implanted with something else? Why wouldn't he tell us that? Why didn't Raven notice it?"

Auric shrugged. "Perhaps because it had nothing to do with Sayir, and it might not be transmitting our location. He didn't even know about the tracker."

"Or did he?" I asked darkly.

I waffled back and forth on whether I wanted to believe Kyril or not. His insane claims were hard to swallow—particularly the idea that I was somehow someone else's child and not the Princess of the Nora. Although, the idea of gods and the Noir being the "elite" of angelkind weren't easy tales to believe, either.

We soared from cloud to cloud, all of us keeping alert for any hint of human aircraft. Kyril's stories around the campfire last night had mentioned more kinds of airships and helicopters than I could ever imagine, but the skies remained firmly empty over a vast green landscape below.

Until Kyril announced that we were about twenty miles from our destination.

I heard the motors first. There were two of them, loud enough to wake the dead, buzzing and whirring through the empty sky like some kind of atmospheric earthquake.

It was a massive airship, larger than any plane I'd ever seen—even the Noir Reformatory jet that had carried me to prison. Long and sleek with wide, straight wings and some kind of foreign lettering on the side.

"Drop!" Kyril barked, his voice more commanding than I'd ever heard it.

Even Auric obeyed. We all shot down, disappearing into the thick white clouds below the plane. I spread my wings and glided, waiting with bated breath as the shadow passed above us like a shark beneath the ocean.

"Have we been spotted?" Auric asked, his tone irritated that we might have already been caught.

Were there people on that plane? The idea sent a little shiver of excitement up my spine.

"No," Kyril said with a glance over his shoulder. "That was a commercial airliner. They don't have the technology to see past our jammer."

I let out a breath and craned my neck to find the airship, but it had already disappeared into the clouds.

So fast, I marveled.

My focus fell to the land below, a gasp climbing up my throat. *Nothing* could have prepared me for my first glimpse of human civilization. Not Kyril's stories. Not my textbooks back home. Not even my private instructors.

Because *wow.*

The clouds parted, revealing a riot of colors and blocky buildings that stretched far ahead of us, all the way up to the vastness of the deep blue sea beyond. My heart lodged in my throat when Kyril forced us higher to fly through the clouds, and I only caught tantalizing little glimpses of the amazing view below.

Kyril hadn't been kidding—the buildings were colorful and full of life. There weren't any tall, mountain-sized ones like he'd mentioned, but they were mesmerizing just the same.

Sunlight illuminated their roofs and bounced off the

metallic vehicles carefully winding through the maze of streets below. It was breathtaking, and I wanted nothing more than to forget why we'd even come here so I could go experience the human realm and everything it had to offer for myself.

We landed on a brightly colored, multilevel building covered in balconies that overlooked the ocean. The beach only held a few figures spread out on towels beneath the sun, but we couldn't take any chances of being seen. Kyril ushered us across the pavement and behind an orange wall. We weren't exactly inconspicuous, so we gathered against the cool siding, tucking our wings behind us.

However, I couldn't help but peek around the corner back at the beach.

A crowd of young humans gathered around a nearby patio, sitting in colorful chairs with drinks in hand. A sensual tune filled the air, the hum making my lips curl.

Two girls with tan skin wearing vibrant dresses swayed on the patio, their hips moving slowly to the beat. It created an inviting scene I longed to experience but knew would never happen.

"Is that a party?" I asked Kyril, unable to drag my gaze away from the humans. They were just... *beautiful*. All manner of skin tones, all of them dressed so brightly, so vibrant and loud. Their voices drifted our way, but I didn't understand the language. Something fast and melodic.

Kyril glanced at the humans. "That's a restaurant."

"It's so casual," I said, thinking back to the many dinner gatherings my parents had thrown at the palace. Males and females in stiff formal wear doing choreographed dances, sipping champagne, and keeping their voices respectfully low.

Nothing loud.

Nothing so exciting as this.

"Human life is fleeting," Kyril explained. "They live to the fullest every chance they get."

"I love that." I watched a handsome young male sweep a dark-haired beauty off her feet and race toward the water. They splashed into the waves, the girl's shrieking laughter carrying back to us on the warm, salty breeze. My body swayed toward them, drawn by the emotion they wore so plainly on their faces.

Kyril brushed his fingers over my arm, reminding me to stay in place.

"There are enchantments that allow us to walk among mortals," he promised. "Our people, the Noir, have developed many magics. Unfortunately, I don't have an elixir with me right now because we couldn't risk Sayir taking the potion from me upon my arrival. He might be an ally, but not all allies can be entirely trusted. However, we'll have access to the enchantment soon."

I bit my lip and nodded.

Kyril motioned for us to follow him. "Come on. There's an area nearby that will be large enough to hide in."

He led us down an angled alleyway beside the building. The road ended at a shiny silver overhead door. Kyril stepped aside and held out a hand for Clyde to perch atop his palm, and the two of them proceeded to have a silent conversation. A moment later, the Blaze disappeared and Kyril went to speak to Auric and Novak, while I joined Raven halfway up the alleyway.

"Now what?" Zian asked.

Novak's intense gaze landed on Kyril, demanding an immediate response.

"We wait," Kyril said, relaxing against the wall. "Clyde will return with news." He glanced in the direction of the humans. "Until then, we need to stay out of sight."

The males continued to talk while Raven and I drifted closer to the mouth of the alley, both of us drawn by the foreign scene.

"They're beautiful," she said, her gaze locked on the humans. We could still see them through the break between buildings. "It's like some kind of technicolor dream."

I nodded. It occurred to me that Raven—like me—hadn't been offered much in the way of "choice" in her life. While I'd been raised to be a princess, to obey orders and live my life doing what was best for Nora kind, Raven had been raised in the prison system, learning to fight for her life.

We both were a kind of prisoner.

The idea made me look at her in a new light.

"Hey," I said, "maybe after we find the Noir king and acquire some of those enchantments Kyril was talking about, we could go to a beach party like this."

She raised a dark brow. "You think our mates would be up for that?"

I scoffed. "Either they join us, or they can get out of our way."

Raven burst out laughing. "You're insane if you think Auric and Novak are going to let you within ten feet of those gorgeous human males."

I followed her gesture to a group of young males walking in the distance. Sure, they were cute, the way puppies and fawns were cute. An oddity. Something I could enjoy observing without thinking too hard about why it was enjoyable.

Because the fact of the matter was, nothing and nobody could ever stand up against Auric and Novak.

Time passed as we hung out in the hidden alley, watching the humans move through the motions of their afternoon and evening. They became even more lively as the sun descended.

Then our mates took out the remainder of the boar for us to enjoy for dinner while we continued to wait.

Clyde finally returned a couple of hours later with news.

Kyril turned to us, the demon perched atop his thin shoulder. His grin settled on me as he said, "Your parents are sending an emissary to retrieve us. He'll be here by midnight."

I swallowed hard and nodded.

Suddenly, the situation felt all too real again.

One way or another, I was about to learn the truth.

CHAPTER TWENTY-EIGHT

LAYLA

Kyril led the way, taking us to a dark human park that didn't look nearly as cheerful as the beach. It was too quiet here, too muted.

Kyril paused every few minutes as he tilted his head toward Clyde, then he turned to a new path and resumed the trek.

I glanced at Auric, who seemed to be thinking the same thing.

He can talk to Clyde.

Not only was the Blaze demon close to the strange Noir, but he also seemed to be able to communicate, something he only did with a few others.

I wondered if it was an innate ability, something that set him apart from the rest, like Novak, or if the little demon just decided whom he liked to talk to.

I wasn't sure I liked either answer.

I almost asked Raven since I knew she could speak to the Blaze, but I was too distracted by our surroundings to focus on much else.

A warm breeze brought in the distant salt from the sea, causing my feathers to lift on the current, eager to leave this dreary place. We'd followed Kyril into the thick overgrowth of an unkempt part of the park, where I felt cramped and isolated. I glanced up, unable to see the stars through the canopy of dark leaves.

"How much longer?" Auric asked, resting his hand on his dagger.

Kyril leaned against a tree and stroked Clyde's back. "Not long."

Zian dropped the backpack that held the last of our reserves into the dirt. "You wouldn't be leading us into a trap, would you?"

Kyril chuckled. "It would be a poor trap since I would be ensnared myself. I assure you, the emissary is loyal to King Vasilios."

Zian frowned. "And how do we know that King Vasilios isn't in league with the Reformer?" He glared at Novak. "If you've led us into a trap, cousin, I will not forgive you for dragging us all the way out here."

Novak only narrowed his eyes in response.

However, I could read the taut lines in his face.

He didn't trust Kyril, either.

His pale blue irises shone like little stars, capturing my gaze as his wings brushed mine.

He'd come here for me, not for Kyril or anyone else.

I just hoped that it hadn't been a mistake.

A dark figure split from the shadows, and Auric drew his blade. He might have attacked if Clyde hadn't growled a short reprimand for Auric's hostility.

Novak's feathers relaxed against mine. He trusted the Blaze demon, at least, which provided a small comfort.

A tall, willowy male stepped into the clearing. His pale skin contrasted against his dark feathers, but he had a regal quality to him that the majority of the Noir at the prison lacked.

Well-kempt, long, dark hair glided over his shoulder, kept even tidier by a ponytail at the nape of his neck. Silky black slacks matched a dark button-up dress shirt that rippled in the warm breeze. Even his steps had a measure of grace to them that clashed against what I knew of the dark-winged angels.

The emissary clearly was a different type of Noir, evident by the stretch of a soft smile on his lips when he found me. "Princess Layla," he greeted, his wings sagging in relief. "At last."

I flushed as he knelt on one knee. While not uncommon behavior, I hadn't been treated like royalty in quite some time.

He took my hand, his grace one that would have matched even my most respected suitors back home, and pressed a light kiss to my knuckles.

"Hey," Auric snapped while Novak released a threatening growl. "That's enough."

The Noir glanced at Auric, then at Novak, and raised a dark brow. He released me before either of my mates mauled him.

Novak's gaze made his intent clear. *You are not allowed to worship my mate.*

The emissary glared at Auric, singling out the Nora among us. "Do you think I wish her harm, *Nora*?" He glanced at Kyril as an unspoken conversation seemed to pass between them. Clyde chirped and Novak glowered.

"I don't know what to think," Auric remarked flatly. "So you'd better start giving us answers."

The emissary glided to his feet, and Auric's wings flared.

I shot up a hand, not interested in watching the two males square off with each other. "Enough," I said. "Both of you." Auric's feathers ruffled, but he backed off. I waved a hand at the Noir. "Perhaps you could introduce yourself?"

"Iston," he replied, his wary eyes still leveled on Auric. Then his gaze swiveled to me. "I've come to accompany you. The king and queen are eager to see their daughter again." He reached out his hand, then thought better of it and curled his fingers into a fist. "If you are ready, it'll just be a short flight."

I glanced at Novak and Auric, who both appeared suspicious of the statement. But upon meeting my gaze, they each gave a subtle nod in agreement to proceed.

So I waved at the darkness. "Very well. Lead the way and we'll follow."

Iston glared at the rest of my party, his distaste landing hardest on Auric. "You intend for all these angels to join you? I assure you, you're safe here. Such protection is no longer necessary. More angels only increase our risk of detection."

Raven scoffed. "If you think we're splitting up after the hell we went through to get here, you're insane."

He raised a dark brow. "And you are?"

She straightened. "I'm the girl who'll stab you if you don't hurry up and show us where Layla's parents are."

Iston frowned as Kyril chuckled. "I can vouch for them all," he said as Clyde chirped his agreement. "The princess has made many friends during her time at the prison. They could prove useful."

Iston's gaze darted to Auric, who still loomed protectively over me. "Perhaps it would be best to leave the Nora behind, at least. He won't be trusted or welcomed among our kind."

Auric growled, taking one threatening step forward.

I rested a hand on his arm and glanced at Novak for assistance. My dangerous mate only watched with his arms crossed, the faintest amused smirk painted on his lips while a lock of dark hair brushed into his eyes. The jerk probably wanted to see a fight. Any excuse to spill blood was a good enough reason for violence for the Prison King.

Ugh. Males.

"Nobody's staying behind," I said firmly, squeezing Auric's arm to indicate he should remain silent. I gave Iston a level stare. "Especially not Auric or Novak. They're my mates."

Iston jolted as if I'd punched him, and his jaw slackened.

"Is there a problem?" I asked.

Iston's throat worked, no sound coming out as if he'd lost his voice.

I exchanged glances with Novak, who offered an ambivalent shrug.

Kyril, however, acknowledged the emissary's overly dramatic reaction with a brief nod. "Yes, I imagine her parents will feel the same, considering."

"Considering what?" I asked, confused. "It's not like it's strange for me to have mates. I'm twenty-one."

The emissary jerked out of his bizarre stupor, his black gaze swiveling to Kyril. "She doesn't know?"

"Not my place," Kyril said evenly.

"Know what?" I demanded.

Kyril held up a calming hand. "Your parents just expected you to be unmated, is all." Before I could respond to that, he smiled benignly at Iston and asked, "Are we ready to depart?"

I wasn't an idiot—Kyril was hiding something that he had no intention of telling me.

Why would they expect me to be unmated? What did that have to do with anything?

"Yes." Iston launched into the sky, finding a dark spot in the canopy I'd missed, and the rest of us followed.

The city stretched beneath us like a vast glittering

blanket of jewels. More than once, I found myself falling behind, mesmerized by the lights and the movement, before Auric or Novak grabbed me and pulled me back on track.

Luckily, we didn't have to fly far, just like Iston had said. We descended on the other side of the city, outside the bustle. A small airfield stretched darkly into the distance, punctuated by pulsating red lights and vertical lines of lights marking the runways.

Seeing an airplane sent the wrong kind of thrill through me. The last time I had been on one of those things, it hadn't ended well.

And that one in the sky earlier had felt almost predatory.

Iston landed on the tarmac next to a large luxury jet before his black wings ruffled close to his back. A smiling female clasped her hands as she stood next to a stairway propped onto the side of the plane.

I alighted on the ground next to the Noir emissary, surprise making me stumble. He caught me with a deft hand and righted me, swiftly pulling away before either Auric or Novak could chop off his hand. Luckily, my mates were focused on the wingless female beaming at us. "Iston, isn't she human?" I asked in a whisper, concerned.

"No, Princess. She's one of us," he said with an indulgent smile.

"But her wings…?"

"An enchantment," he explained, and I recalled Kyril's promise of magic that could hide my wings and let me roam amongst the humans. "Come. You'll receive your own dose once we're in the air." He glanced skyward. "We don't want to remain in one place for too long." He moved for the plane, then hesitated as he turned. "You can leave your weapons with Netiri. She'll keep them safe for you."

The indicated female opened up the suitcase and stepped away.

"We're not setting one foot inside that thing," Auric said, echoing my reluctance. "Especially not without our weapons."

"Finally, he has some sense," Zian muttered.

I glanced at Novak, wanting to hear his input. His focus remained on Clyde, who scampered up the stairway before he disappeared into the plane.

Novak glowered before meeting my gaze.

"It's your decision, little blossom." He flexed his wings, reminding me that he *was* a weapon.

I swallowed hard. Clyde hadn't led us wrong yet, and I knew in my gut we were on the verge of finding real answers. Sayir hadn't caught up with us yet, but it was only a matter of time.

I took Novak's hand. "I need answers," I said honestly.

And this was the only way to acquire them.

Auric sighed but joined Novak as the group produced their daggers and knives, Raven surprising us when she pulled five short daggers from gods knew where and clattered them into the suitcase with a smirk.

I felt naked without a weapon, and I imagined that the rest of the group felt similarly.

My mates flanked me as we ascended the staircase to the plane's door. We passed into a surprisingly cool interior and made our way down the narrow aisle.

I trailed my fingertips over the lush seats.

Unlike the plane that had carried me to Noir Reformatory, this one had cushions and amenities. Each row held a pair of seats, two on either side with ample legroom. Except they didn't seem to account for wings.

I settled into one chair and crammed my wings against the sides, not sure how we were all going to fit like this.

"It'll be more comfortable once we receive our doses of the enchantment," Kyril assured me.

Raven flopped into my neighboring seat before Auric or Novak could sit beside me. She grinned at me and reached for her seat belt. "You hear that? This flight comes with drinks."

Auric and Novak both stood over her for several seconds, frowning and none too pleased that she'd taken the only open spot. In the end, though, they settled into the seats in front of us, while Zian and Sorin settled across the aisle.

Raven and I had gone through an ordeal together on this trip, and perhaps she had something to talk about. Fine by me, because I didn't want to deal with two mates being overprotective the entire flight.

"I don't suppose you'll tell us where we're headed?" Auric drawled.

Iston merely looked at him while Kyril said, "Home."

Raven and I shared a look.

Home didn't tell us anything at all.

The takeoff was uneventful and smoother than my last flight experience.

After we leveled out at cruising altitude, Iston came around with a tray of shot glasses and held it out to us.

"The enchantment to hide your wings," he explained.

I almost refused.

But after seeing the other female, I was curious to see if it was real.

However, both Raven and I waited as Kyril demonstrated with his own glass from the tray.

When his wings disappeared, we gasped. I half expected him to fall over in shock, but all he did was shake his head a little and sit back down.

Raven and I shared another glance.

Then I pinched a tiny glass between my thumb and forefinger, and Raven did the same.

Holding it out to her, I said, "Cheers."

We clinked glasses, then tossed back the dose.

A weight lifted from my back, and a slight sense of panic rushed through me when my shoulder blades rested against the seat.

My wings were *gone*. Which I'd expected. But to experience it was something else entirely.

"Breathe," Iston instructed me. "They're still there. Do you feel them?"

I... I did, but it was as if they were far away.

Raven snuggled against the seat and sighed, clearly far more okay with this sensation than I was. "This is kind of amazing," she mused.

Iston chuckled and collected our glasses.

"Iston," I said before the emissary could walk away, deciding to try something. "Will you please tell me where we're going within the human realm?"

The slender man grinned. "Milady, we're on our way to Rome." He nodded to our laps. "Put on your seat belts. It'll be a long ride."

Auric glanced back at me with a grateful expression.

I smiled in response.

Then I buckled my seat belt for the flight and wondered what answers waited for us in Rome.

CHAPTER TWENTY-NINE

NOVAK

I DID NOT LIKE THE SERUM OR THE SENSATION OF LOSING my wings.

My sharp feathers were my ultimate weapon, and I instinctively knew that Kyril's tonic suppressed that ability to some extent. They were still there, perhaps I could still even fly, but I couldn't shake the sensation that I had been diminished somehow.

Was this all a ruse to weaken me? Weaken *us*?

Or was this the only way to find Layla's answers?

Darkness fled from the cabin as the plane jolted onto a private airstrip. I'd been watching from the window after a brief nap—one I hadn't meant to take, but my exhaustion had won at some point during our journey.

However, while I'd been aware and observant, we'd been the only ones in the sky and on the ground.

Which meant that whoever these Noir were, they had not only successfully mingled with humans, but had *thrived*. They didn't seem like the hobbled, nearly extinct race they painted themselves out to be.

I silently observed as the wingless Noir female opened the hatch, revealing clear blue skies. I wasn't sure how long we'd flown but knew several hours had passed.

The female's wings were visible when I scrutinized her

hard enough. A faint, delicate disturbance in the air accompanied by a subtle scent distinct to Noir. Although, the Noir we'd encountered so far had a different scent. Sharper, not unpleasant, but definitely unusual.

And nothing like Layla's cherry blossoms.

It didn't prove anything, but I knew the instant I'd set eyes on the emissary that Layla's world was about to be blown apart.

I'd be there for her when she needed to put it back together.

"We're up," Auric said, shoving out of the seat.

I waited for Layla as she disentangled herself from her buckle. Her fuchsia hair curled around her pixie face, her sapphire eyes darting to me when she stood. She wobbled, unbalanced without the weight of her wings.

Yeah, I was struggling with that part, too.

I glared at Raven because I would have liked to have been able to comfort my mate throughout the flight. However, I'd overheard their conversation earlier.

Raven obviously wanted to make amends. To be friends. To find answers together. She understood that Layla was the key to all of this, and it seemed she was finally showing some respect. I couldn't exactly fault her for trying to be a decent angel.

I held out a hand and guided my mate in front of me, then crowded in behind her as we headed for the exit with Raven and her mates at my rear. Auric was already several steps ahead, scouting the way.

In the too-bright sunshine, a group of males in military uniforms stood at the ready on the runway, forming a semicircle in front of two black vehicles. There a dozen men, all of them wingless, though their sharp floral scent told me they were the strange earthly breed of Noir.

A quick survey of our surroundings confirmed an open sky providing plenty of opportunity to flee.

Assuming we could fly. I hadn't tested that part of the enchantment yet.

Layla rubbed her arms, and I pressed my palm to the small of her back, wishing I could fan my wings over hers in a sign of solidarity and comfort. Instead, my touch would have to do.

As we halted in front of the waiting soldiers, every single one of them bowed so deeply they nearly doubled over.

I glanced over Layla's head at Auric, who looked less than amused himself. But he simply clasped his hands behind his back. He would portray himself as nonthreatening, for now. While we were outnumbered, that didn't concern me. I'd faced far worse.

The emissary stepped forward to greet one of the men in a strange language. The two shook hands and exchanged words, while the rest of the stone-faced soldiers openly studied Layla with gazes of adoration and awe.

Only Auric and I have permission to worship her, I thought, growling.

I put my arm around her waist, dragging her against my side. She sighed and fell against me, her hand resting on my chest.

I glared at the soldiers. *Fuck off. She's mine.*

The emissary finished his brief conversation with the leading soldier I'd heard him call "Sergeant," then turned back to us.

Iston motioned to the vehicle on the right. "Princess, if you and your, erm, mates will join Kyril in this vehicle, I'll accompany your other companions in the second SUV." When we stared at him, he added, "Sport utility vehicle. It means it'll handle any rough road conditions we might encounter."

Layla nodded, but she looked stricken at the thought of our party being separated. I wrapped my fingers around her slender hip and squeezed.

A reminder that she wasn't alone.

If anyone tried to test me, they'd receive a one-way ticket to the afterlife.

Without speaking, Kyril chose the front passenger seat so that the three of us could pile into the back.

Normally, we wouldn't have been able to fit due to the size of our wings, but the elixir made them invisible. Physically, they were still there, in a sense, but they weren't impeded by objects around us while enchanted.

Once I settled into the back seat, I was able to fully press my shoulder blades into the leather as though my feathers weren't there at all. Layla and Auric seemed to share the same experience as they joined me, their gazes holding a touch of wonder mixed with panic.

None of us enjoyed this sensation.

And yet, we couldn't deny the uniqueness of it.

We left the airport on a busy highway and headed away from town.

After only moments on the road, Layla drifted off to sleep on my shoulder. But once we left the motorway, the roads became a little rougher. She didn't seem to mind, her lips parting on a sigh as she slept easily between us. She clearly hadn't rested well on the plane.

I anchored my arm around her and held her tight, and Auric rested his palm on her thigh.

She mumbled something incoherent, snuggling deeper into us just as Kyril glanced back at us.

With a look, I dared him to comment.

He didn't. Instead, he righted himself and stared out the window.

Auric smirked, amused.

But I didn't share the emotion. We were on the cusp of something big, and I worried about what it would do to Layla. What it might do to *us*.

An hour later, the turquoise glimmer of the Mediterranean Sea spread out before us, the name Kyril helpfully supplied from the front seat as if we were on a tour.

We took a coastal road alongside pearly white beaches for another half hour before we passed into a small seaside town. Several more turns took us into a manicured tree-lined area of homes set back off the road, and the farther we drove, the farther apart and less visible the houses became.

Until, finally, we turned into a gated driveway.

Thriving, I repeated to myself. *Definitely thriving.*

The gates were painted beige and flanked by thick trees. I couldn't see beyond them, but everything about the setup screamed *wealth*—from the guard gate nearly hidden next to the driveway, to the electric panel within arm's reach of the car, to the secluded location along the coast.

The driver rolled down his window and entered a code on the PIN pad. A split second later, the gate let out a series of monotone beeps, then began to swing open.

Layla jerked awake as the car started to move again. She straightened and peered blearily around while we passed through the gates. When she realized we'd arrived at our destination, a tinge of fear slipped into her blue eyes.

I removed my arm from her shoulders and reached for her hand to lace my fingers through hers. Then I leaned in to kiss her temple. On her other side, Auric squeezed her thigh as his gaze remained riveted on the world outside the tinted windows.

We really had no way of knowing exactly what we were walking into, but in this, I was glad to have my former commander at my side.

The trees broke, and the driveway curved in a semicircle in front of a lavish mansion. A strip of sand and the ocean formed a picture-perfect background for the mansion.

Shallow steps led up to a columned portico, and the double doors—red like the roof—stood wide open.

A shadowy figure waited at the top of the stairs. As the SUV curved around and came to a halt on the drive, the figure stepped out into the sunshine, the faintest glimmer of dark wings behind her, a mirage I knew I hadn't imagined.

Layla stiffened with a small, sharp gasp.

The woman wore her hair long, and it tumbled around her shoulders in brilliant fuchsia waves. I recognized her—not only because she was the spitting image of Layla.

But because she was the same Noir female I'd seen from afar over a hundred years ago.

The female the rogue Noir had avenged when he'd killed all those Nora guards.

On the day I'd Fallen.

Kiss of the Gods.

"The rogue Noir," I whispered. "It was the rogue Noir."

"What was?" Auric asked, meeting my gaze with a sense of alarm. "Novak?"

"Who is she?" I asked instead, my focus on Kyril. "The female?" I already knew the answer, but I needed to hear him say it. To confirm the chaos roaring through my mind. To add context to a memory I would never forget.

Kyril smiled fondly as he gazed upon the female at the door. "Queen Gaia."

Which could only mean one thing.

"The rogue Noir…" I swallowed. "The rogue Noir was King Vasilios."

And the way Kyril turned to look at me now confirmed it.

"You knew," I realized out loud. "The Kiss of the Gods." He'd been the one to mention it, to say someone had marked me for greatness.

Because I let King Vasilios live that day.

I watched as he annihilated all those Nora.

And I never once tried to stop him.

Kyril's smile turned sympathetic. "I don't know the details. But yes, I recognized his mark."

Something he could have told us before. But I understood why he hadn't.

I wouldn't have believed him.

However, I sure as fuck believed him now.

Because my past, or a part of it, was standing on that front step. Alive. Healed. And smiling at our approaching SUV.

Layla was born after I saved her parents, I marveled. *Just as I Fell because I saved her parents.*

I looked at Auric and found him staring at me in awe, likely because he'd just realized the same connection.

Everything I'd endured since the Fall had all served a greater purpose.

Because without my sacrifice and ability to be compassionate for that mated male all those years ago, Layla wouldn't exist today.

Those Nora would have finished the job, killing his mate. *Layla's mom.*

And I would have handed the male over to be "reformed."

I felt the truth of it in my bones, down to my very spirit.

No wonder I felt so connected to Layla.

I'd been protecting her before she was even born.

Because she's always been mine to protect.

I met her wide eyes now, caught the questions floating in her gaze. "Your father is the rogue Noir that I let go," I whispered. "He's the reason I Fell."

I'd told her the story, though I'd kept most of the details to myself.

Such as the brutal way those Nora angels had raped her mother.

But she knew enough.

And now she gaped at me with startled understanding. "My parents…" She trailed off, her pulse a frenzied echo throughout the small space between us.

"They're your real parents," I told her, certain of it. I could *feel* the truth even before the doors opened.

This was exactly where we were meant to be.

The path we were always intended to walk.

Together.

We would face this future united as one.

Auric. Layla. Me.

A force to be reckoned with.

A power triad that would make others bow.

Because our mate was the heiress to a much greater throne.

And the daughter of a god.

CHAPTER THIRTY

LAYLA

They're your real parents.

Novak's statement rolled through my mind on repeat.

Somehow, his belief made it all more real. It deepened the sense of tightness swirling through my veins. Confirmed what my eyes already knew. Told me that the female waiting on that stoop was indeed my spitting image.

My mother.

Some hidden part of me recognized her immediately, as though my soul automatically knew the identity of my true blood.

I didn't need anyone to confirm it or to tell me who this female was to me.

Yet Novak's comments cemented that knowledge as fact because he knew it was true, too.

Everything Kyril said… is real. And he knew that the moment I met this Noir, I would believe him. *That* was why he'd been so adamant about bringing me here.

My mother and I could have been twins. We even appeared to be roughly the same age. Except she boasted a power that could only be described as ancient. It rolled off her in waves. More powerful than any of us, even the warriors. She carried herself with the weight of the ages, and I had no doubt that if threatened, she could destroy us all.

Which meant those Nora who'd hurt her a hundred years ago must have tricked her in some way.

But my father had avenged her.

Because my mate had let him live.

I glanced at him again, catching the reassurance in his gaze. I felt a similar emotion radiating from Auric as he squeezed my thigh.

They were here for me.

They would follow my lead.

They would never leave me behind.

That was what their presence said, their auras providing me with my own kind of protective shield. My mates would do whatever it took to keep me safe. And they'd let me take control as I saw fit.

Like right now.

My mother watched silently from atop the stairs as we stepped out of the SUV. Raven and her mates were just behind us as the security team guided our party toward a final checkpoint.

My mother continued observing us as the guards began sweeping our entire party for contraband, too.

Novak's wings were enough of a weapon for all of us, but I sensed his subtle unease at having them cloaked by the elixir.

Do they no longer possess the same potency? I wondered. It hadn't occurred to me before that the enchantment that affected our wings might impact him.

Fortunately, I didn't think his blades would be needed.

Besides, no manner of enchantment would ever weaken him.

The solitary female guard released me before the others, moving on to Raven next while the males continued their thorough pat-down of the males in our party.

I barely had a chance to lift my head before the woman who looked like me tapped delicately down the stairs and came right for me.

I didn't wait.

I moved toward her as well, some sort of bond snapping into place with every step we took toward each other.

Like our souls required this joining.

A daughter running into the arms of her long-lost mother.

It was so natural. So *right*.

This sensation had been missing my whole life, and I only realized it now as her arms came around me. My nostrils flared as her sweet, floral scent hit my senses. *I remember that smell*, I marveled. *I remember* her. But I couldn't pinpoint the exact memory. Because my fath—

I cut off the word, replacing it with *King Sefid* in my mind.

King Sefid must have altered my mind, taking this memory from me. But my body knew. My soul remembered. And my heart recognized the truth.

It's true.

All of it's true.

"Oh, my darling," my mother said, her tearful voice muffled by my hair. "I thought I'd never see you again."

I buried my nose against her neck and inhaled, unable to speak as my throat closed with emotion. A powerful and immediate current swept between us—a connection I never knew I was missing but would never be able to live without again.

My mother.

My real mother.

She released me and pulled away, brushing her fingers

through my hair as she studied me with glittering eyes. "You're so beautiful."

"Of course she is," a deep voice replied from behind her. "Because she looks like her mother."

She swiped at her eyes—the same color as my own—and stepped away, turning an adoring grin to the new arrival.

A faint, familiar salty-ocean scent tickled my nose, touching another deep and buried—*magically distorted*—memory. While childhood recollections could be generally foggy and fleeting, I never forgot a scent.

This is my father. The rogue Noir. King Vasilios.

His tall, muscular stature radiated an ancient power similar to my mother's. And he moved with the quiet danger of an approaching thunderstorm, the ground seeming to vibrate in his wake as he made his way to us on the sidewalk in front of the palatial estate.

He held out a hand, palm up, and gave me an indulgent smile. "Layla. At last."

Even though Novak and Auric were still being searched, leaving me without protection, I couldn't help myself. I set my hand in his, trusting him immediately. His fingers wrapped around mine and gave a gentle squeeze while his expression softened with affection.

"Welcome home, daughter," he said, his voice thick with emotion.

Auric's wintergreen scent washed over me, his approach one I sensed more than saw. He'd clearly finished up with the guards and had started making his way toward me.

To my parents.

To my home.

But my father's expression changed, his smile turning into a tightened line. "Why the fuck is there a Nora on my lawn?" he demanded, searching for someone over my shoulder.

"He's with Layla, my king," Iston informed him in that cultured tone of his. "Apparently, he's one of her mates."

"One of...?" my mother began to repeat, her fingers lifting to cover her lips as a shocked calm fell over the group.

My parents gaped at me with twin expressions of horror.

Is it that strange that I mated a Nora? I wondered.

Although, based on Iston's flat stare as he joined my father's side, perhaps it was a surprise to them that I'd *mated* at all.

It occurred to me that I hadn't found any compatible mates during my courtship season. I shouldn't have found one in King Sefid's court, because in truth, I wasn't a Nora.

Which made Auric's compatibility with me extraordinary. Nora and Noir never mated for obvious reasons—Noir were sent away to reform. But we'd been operating under the assumption that Noir were Fallen Nora.

However, Kyril claimed we were different races entirely. That Nora were created to protect and guard Noir.

So I doubted it was very common, even here, for a Noir to take a Nora mate.

Perhaps our kinds weren't biologically suited?

That was why the Valkyries didn't have any qualms about killing their mates, and in fact, they preferred it that way to keep their female offspring "pure." They weren't often truly compatible with anyone, at least in terms of a relationship. But they were able to procreate with anyone they deemed worthy, no mate-bond required.

Regardless of the rules or the norms, Auric and I were bonded on every level. I couldn't imagine life without him. Not now, not ever.

And my other mate, well, my family certainly wouldn't have expected me to take an inmate to my bed, much less the dangerous shadow at my back who was Novak.

Although, he had helped my father all those years ago. He now wore his mark, according to Kyril.

So maybe my parents would find him worthy after all. Perhaps—

"I'm missing the party, it seems," an unfamiliar male voice said, interrupting my thoughts and captivating my complete attention with his sensual tone.

My nostrils flared as a new scent hit my senses. This one a floral aroma that overpowered anything I had ever encountered, even my mother's.

Ambrosia.

I knew it on instinct, even though I had never experienced it, and my gaze snapped up to a gorgeous male with dark violet eyes. He stood just outside the door of the home, his presence palpable and intoxicating.

The enigma started toward us, his movements hypnotically elegant.

Oh…

His dark brown hair fluttered around his ears, caught in some sort of invisible breeze.

Like a god…

Each step punctuated his otherworldly appeal, his aura underlined in magnificent power that made my mouth water for a taste.

Stunning.

Gorgeous.

Decadent.

And he smelled… *delicious.*

His gaze met mine, and in one look, he offered everything my body could possibly desire and more.

My tongue slipped out to dampen my lower lip. His gaze dipped, following the motion, and a slight smile formed on his perfect mouth.

Novak growled.

Auric caught my hip, his touch possessive and clear. *Mine.*

Part of me wanted to protest, but I clamped down on the instinct at once, not having been prepared for a compatible mate to intrude on my family's reunion.

Not just compatible.

It was as if this male had been sculpted exactly for me, his floral scent designed to make me weak in the knees.

His backless black suit opened up at the collar as he ran a hand over his neck, revealing perfect porcelain skin and delicious lines. His chocolate hair moved with him in tousled waves, framing a strong jaw and an aristocratic nose. He carried himself with confidence and ease as feathered, silky sable wings edged with beautiful golden tips wafted behind him.

No elixir for him, I mused, admiring his thick plumes.

Kyril cleared his throat, breaking the charged silence as he approached from the side to stand next to the godly male.

"Princess Layla," Kyril said. "Allow me to introduce Prince Ketos. Your betrothed."

My lips parted. *My betrothed?*

But I didn't have a chance to respond.

Because, in the next breath, Auric punched my betrothed. *Right in the face.*

The Story Continues with *Noir Reformatory: Third Offense...*

Thank you for reading! We love writing complex worlds with a sensual bite. For some of our other cowrites, check out Elemental Fae Academy, a reverse harem romance.

Or venture into the dark worlds of Lexi's mind with the Immortal Curse series. For more dark angelic romance with a fae twist, check out J.R. Thorn's *Sins of the Fae King*.

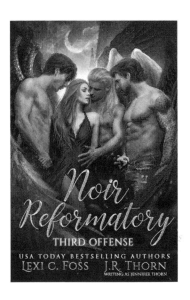

NOIR REFORMATORY: THIRD OFFENSE

So, I have a third mate.
No big deal.

Except, Auric punched my royal—descended from gods—
betrothed right in the face.
Novak has murder in his eyes, more so than usual.
And my body is screaming at me to take all three males
and teach them who's in charge here.

Because I believe the truth now. I'm a Noir royal,
descended from the gods themselves and destined to fix the
history my fake father forged. The one where black-winged
angels were the result of sin and scandal instead of the
truth.

My black wings mark me as a superior being, one that will
reunite angelkind to the glory they once were.

But first, I need to get my three mates in line and keep them from killing each other.

Ketos, a prince with gold-tipped wings, has a legion of Noir on his side, along with the technology and power that we'll need to play Sayir's game. Not to mention he has always been destined to be my mate, a fact I know is as true as the sun and the stars.

Novak, my lethal weapon, has been blessed by the gods, chosen to stand with us and slay our enemies.

And Auric, my commander, my Nora, represents everything I want for a new world, one where Nora and Noir work together like they were meant to.

It'll take a miracle, or divine intervention, to convince these three males to work together.
It's my ultimate test.
A trial that I must pass.
Because if I can't bring my mates together, how am I supposed to unite a lost world?

Note: *Noir Reformatory: Third Offense* is a "why choose" paranormal romance with a plot that spans six novels. There will be cliffhangers, adult situations, violence, and MM/MF/MMF/MMFM content.

CURIOUS ABOUT HOW RAVEN MET SORIN AND ZIAN? FIND
OUT IN THE STANDALONE PREQUEL, NOIR REFORMATORY:
THE BEGINNING

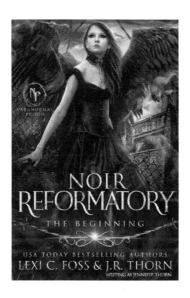

Trapped in a world of sin and sexy alpha angels.
Forever defined by my black wings.

My father, King of the Nora, sent me to Noir Reformatory
to atone for crimes I didn't commit.

So what's a girl to do? Escape, obviously.

Except I need allies to accomplish that feat and no one
wants anything to do with King Sefid's daughter. If
anything, my claim to the throne has only made running
that much harder, and worse, I'm stuck with two hot angels
standing in my way.

Auric is my supposed guardian, his white wings marking him as my superior in this deadly playground. Only, I'm his princess and I refuse to bow to a warrior like him.

And Novak, the notorious *Prison King*, is hell-bent on teaching me my place. Which he seems to think is beneath him. In his bed.

This prison resembles a training camp for soldiers more than a reformatory for the Fallen. I suspect something nefarious is at play here, but of course no one believes me. I'm the guilty princess with black wings. Well, I'll prove them all wrong. I just hope it isn't too late.

My Name is Princess Layla.
I'm innocent.
And I do not accept this fate.

Noir Reformatory: The Beginning

USA Today Bestselling Author Lexi C. Foss loves to play in dark worlds, especially the ones that bite. She lives in Chapel Hill, North Carolina with her husband and their furry children. When not writing, she's busy crossing items off her travel bucket list, or chasing eclipses around the globe. She's quirky, consumes way too much coffee, and loves to swim.

Want access to the most up-to-date information for all of Lexi's books? Sign-up for her newsletter here.

Lexi also likes to hang out with readers on Facebook in her exclusive readers group - Join Here.

Where To Find Lexi:
www.LexiCFoss.com

ALSO BY LEXI C. FOSS

Blood Alliance Series - Dystopian Paranormal

Chastely Bitten

Royally Bitten

Regally Bitten

Rebel Bitten

Kingly Bitten

Cruelly Bitten

Dark Provenance Series - Paranormal Romance

Heiress of Bael (FREE!)

Daughter of Death

Son of Chaos

Paramour of Sin

Princess of Bael

Elemental Fae Academy - Reverse Harem

Book One

Book Two

Book Three

Elemental Fae Holiday

Winter Fae Mates

Hell Fae - Reverse Harem

Hell Fae Captive

Immortal Curse Series - Paranormal Romance

Book One: Blood Laws

Book Two: Forbidden Bonds

Book Three: Blood Heart

Book Four: Blood Bonds

Book Five: Angel Bonds

Book Six: Blood Seeker

Book Seven: Wicked Bonds

Immortal Curse World - Short Stories & Bonus Fun

Elder Bonds

Blood Burden

Mershano Empire Series - Contemporary Romance

Book One: The Prince's Game

Book Two: The Charmer's Gambit

Book Three: The Rebel's Redemption

Midnight Fae Academy - Reverse Harem

Ella's Masquerade

Book One

Book Two

Book Three

Book Four

**Noir Reformatory - Ménage/Reverse Harem
Paranormal Romance**

The Beginning

First Offense

Second Offense

Third Offense

Underworld Royals Series - Dark Paranormal Romance

Happily Ever Crowned

Happily Ever Bitten

X-Clan Series - Dystopian Paranormal

Andorra Sector

X-Clan: The Experiment

Winter's Arrow

Bariloche Sector

Hunted

V-Clan Series - Dystopian Paranormal

Blood Sector

Vampire Dynasty - Dark Paranormal

Violet Slays

Crossed Fates

Other Books

Scarlet Mark - Standalone Romantic Suspense

Rotanev - Standalone Poseidon Tale

Carnage Island - Standalone Reverse Harem Romance

ABOUT JENNIFER THORN

Jennifer Thorn is a Paranormal Romance Author specializing in M/F and M/M/F (ménage) and the pen name of USA Today Bestselling author J.R. Thorn.

Learn more at www.Jennifer-Thorn.com

ALSO BY JENNIFER THORN

Sins of the Fae King

(Book 1) Captured by the Fae King

(Book 2) Betrayed by the Fae King

Noir Reformatory

Noir Reformatory: The Beginning

Noir Reformatory: First Offense

Noir Reformatory: Second Offense

Reverse Harem Books

Elemental Fae Universe Reading List

Lexi C. Foss & J.R. Thorn

• Elemental Fae Academy: Books 1-3 (Co-Authored)

• Midnight Fae Academy (Lexi C. Foss)

• Fortune Fae Academy (J.R. Thorn)

• Fortune Fae M/M Steamy Episodes (J.R. Thorn)

• Candela (J.R. Thorn)

• Winter Fae Mates (Co-Authored)

• Hell Fae Captive (Co-Authored)

~

Blood Stone Series Universe

Recommended Reading Order is below, all series in the Blood Stone Universe are written in the same world in consecutive order. This is the recommended reading order.

Seven Sins

• *Book 1: Succubus Sins*

• *Book 2: Siren Sins*

• *Book 3: Vampire Sins*

The Vampire Curse: Royal Covens

• *Book 1: Her Vampire Mentors*

• *Book 2: Her Vampire Mentors*

• *Book 3: Her Vampire Mentors*

Fortune Academy (Part I)

• *Year One*

• *Year Two*

• *Year Three*

Fortune Academy Underworld (Part II)

• *Episode 1: Burn in Hell*

• *Book Four*

• *Episode 2: Burn in Rage*

• *Book Five*

• *Book Six*

Fortune Academy Underworld (Part III)

• *Book Seven*

- *Book Eight*
- *Book Nine*

Crescent Five: Rejected Wolf Shifter RH

- *Book One: Moon Guardian*
- *Book Two*
- *Book Three*

Unicorn Shifter Academy

- *Book One*
- *Book Two*
- *Book Three*

Learn More at www.AuthorJRThorn.com